"We belong together, you, me and the baby. If you let it happen, Chris could be the son I never had."

Eden reached for his hand. "You don't understand. Chris is the son you *did* have. He's yours, Nick."

Nick stared at her, a stunned look on his face. "But you said I wasn't..." He looked down at Christopher.

A lump formed at the back of Eden's throat as Nick touched the baby's soft skin almost in awe. Surprise had turned to wonder, and now to gentle love that all but tore her breath away.

"Why didn't you tell me the truth before?" he asked. "I want the whole story, Eden."

Dear Harlequin Intrigue Reader,

Your summer reading list just wouldn't be complete without the special brand of romantic suspense you can only get from Harlequin Intrigue.

This month, Joanna Wayne launches her first-ever miniseries! You loved the Randolph family when you met them in her book *Family Ties* (#444). So now they're back in RANDOLPH FAMILY TIES, beginning with Branson's story in *The Second Son* (#569). Flesh and blood bind these brothers to each other—and to a mystery baby girl. All are her protectors...one is her father.

Familiar, the crime-solving black cat, is back in his *thirteenth* FEAR FAMILIAR title by Caroline Burnes. This time he explores New Orleans in *Familiar Obsession* (#570).

It had been Hope Fancy's dream to marry Quinn McClure, but not under a blaze of bullets! Are *Urgent Vows* (#571) enough to save two small children...and a lifelong love? Find out with Harlequin Intrigue author Joyce Sullivan.

With her signature style and Native American characters and culture, Aimée Thurlo revisits the Black Raven brothers from *Christmas Witness* (#544). In *Black Raven's Pride* (#572), Nick Black Raven would die to protect Eden Maes, the one-time and always love of his life. And he'd be damned before anyone would touch a hair on the head of *their* child.

So if you can handle the heat, pull the trigger on all four Harlequin Intrigue titles!

Sincerely,

Denise O'Sullivan
Associate Senior Editor
Harlequin Intrigue

Black Raven's Pride
Aimée Thurlo

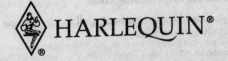

HARLEQUIN®

TORONTO • NEW YORK • LONDON
AMSTERDAM • PARIS • SYDNEY • HAMBURG
STOCKHOLM • ATHENS • TOKYO • MILAN • MADRID
PRAGUE • WARSAW • BUDAPEST • AUCKLAND

ISBN 0-373-22572-5

BLACK RAVEN'S PRIDE

Copyright © 2000 by Aimée and David Thurlo

ABOUT THE AUTHOR

Aimée Thurlo is a nationally bestselling author. She's written forty novels and is published in at least twenty countries worldwide. She has been nominated for the Reviewers' Choice Award and the Career Achievement Award by *Romantic Times Magazine*.

Aimée was born in Havana, Cuba, and lives with her husband of twenty-eight years in Corrales, New Mexico. Her husband, David, was raised on the Navajo Indian reservation.

Books by Aimée Thurlo

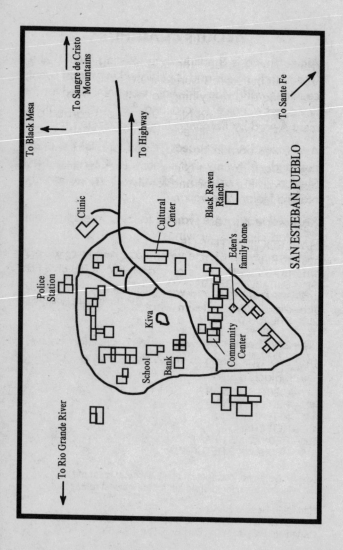

SAN ESTEBAN PUEBLO

To Sangre de Cristo Mountains

To Black Mesa

To Highway

To Santa Fe

To Rio Grande River

Clinic

Police Station

Kiva

School

Bank

Community Center

Cultural Center

Eden's family home

Black Raven Ranch

CAST OF CHARACTERS

Nick Black Raven — The past had caught up to him. But the secrets buried there could destroy everyone and everything he loved.

Eden Maes — Loving Nick had always carried a price. This time, with even more to risk, she was determined not to repeat the mistakes of the past.

Jake Black Raven — Nick's twin brother stood to lose it all. But honor and family loyalty were everything.

Rita Korman — She wanted to be a free spirit, but life had clipped her wings.

Wayne Sanders — He was Rita's brother and best friend. But he had his own agenda.

Patrick Korman — He was his own man, and no one would ever tell him what to do, including the tribe.

Deputy Torres — He was up for promotion and nothing was going to stand in his way — including Nick Black Raven.

To Evelyn who will always walk beside Christopher.
And to Camilla and Natalie, two very helpful babies.

AUTHOR'S NOTE

San Esteban Pueblo is a fictional composite of the
Tewa Pueblos in New Mexico. The religious rites
depicted herein have been abbreviated in order to
avoid offending those whose religious beliefs
depend on the secrecy of the rites.

Chapter One

Nick Black Raven held on tightly to the reins of his mount as lightning flashed across the night sky and thunder shook the earth. Restless, the black stallion stomped at the ground, eager to get going.

"You're getting soft, Bravo. Since when do you care about storms?"

Bravo pinned back his ears and tossed his head as if annoyed by Nick's comment. Then, suddenly, he focused on something ahead he alone could sense, and dipped his head hard twice, hoping to loosen Nick's hold on the reins.

"Stop that. The last time I gave you your head, it took me twenty minutes to bring you to a halt, and I had to run you into a circle to do that. This time we're going to play by my rules."

As soon as he'd spoken, the harsh gusts of the leading edge of the storm struck, bringing with them a torrent of swirling dust and grit. Cold rain was likely to follow.

"Okay, maybe you're right. Let's head back. It's really a miserable evening." Nick lifted the bandanna he wore around his neck and covered his mouth and nose, hoping to avoid another lungful of dirt. "Let's race the storm back to the ranch before we get drenched."

Nick loosened his hold on the reins and touched the animal's flanks with the heels of his boots. In an instant, Bravo leaped forward, galloping across the desert canyon at a speed worthy of the lightning flashing overhead.

The cool September wind and the rumbling chaos of the brewing storm incited both horse and rider. Here, just a few miles outside the pueblo, the only rules that mattered were nature's own.

Dark laughter escaped his lips as he raced like the wind just ahead of the stormy maelstrom.

EDEN MAES opted for a shortcut back to her house at the pueblo in hopes of beating the rain. She'd been visiting a friend of the family but had soon lost track of time. Now, the massive cumulonimbus clouds overhead obliterated all traces of the moon, and thunder raged from the steady barrage of lightning.

Moving carefully, Eden climbed over the stepladder stile in the cattle fence and headed out cross-country, avoiding the pueblo's main road, and hoping to cut at least fifteen minutes off her walk.

The wind howled, lifting clouds of sand and sending waves of it against her until her skin stung from the onslaught. As lightning illuminated the landscape like a Fourth of July fireworks display, Eden checked her watch and quickened her pace. Mrs. Chino, the baby-sitter, had told her that she'd have to leave at seven to attend a meeting of her religious society, and it was nearly that time now.

This was turning out to be a lousy shortcut after all. Earlier in the monsoon season, heavy afternoon storms had cut new arroyos into the sparsely covered ground, and now she was spending too much of her time finding alternate routes across the dry channels between her and the pueblo.

She made progress slowly. Then, two or three miles from her home, through the howls of the wind and the angry storm, she saw the headlights of an approaching vehicle. She turned around, hoping it would be someone who could give her a ride back. Surely no one but a local pueblo resident was likely to be driving around out here in this weather.

Unfortunately, not all the people at the pueblo were her friends. Her parents had been labeled as thieves and although neither was still living, that dishonor and stigma now followed her. It was one more factor that worked against her, adding to the determination of those opposed to having a half blood like her claim a place on pueblo land.

Suddenly, the truck driver turned off his headlights, though she could hear him still accelerating toward her.

Instinct and logic warned her that the driver wasn't behaving like a friend or neighbor. As the vehicle bore down on her, Eden took off running. She chose her path carefully, going uphill across a rocky slope. The boulder-laden terrain would slow the vehicle down.

Yet the truck continued to move relentlessly forward. Instead of accelerating to full speed and catching up quickly, however, the driver was toying with her, closing the gap and forcing her to sprint, then slowing down again, but remaining close.

Climbing farther up the slope was her only chance, but her lungs felt as if they were about to burst, and her legs were giving out. Ahead, she could see the lights of several buildings near the pueblo. If she could only make it a little farther, she'd be within shouting distance of Black Raven Ranch. Although she'd sworn a long time ago never to ask any Black Raven for help no matter what happened, she had no choice now.

Fear prodded her forward. As she glanced back, she realized that the hill was flattening out now, and the vehicle could outmaneuver her easily when they reached level ground. With no other choice, she kept running, though she knew it was a race she couldn't win. The outcome would be entirely in the hands of the driver pursuing her. She thought of her son, still just an infant. He'd never even seen his father, nor did his father know about him. She wouldn't leave him alone. Somehow, she'd make it through this, no matter what lay in store for her.

BRAVO PRANCED excitedly as Nick held the stallion in check for a moment, trying to determine the best path downhill. He had to get off the high ground. Lightning made the mesa he was on now one of the most dangerous places around, especially for a rider. The large black horse tossed his head impatiently.

"The rain's dealt us a bad hand, Bravo," Nick said. "We can't go down the usual way. With all those new arroyos, you'll break a leg for sure. Let's try circling around to the north," he said, turning Bravo's head.

It was then he saw movement below. He squinted, trying to see through the haze of dust and sand raised by the angry wind. A long-haired woman was being chased by someone in a tan or yellow pickup. In another minute the truck would overtake her, and the woman would pay dearly if the driver meant to do more than intimidate her.

"I thought it was cowboys who were supposed to ride to the rescue, not Indians," he muttered. "Let's go, Bravo," he said, applying pressure to the stallion's flanks with his legs.

The horse, obeying the cue, bolted forward, hurtling across the slope, heading down at an angle to intercept her. As they drew closer, Nick tried to get a good look at the driver inside the truck. He appeared to be alone, but the dark hampered efforts to make out a face.

Nick focused on the woman. She was his priority now. Asking his horse for even greater speed, he leaned back, trying to make it easier on Bravo by keeping his weight centered. They'd get to her first, he knew that, and although Bravo wouldn't be able to outrun a pickup, he could go places that the truck would never be able to handle.

Hearing hoofbeats behind her, the woman turned her head, glancing back. He couldn't see her face clearly through the gathering shadows of night, but he could sense her fear. He slowed Bravo to match her stride, then reached down. "Let me help you."

He grasped her by the waist and pulled her up before him onto the saddle. Smart enough to realize cooperation was her only hope, she shifted quickly, straddling the horse. Only then did she turn to look back at him. At that moment, he remembered the bandanna that still covered his face.

"It's okay. Stay still," he said, trying to keep his voice sure and steady. "Bravo's not used to taking double, but he'll adjust fast."

The storm and the danger from their pursuers were nothing in comparison to the savage emotions that suddenly ripped through him as she eased against him, settling against his parted thighs. Familiar memories flooded his brain. He'd held this woman before—intimately. Although he hadn't seen her face clearly, in his heart, the feeling was nothing less than utter conviction.

"Get me away from that pickup, please," she managed, breathlessly.

Her gentle voice, so filled with fear, touched him deeply. The need to protect her pounded through him with every beat of his heart.

Glancing back and seeing the pickup now gaining ground, he forced himself to concentrate. "We're going to have to jump that arroyo ahead. It's our only chance. The landing will be rough, but don't worry. Just hang on and let the horse do all the work. I won't let you fall.''

''I'll be okay,'' she said, tightening her legs around the horse.

Together they galloped as one, the thump of pounding hooves and heartbeats and the creak of leather competing with the howl of the wind.

She did know how to ride. Nick was certain of that now. She moved with Bravo instead of against him and was shifting to a jumping position now, leaning slightly forward as she held on to his mane.

As her long, chestnut brown hair caressed his arms, dark whispers echoed in his mind. In a heartbeat, they were flying through the air and, in those precious moments, fantasy and reality merged. Their bodies, weightless, flowed into each other's. As a union of purpose held them, a longing for something elusive and unnameable wrapped itself around his soul.

Tightening his grip around her waist, he pulled her back toward him just as Bravo landed on the other side of the wide chasm. They continued on for another fifty feet before Nick could safely rein in his mount.

As he spun Bravo around and faced the pickup, his breathing was as ragged as that of the animal's. The challenge of danger, and the fire this woman had created in him, made him feel powerfully male and alive. Memories of another time and the only woman he'd ever loved whispered warnings from the edges of his mind.

The pickup slid to a stop just before reaching the rain-carved ditch, engine running, but unable to cross. Quickly, the truck was thrown into reverse, and the vehicle spun around, roaring away in a cloud of dust.

Nick smiled with satisfaction. They'd won the battle. Unwilling to linger out in the open, so far away from cover,

Nick made a clicking sound and Bravo began a slow lope toward the gates of Black Raven Ranch.

Once they reached the main entrance, Nick stopped the tired animal. "Good job, Bravo."

"I'll get off here," the woman said, then surprised him by swinging her leg over Bravo's neck and dismounting with ease.

He slipped off next, and stood right by her. Seeing her face clearly for the first time, he sucked in his breath. After years of wondering if this moment would ever come, he was finally face to face with the girl who'd claimed his heart so many years ago—and, later, the only woman who'd ever walked out on him.

She looked up at him, and seeing the bandanna that covered his face, reached up tentatively. "I'd like to see who I'm thanking," she said, her trembling voice betraying her uncertainty.

"You know who I am, Eden. Just as I knew, deep down, who you were from the moment you were back in my arms." He covered her hand with his as she pulled the bandanna down.

Her eyes shimmered with excitement and desire as she saw his face. Following an instinct he couldn't deny, Nick pulled her against him and, in a heartbeat, covered her mouth with his own.

His kiss was harsh, demanding everything she'd ever denied him. He'd expected her to resist and maybe slap his face, but her surrender was sweet and filled with passion. Her body softened against his, and her gentle sighs ripped him apart. Shock waves spiraled down his body.

Nick knew he was playing with fire. He should have let Eden go right then, but he couldn't bring himself to do it. She'd been a part of his dreams, of his heart, from the very first day he'd laid eyes on her.

His arms tightened around her. She was as beautiful and as sensual as he remembered. Passion rocked him to the core. The love they'd shared had always been like this—fierce and wild.

She moaned and the soft sound, so familiar to him, took him back to the last night they'd spent together. He'd loved her then in every way a man could love a woman, and she'd given herself completely to him in return. But the next morning she was gone, without even a goodbye.

Nick eased his hold on her, then stepped back. The memory of Eden's betrayal still felt like a knife to his gut. As he gazed down at her, and saw the passion that still burned in her eyes, he felt himself drowning in the amber depths, despite his efforts to resist her.

"Of all the people I could have run into, I never expected…" Her shaky words trailed off.

"You're welcome, Eden," he said gruffly.

"I didn't mean to sound ungrateful. I really appreciate what you did, Nick. I'm just…surprised."

Nick led Bravo through the gate and waited as Eden shut it behind them. "What was that all about out there?" he asked, leading Bravo toward the stalls.

Eden didn't meet his gaze, or answer right away. At long last, as if finally making up her mind, she spoke. "I really appreciated your help tonight, but I'll handle things on my own from here on. Don't worry about it."

He searched her face for answers, but drew a blank. The only thing he could see there were echoes of the fear that had gripped her.

"Don't shut me out," he said quietly. "You're in trouble, and it looks to me like you're in over your head."

"It's my problem, Nick, not yours," she said firmly.

Her polite brush-off stung and he grew stone-cold. Eden had betrayed him once, tearing his heart out in the process.

That was not something any Black Raven forgot or forgave easily. But he wouldn't back off. "I'm not asking you as an old friend. I'm a deputy now," he added.

Surprise, then a coldness he couldn't miss flashed in her eyes, and her expression became suddenly guarded. "Somebody has been letting me know since I returned two weeks ago that I'm not welcome here. But what happened tonight won't happen again. I'll be more careful from now on. I'd been visiting Lena Ortiz, a friend of my family's, and stayed too late. I won't let time slip away from me that way again. The driver of the truck played a lot rougher than I expected. My guess is that the guy who chased me tonight is probably the same one who has been sending me unsigned notes telling me to get off pueblo land. I don't think he would have run me over. I just got scared and panicked, so he chased me."

He studied her expression pensively. "Give me the notes. Let me see if I can track down the sender."

"I didn't keep them. But having you get involved isn't going to change anything, Nick. As I'm sure you know, there are many people who oppose anyone of mixed blood claiming a place on pueblo land. My father was Tewa, but my mother was Anglo, and that makes my return home something that many haven't exactly welcomed. I realize it's not really a racial thing. They're just trying to insure that the whites don't take away the land our tribe has left, one concession at a time. And they're willing to fight to preserve the little they've got. I understand it because in my heart, I *am* Tewa." Eden checked her watch. "Oh, I'm really late now! I've got to get home. We'll talk another time, okay?"

"Let me give you a ride."

She hesitated, emotions flashing across her face at lightning speed. More intrigued than ever, he continued to press her.

"What's the problem? You're in a hurry and I'm offering you a ride. And, this time, we can take my four-wheel drive instead of Bravo. That's my old Jeep parked by the stables."

She gave him a thin smile. "Sorry. I'm still jumpy. The truth is I really would appreciate a lift," Eden said, at last.

"What's your hurry tonight? What are you so late for?"

She hesitated for several moments, then reluctantly answered him. "I left my son with a sitter, and she warned me that she had to leave at seven. It's almost eight now."

"Your...son?" His jaw clenched as he struggled to control his emotions. Surely it couldn't be... "How old is he?"

"Six months," she said, after a beat.

Nick stared at her. "Is it...am I..." he said, his voice a blur of sound.

"The father?" She shook her head. "There was another man in my life after I met you in Arizona. But let's not talk about this now. That's all ancient history."

Dawning came then, a slow realization that left him numb. "So that's why you ran out on me?" His voice sounded hard and bitter, even to his own ears. "No, never mind. You don't have to answer that. It's clear enough."

A coldness unlike anything he'd ever felt filled him, numbing him from any more pain. Her betrayal had been absolute—more so than he'd ever dreamed—and it became the last nail in the coffin of their ill-fated love affair.

"Let me put Bravo away," he said tonelessly, gesturing to the stables. "Then we'll get going."

They removed the horse's tack and placed him in his stall. While she brushed the stallion down, Nick filled the feeder with hay and made sure he had fresh water.

"Are you home to stay?" he asked. No matter what had

happened between them, he was a cop and it was his job to maintain law and order on the pueblo. The fact was it was his duty to find out what was going on, and he would honor that.

"I accepted a temporary teaching position so I'll be around for a while at least. But I've got to tell you, you're the last person I expected to see here at the pueblo," she said. Then slowly added, "And now, to find out you've become a tribal cop... You're certainly one for surprises."

"Why do you say that? It's not that much of a leap, really. I've always known that I was meant to work with people. I couldn't run a job placement center here like I did in Arizona since the tribe now has an agency that takes care of that. But that left me at loose ends. My father's will stipulated that in order for any of us to inherit, we'd all have to live at the ranch for one year, so I had to stay. But ranching full-time just wasn't for me. Then I found out that one of Captain Mora's two deputies was about to quit and that the department was searching for a replacement."

"The police department here is very small. The loss of one man can be a crisis."

He nodded. "Our entire police force consists of Captain Mora, two deputies and a civilian dispatcher. I figured I could be of use to the tribe, so I applied for the second deputy's job and was lucky enough to get it." He glanced over at her. Somehow, he had to make Eden see him as a cop who could help her, not just as a former lover. It was the only way she'd ever confide in him and finding out what trouble was hovering on the pueblo was his first priority. "This job really gets under your skin. It's the best thing that ever happened to me. But you know a little about what it means to be a cop. Your father was an officer for the Bureau of Indian Affairs."

"A cop's family views his job in a very different light,

Nick," Eden answered, her voice taut. "What I remember most is my dad's long absences and the way he was totally dedicated to his job. He almost never made it home for my birthdays or most holidays. It was hardest on my mom, though. She spent most of her life worrying about him. Being a cop may be a great job, but not for a man's family."

He nodded thoughtfully. "Well, I've got no plans to marry. The bachelor life suits me."

She didn't comment. "How are you and Jake getting along trying to run a ranch together? You two never used to agree on anything."

"Jake and I will never see eye to eye on a lot of things," he answered, "but we're working it out." He paused, studying her expression. "But let's get back to what's going on in your life, Eden. People have the right to their opinions, and they're not required to like the fact that you're now living here. But no one has the right to threaten you physically, or harass you. It looks like you're caught up in something that might be too big for you to handle alone. You're a mother now and have other responsibilities to take into account. Let me do my job as a cop and help you out."

She hesitated, then forced a smile. "What happened out there won't happen again. I'm sure of it."

"I don't believe that any more than you do."

"Don't put yourself in the middle of this, Nick. It'll only make things tougher for me," she said. "I've always taken care of myself and I know what I have to do. I'll handle it."

"I'm sorry, Eden, but I can't let this go. This trouble is taking place on pueblo land, and that's my turf."

As he pulled up in front of her adobe home, she mumbled a quick goodbye, let herself out, and began walking up to the door.

Nick knew he hadn't been invited, but he parked the Jeep and decided to go inside with her. He had a job to do, and, as long as she was at the pueblo, it was his duty to help her fight whoever was trying to drive her off.

Like star-crossed lovers destined to keep meeting, Eden was back in his life again. But, this time, it was different. Eden, the woman he'd loved, was gone for good. In her place was this stranger who was bringing trouble to the land he was sworn to protect.

Chapter Two

Eden knew Nick Black Raven was right behind her as she stepped up to the front door. She could sense him as clearly as she could the wind that swept her long chestnut hair across her face. She'd never wanted to bring Nick here. It was too hard to be with him. There were too many memories. Every time she looked at him, her heart remembered the only man who had ever made her blood sing. But he was not for her.

She could still remember every detail of their last night together. She'd loved him with all her heart, but afterward, as he'd held her, he'd bared his soul to her. What she'd seen there had made it clear that they couldn't have a future together. A fierce agony had gripped her as he'd shattered her dreams one by one with each word he spoke.

He'd asked her to stay with him, but he'd never spoken of marriage. He'd told her that they'd make a life together, away from the pueblo, and never set foot on Tewa land again. They'd make a home in Arizona, just the two of them. Kids would never be a part of the picture. As far as he was concerned, the world didn't need more children.

His vision of their future had been so different from hers! The knowledge had broken her heart and she'd realized then that she'd allowed things to go too far. The inescapable truth had been that she'd sworn to return to the pueblo to clear her parents' name. She had hoped he'd go with her, but knew suddenly that it would never be. And then to learn that he never wanted children to become a part of his life… The prospect had chilled her soul.

Although she'd loved Nick, she'd realized that what they each needed to be happy went beyond their ability to make compromises. Although it was clear that circumstances had now brought him home to stay, it was just as evident from his earlier reference about his bachelor lifestyle that he hadn't changed his mind about that part.

As it had been in the past, fate brought them together but continued to put obstacles in their way. To make matters even worse, Nick was now a cop. As the daughter of a man in law enforcement, she knew the high emotional cost that would carry for anyone close to him. Childhood memories made her hand tremble as she grasped the door and stepped inside.

Suddenly her son, Christopher, let out a delighted cry. The dark-haired baby crawled toward her from across the room, leaving his activity blanket behind in a heap. Her heart melted. "Come here, little guy. Did you miss me?" She scooped Chris up and held him against her, shutting out Mrs. Chino's scowl for a few moments longer.

"You're *very* late, Eden. I told you I was expected at my daughter's, so you had to be back by seven, not eight forty-five. I almost left and took Christopher with me."

"It was entirely my fault, Mrs. Chino." Nick stepped around Eden and gave Mrs. Chino a mischievous grin that could have melted a dozen women's hearts. "The weather was lousy and we were only trying to get out of the rain. Isn't that what you were always telling us to do when Jake and I were kids?"

She smiled back at him, her anger vanishing in an instant. "I did do that, didn't I? I'm surprised you remember!"

"How could I forget? Remember that big storm in October of 1985 that broke all those branches off the cottonwoods around the Plaza?"

In a matter of seconds, Nick had her talking about old times. By the time the elderly lady left, Eden was amazed to see Mrs. Chino was in a better mood than she'd been in days.

Eden sighed softly as she stood at the window, watching Nick walk the sitter down the street toward her house. Nick had a way about him. As far back as she could remember, he'd always had at least half of the women in the pueblo madly in love with him. But the time she remembered most was when he'd only had eyes for her.

A delicious warmth spiraled through her as her thoughts drifted back to those days. Suddenly aware of what she was doing, she squelched that sentimental memory. Their time had come and gone, though destiny still toyed with them.

She remembered what she'd told Nick earlier tonight about her baby when he'd pressed her. She hadn't lied. There *had* been another man in her life after she'd left Nick—the child he'd fathered, their son Christopher.

Nick came back inside after having shown Mrs. Chino to her own door. Moving with purpose, he strode across the room toward her, all masculine power and confidence.

Eden's heart was racing as she cradled Christopher closer in her arms, bracing herself for what she had to do. Nick was only a part of her past. All he represented to her now was another complication she'd have to deal with. Christopher and Nick would eventually have to know each other as father and son but, first, she wanted to make sure Nick would welcome that news. Everything she knew about him told him he would not.

For now, the best thing she could do was concentrate on what she'd come home to do. She had returned to clear her family's name and that had to remain her first priority.

"Thank you for bringing me home, Nick, but I don't want to keep you," she said. Placing the squirming baby down on his special blanket, she started toward the door.

"So this is Christopher," Nick said, ignoring her hint. Picking the baby up off the floor, he went to the couch. To Eden's surprise, Christopher didn't let out the usual ear-piercing shriek he was famous for when a stranger held him.

Nick raised the baby up, holding him in a standing position on his lap. "What a great kid! And, hey, I think he likes me."

"Don't be too flattered. He's not picky. He also loves eating lipstick and crawling backwards down the hall."

Nick looked up at her and smiled warmly, shaking his head. "Well, you certainly won't win Miss Congeniality tonight."

Forcing herself not to even crack a smile, she stared at him coldly. "I hate to be a poor hostess, but I've *got* to put my son to bed."

"Let me help you. Then we can talk," Nick said, refusing to be put off.

Her chest constricted. This had been a favorite fantasy of hers—one she'd harbored in the deepest recesses of her heart.

"I'll take care of it," she said.

Eden tried not to look Nick in the eye as she silently took Christopher from him and started down the hall. Thankfully, Mrs. Chino had already bathed Christopher and he was in his pajamas. Giving her son a kiss on the forehead, she laid him gently in his crib and watched him for a moment. Christopher was her miracle, the only thing life had brought her that held nothing but good.

As she turned away, she noticed that Nick had followed her and was now standing just an arm's length behind, watching the baby.

"You're a lucky woman," he said, following her out of the room. "That's one special little boy."

His words of praise only made her more nervous. Nick and Christopher had responded to each other in a way that had taken her by surprise. And that served to remind her of the need to be cautious.

"You've made a good life for yourself, Eden." He brushed her face with his hand. His work-hardened palm made a shiver course through her. His body was all steel and muscle but, as it always had been, what made her melt inside was his gentleness.

Forcing her feelings aside, she walked to the door. "You have to go now, Nick. You don't belong here. You're not part of my life anymore." Eden could see the impact her words had on him.

His eyes became hooded, his expression cold. "I know you want me to keep my nose out of your business, but any trouble that touches this pueblo *is* my business. If someone is trying to drive you out of town, I need to know. So, whether you like it or not, that makes *you* my business."

Eden watched him from the living room window as he strode away. The attraction she felt for him was as strong as ever and that spelled big trouble. She'd have to protect herself or heartbreak would be sure to follow.

NICK DROVE AWAY, heading across country, pushing the Jeep through the worst terrain around. The rocky ground, full of risk and uncertainty, suited his mood.

Finding Eden after all this time had thrown him one heck of a curve ball. Not that his life had ever been simple. After his father had kicked Jake and him out of their home the day after high school graduation, nothing had ever come easy. His father's brutal attempt to force their transition from boys into men had taught him many hard lessons. Never Count On Anything and Never Trust Anyone had become his motto. He'd learned all about hopelessness and fear back then, and what it could do to the human soul.

In time, he'd made a life for himself away from the pueblo, and had achieved a measure of success. He'd proven to himself and everyone else that he didn't need his father's support to make it in the world.

Yet, even though he'd thought he'd left his old life behind him forever, it eventually had called him back. After his father's murder, he'd been forced to return to the pueblo. At first, it had been the last place he'd wanted to be, but things had changed over the last few months. He served a purpose here now, and he was exactly where he belonged. Nick knew he was home for good.

Moments later, he pulled up to the tribal police station, parked and went inside. The small, former residence was equipped only with the bare necessities. Crime had never really been much of a problem on the pueblo. For the most part, a San Esteban cop needed to know how to lead a wayward horse out of the road, or write a speeding ticket far more than he needed to know how to shoot. Of course, he'd had the required courses in self-defense and weapons, but it had only been a formality as far as he was concerned.

As he came in, Nick waved at Angelina, the civilian dispatcher. The desk against the wall that he shared with Deputy Torres was unoccupied at the moment. Torres was out on patrol somewhere. Walking to the back of the room, he knocked on Captain Mora's open door. The man looked up, leaned back in his creaky old office chair, and waved him in.

Captain Daniel Mora was built like a safe—short, stocky, and nearly impossible to break. People often compared him to a pit bull because he had a reputation for never backing off once he was on the trail of a criminal. "What brings you here, Nick? You're off duty tonight."

"There's a problem," he said, then sitting across from Mora's desk, related what had just occurred with Eden and the man in the pickup.

"You say she won't file a complaint?"

"That's right. She chalked it up to one of our tribe trying to scare her. She's also been getting some unsigned notes demanding she move off the pueblo, but apparently she tossed them out. I told her that nobody had a right to make any threats, but in spite of what happened tonight, she doesn't think she's in any danger."

"Was she in danger this evening?"

"I sure saw it that way. The person chasing her in that pickup wasn't kidding around. He could have easily run her over, or caused her to injure herself."

"Did you get a plate or an ID?"

"No, it was too dark."

"Then, until she wants to file a complaint, our hands are tied."

"My gut tells me to get to the bottom of this before whatever trouble she's in poses a danger to the rest of the pueblo."

Mora regarded Nick silently, his eagle-sharp gaze cutting through to the heart of the matter. "Are you worried about the woman, or about the tribe?"

"Both," he admitted, grudgingly. The direct approach was the only way to work with a man like Mora.

"There's something I want you to see. I think it'll give

you some insight into what's going on with Eden Maes. It all goes back to when her parents were alive.''

Captain Mora reached inside the file cabinet, extracted a letter from one of the folders and handed it to Nick.

"Keep what this says to yourself," he said. "Eden brought the original letter to me the day she moved back into her parents' old house. She'd wanted me to know why she'd returned and what she hoped to learn by being here. Take a minute to read it then give it back to me.''

Nick saw the letter was to Eden from her grandmother. The text was handwritten and difficult to read, but he persisted.

Dear Eden,

If you're reading this, I have gone on to the Lake of our Ancestors and you are now alone. You always said that someday you'd clear your parents' name, and if that's what you choose to do now, there are things you have to know.

Your father told me everything. Your mother was carrying trash out of the Cultural Center at the end of the day, as was her custom, when she accidentally discovered that one of the boxes contained ritual items. She realized then that one of the employees had used her to take the artifacts outside where the real thief could take them easily without leaving a trail. But she couldn't figure out who hated her enough to implicate her in something like that. She decided to go to your father because he was a BIA cop. But the thief photographed your mother putting the sacred objects into her car, and used that to blackmail her. Shortly after your mother got home and before your father could go to the police, the thief called them. He ordered your father to get the objects off the pueblo and leave them at a specific place.

My son put his own plan in motion and led the thief on a wild-goose chase while your mother hid the artifacts elsewhere. Realizing that he'd been tricked, the thief turned on Isabel and gave the police the photos that incriminated her. Isabel went into hiding but the thieves found her and kidnapped her. Then they called your father, and offered to exchange Isabel for the artifacts.

I know that James tried to free your mother. He went alone because they told him Isabel would die if the cops got involved. Later, when they were both found dead by the side of the road, I knew right away what had happened. There was no evidence that could explain the crime, but I knew where my son had gone and why, and that was enough for me. I told the police, but they never found anything that would solve their murders.

Afterward, I was told by people I trust that the man behind the scheme was Tall Shadow. He was well-known for wanting to keep non-Tewas off our land, and he particularly opposed your mother who was a white woman.

That's all I know. Isabel's mother disowned her when she married your father, so she never confided in Beth. I spoke to her before her death years ago, but she didn't know anything more than what I've told you. If you choose to pursue this, you'll be on your own. Be careful who you trust.

Grandmother

Nick read the letter over again, fighting the urge not to look up at Mora and see his reaction to the mention of Tall

Shadow. Nick knew the nickname. It had been an old, rarely used one for his father, Paul Black Raven.

Nick finished the letter and handed it back to Captain Mora, searching Mora's face to see if he also knew who Tall Shadow was, but finding no answers.

"James must have been up against the ropes if the thief had photos of Isabel putting the artifacts in her car," Nick commented. "Incriminating evidence like that is very effective blackmail."

"According to the statement James Maes made, the thief stayed one step ahead of them. And that eventually cost James and Isabel their lives," Mora said. "Of course, Eden's seeing far more in her grandmother's letter than she should. She's always wanted to clear her parents, and thinks that the information in this letter is a solid starting point." Mora leaned back in his chair.

"What did you tell her?" Nick pressed.

"Without more to go on than an old woman's memories—a woman who is now dead and can't be questioned—we really don't have anything solid. I also can't remember anyone by the nickname 'Tall Shadow' but, of course, all this happened when we were both kids." Mora put the letter back into the file folder.

"Eden won't back off," Nick said slowly.

"Of course not. I know for a fact that she's actually been busy asking people all kinds of questions about the past and her parents' lives here. I think she's determined to gain acceptance here by finding the stolen religious objects. Unofficially, of course, I wish her luck on her search. The two missing items are a crucial part of our rites."

"I'm not up on all that. Can you fill me in on what was stolen?"

"One of the two *Tsave Yoh* masks used for the Turtle Dance, along with its accompanying bear fetish, have been missing for almost twenty years now. The *Tsave Yoh*, as you probably remember, are supernatural beings entrusted with keeping the people's ties to our gods strong. They're said to be brought to life when specially appointed men wear the masks representing them. When one of those masks and the fetish were stolen, the power of the remaining *Tsave Yoh* was weakened. Our people believe that all the bad times that have befallen the pueblo since then—years of drought followed by persistent flooding and crop failures—prove that our people have slowly been losing the protection of our gods.''

"If she's trying to find the artifacts, how come our people don't support her?'' Nick asked.

"I don't think anyone believes she'll get anywhere. She was only nine when her mother took the artifacts, so what can she possibly do now for the tribe except create division and more problems? To most, she's just the daughter of someone who brought ruin down on us. Everyone already knows how hard our department searched for those objects. If the police couldn't find them, it's highly unlikely she will either. She doesn't have access to any more information than we do. Remember the letter?''

Nick nodded. "Do you have any idea who's trying to run her off, Captain?''

"No, and I can't even begin to guess. She has many enemies here. Official opposition began the moment she applied for a teaching job. Samuel Runningwater, who's been the director of the Cultural Center since it first opened, was dead set against allowing Eden to come back and live among us, let alone get a job as a teacher. But Mrs. Peña had transferred out and we needed a teacher badly. Eden got the matter put to a vote, and the elders decided to hire her and let her move into her old home for the school year.

After her grandmother died, that house had been sitting vacant."

Nick knew that Runningwater was Mrs. Chino's father, and that raised some interesting questions in his mind. "Mrs. Chino is taking care of Eden's son. She's *Apienu,* the head of the women's religious society. No one is more respected than she is. How come that hasn't helped Eden? If Mrs. Chino says that Eden's okay, I would have expected others to fall in line, including her own father."

"Laura Chino *works* for Eden and supplements her retirement income that way. That's all there is to that."

Weighing everything he'd learned this evening, Nick suddenly realized how little he knew about Eden's life. "Thanks, Captain." He stood. "I'm going to head back to the ranch. If you need me, I'll be there."

"See you tomorrow."

Nick drove home slowly. As his thoughts returned to Eden, he felt his gut tighten. Her betrayal had ripped a piece of his heart away. He'd loved her once—more than he'd ever thought possible. He was not a man given to fantasies and daydreams, yet he'd felt closer to her than he had to any other person who had ever played a part in his life. Being with her had been like finding the other half of himself.

He still vividly remembered their fateful meeting fifteen months ago. He'd been giving a guest lecture at the university in Phoenix on the teenage runaway problem. As the head of one of the leading job training centers in the state at the time, his experience had been sought after.

He recalled walking up to the podium and finding Eden sitting in the first row of the auditorium. Their eyes had met, and suddenly their years apart had seemed like nothing more than heartbeats in time.

In high school, his love for her had been all encompassing and absolute—a boy experiencing his first real love. Then suddenly, almost twelve years later, there they'd been as adults. They'd spent every available moment of those glorious days catching up on the years spent apart, and trying not to rush into anything. But his love for her had deepened naturally and the raw power of their emotions had compelled them to follow their hearts.

Now, looking back on it all, he regretted everything that had happened between them that week. But it was over, and looking back wouldn't fix anything.

As he reached home, the old bunkhouse, he felt a bone weariness that only came with mental exhaustion. He didn't want to mull things over anymore trying to figure out what ifs. He didn't want to dissect the situation. He just wanted peace.

He undressed then crawled into bed, wondering if he'd have to stare at the ceiling for a long time before sleep came. Yet, almost as soon as he closed his eyes, gray shadows closed in and images of the day when she'd stepped out of his arms and his life formed in his mind's eye.

In his dream, the scene that had changed him forever unfolded once again…

"This is where you belong," Nick said, holding her close to his side. They'd just made love and they were both feeling sated and at peace.

"I never thought this day would come," she whispered, her warm breath tickling his throat.

"It nearly killed me to leave you at the pueblo when my father kicked me out," he said, his voice soft. "All you had left was your grandmother, and you barely knew her. You needed me, but I had no way to provide for myself or you."

"It was hard to say goodbye," Eden said, settling against

him, her cheek and the palm of her hand resting on his chest.

"The pain our families caused is finally behind us. Let's not look back. We have each other, and that's all that's important."

Only through passion had he ever been able to say everything he felt, and once again he began to show her what he couldn't put into words. As long as they had each other, they'd never need anyone else. He molded her body with his hands, fitting her against him. He fed her soul with his kisses, speaking wordlessly to her of needs that would be shared for a lifetime.

"When you look at me that way, all I see in your eyes is love, steady and sure," she whispered.

Always and forever. The words were in his heart when he entered her again, loving her fierce cries as he plunged deep inside her. Their release was sweet and he lay over her, their bodies still locked together.

Then suddenly Nick's dreams shifted. Another scene unfolded, and Nick's heart began to drum against his chest, anger and pain gripping him. He was standing in the center of his old room, trying to accept the fact that Eden was really gone. The note she'd left for him was balled up in his fist, the words branded in his mind. *I made a mistake. I'm sorry. There's life and there's love, and we'll never be able to make the two come together.*

Black sorrow filled him and, with a sharp, angry cry, Nick jackknifed to a sitting position, coming abruptly awake. He got his bearings slowly as he looked around the bunkhouse and tried to focus on the present.

Back then he hadn't understood what had happened. Afterward he'd wondered if it had been his stand on children, but if Eden had loved him enough, she would have understood. They'd both lived through so much pain as kids on the pueblo that it had seemed inconceivable to him that she might have felt differently from him on that issue.

They'd known each other well as children, but he wondered now how well they'd really known each other as adults. One moment they'd had an entirely new life waiting for them. The pueblo and the sadness in their pasts would have eventually been nothing more than a memory for them. Yet she'd vanished without explanation, taking a piece of his heart.

The love he'd felt for her had been real but the closeness he'd wanted and had thought they'd shared had only been an illusion. It hadn't been anything said or left unsaid that had split them apart. What had really come between them was that there'd been another man in Eden's life.

He took a deep breath. The gut-wrenching pain he'd felt fifteen months ago had not diminished with time. He'd simply filed it away mentally, banishing it to a spot where he could handle it. Now, understanding the depth of her betrayal, a coldness settled over his steel-encased heart.

Naked, he walked to the window and stared out at the stars. He would never again allow anyone to come as close to him as Eden once had. Gone forever was the boy who'd thought love could conquer all, and the faith that had allowed him to give his heart.

The only thing he would do now was protect her. As a cop it was his duty—and as a man who'd once lover her it was his debt of honor to the past they'd shared.

Chapter Three

It was shortly after eight the following morning and Nick was on his second cup of coffee. All night long he'd lain awake, unable to stop thinking about Eden. At one time in his life, she'd been the world to him. But now everything was different except for the way she could make desire twist through him. And, as always, she'd turned his life upside down.

The letter Eden's grandmother had written to her mentioning Tall Shadow had disturbed him deeply. He'd only been a young boy, but he remembered how his father had hated the nickname, thinking that it made him sound like some kind of big boss the pueblo was required to look up to. His father had chewed out Martin, the ranch foreman, for using it, and he'd given orders that he was "Paul" on the ranch. Any ranch hands referring to him as Tall Shadow would be stuck with cleaning out the horse stalls permanently.

Lost in thought, Nick almost didn't hear the phone. On the third ring, he picked up the receiver, half expecting to hear Captain Mora's voice telling him he was needed to go on duty earlier than his originally scheduled shift.

Instead, it was his brother, Jake. "Nick, I need to talk to you. Can you come over this morning?"

"Sure." Nick had moved into the empty bunkhouse several months ago. He'd told his brother and his wife Annie that he wanted to give them more privacy, but the truth was that he'd felt out of place there. "Is something wrong?" he asked Jake.

"You could say that," Jake answered, his voice hard. "But I'd rather discuss this in person."

"I'll be there in five minutes."

Nick put his coffee cup in the sink, then walked over to the main house, which was less than a hundred yards away. Jake's tone had put him on his guard. Whenever Jake sounded this cool and reserved something major was brewing. And on top of whatever was going on, Nick knew he'd also have to tell Jake about the letter, and what Tall Shadow had been accused of doing years ago.

From the second Nick stepped into the main house, the large two-story adobe structure they'd both grown up in, he felt the tension in the air. Annie gave him a quick "good morning" as she met him by the door carrying nine-month-old Noelle in her arms.

Nick gave his niece a kiss. "Hey sweetpea."

The baby smiled and so did Annie. "You're so good with kids, Nick. Why don't you hurry up and get married?"

"It doesn't work that way. Not in my book anyway."

"I thought Black Raven men never went by the book— unless they wrote it themselves."

Nick laughed. "We only play by the rules when it suits us," he said, following her to the library.

As they entered the room, he saw Martin, who'd been the ranch foreman for as long as he could remember, as well as a family friend. He was helping Jake remove books from a shelf, then searching each one.

"What's going on? Lose something important?"

Jake came down the ladder that allowed him to reach the

top of the highest shelf in the wood-paneled library. The ceilings in most of the ground floor rooms were ten feet high. "Our mother's diary is gone," he said flatly.

"Gone? You mean stolen?" Nick asked, his tone now as taut as his brother's had been.

Jake nodded. "Precisely."

That diary had already cost them their father's life. Its loss now made Nick's blood turn to ice. There was no telling what price getting it back would exact this time. The journal was a treasure trove of community secrets, since just about everyone had confided in Saya, their mother, and she'd written down all her private thoughts in that leather-bound book. Last time, as they'd worked to get it back, greed and jealousy over the contents of the diary had nearly claimed Annie's life and that of her baby.

"Did you just leave it in plain sight?" Nick demanded, trying to suppress the anger in his voice. It was just like Jake to think it impossible that anyone would break in now that he was the head of the house.

"I wasn't careless," Jake snapped, sensing the direction Nick's thoughts had taken. "Far from it. I'd intended to start reading it a little at a time each night, so I took it out of our bedroom nightstand and put it down here. I honestly thought mom's diary would be safer in these bookshelves than in any drawer."

Nick paced around the room, his thoughts racing. "Okay, so now we concentrate on getting it back. Any idea who'd want the diary? Before, it was used against our father, but now that he's gone…"

"I don't think this has anything to do with our family's past this time. Those matters are settled," Jake looked at Annie and his daughter, love and relief etched clearly on his face.

"But there are other families—and other secrets," Martin said. "There's a skeleton in almost everyone's closet, if you look hard enough."

"We have to figure out who in this community knew about that diary," Nick said. "This house obviously wasn't broken into by some stranger or you would have seen evidence of it before now. We have to backtrack, and check who's been here recently."

"Everyone knows about the existence of that diary these days," Martin answered with a shrug. "It came out in the trial that convicted your father's killer."

"Then let's narrow down the times when it could have been taken, and figure out who was around then. When was the last time any of you remember seeing the diary?"

Annie spoke first. "I was dusting in here last Wednesday, or Thursday. I would have noticed it missing then...I think."

"You don't take the books out every time you dust, do you?" Nick asked.

"No," she admitted. "I stand on the ladder, and move the books back and forth. But I really think I would have noticed the diary missing. Jake showed me where he'd put it so he wouldn't be the only one to know."

"I'm no help on this," Martin said. "I come in here at least once or twice every day, but I don't pay much attention to what's on the shelves. All I look at are the ranch's business ledgers, the breeding records, and things like that."

Jake took a long, deep breath. "Then I guess I was the last one to see it. I read the first few pages about a month ago, the day before Noelle's naming ritual, to be exact. Then, I put it back on the top shelf, with the book jacket in place."

"Tell me, who came to Noelle's naming ritual?" Nick asked.

"Almost everyone we know stopped by that day—either before, during, or after. And any of the guests could have come in here," Annie said.

"I came at dawn in time to see her presented to the sun," Nick said. "If I remember right, my boss, Captain Mora, arrived right after that. After we all returned to the house, Elsie Mueller, the pueblo's nurse practitioner arrived."

Annie nodded. "Elsie helped us bathe Noelle, and was there when Blue Corn Woman and White Corn Maiden were thanked for bestowing a soul on the baby. After that, everyone else dropped by."

"Think in specifics," Nick persisted.

"Your uncle Thomas was here briefly with his girlfriend, Theresa Redwing. All the ranch hands came, too, even recent part-time help like Daniel Hawk."

"I thought Daniel worked at the Cultural Center," Nick said.

Jake nodded. "Here in the mornings, there in the afternoons." He paused. "Our list of guests that day is almost endless. Martin, of course, was here, and so was Mrs. Chino. Our family lawyer came, the Kormans, Samuel Runningwater, some of our best clients from Santa Fe, the Winter Chief and the Summer Chief. I really think that everyone from the pueblo or connected to it visited that day at one time or another."

Nick weighed the information then, at last, spoke. "As far as I'm concerned, no matter how many came, our uncle should be at the top of our suspect list. Thomas admitted to us months ago that he'd been sneaking into the house for years when our father wasn't around and searched every room, hoping to find that diary. He'd intended to use it to get leverage over people. In my opinion, it's very possible he's gone back to his old tricks."

"Let's go over there and pay him a visit. Knowing

you're a cop should rattle him, even if nothing else does,'' Jake said.

"Slow down, Jake. We don't want to go in there like gangbusters, tip our hand, and let him know the diary's missing. Although we have to know if he's got the diary, we also have to be careful not to give him any more information. If he discovers the diary's gone, even if he didn't take it, he could play on people's fears who have secrets they want to keep hidden. Let's think this through before we take any action.''

"We'll think on the way,'' Jake said, grabbing his keys from the desk. "You always move too slow, brother.'' He gave Annie a quick kiss, and Noelle a tiny peck on her forehead.

"And you always rush out, leading with your chin. That's why it ends up on the ground so often.'' Nick glanced at Martin, who just shook his head, knowing that neither brother would win this perpetual competition.

They took Jake's truck, Nick having decided to keep his presence as unofficial as possible, despite Jake's protests.

As Jake drove past a familiar tree-lined path that led seemingly nowhere, Nick's thoughts drifted to Eden. There was an old house down that lane that had been gutted by a fire decades ago. These days he saw it as nothing more than a burned-out shell, but back then, meeting with Eden there had made it seem like high adventure.

Relationships hadn't seemed so complicated in those days and he'd moved faster then, too often tripping over his heart. But nothing had been more important to him than stealing time to be with his girl. It had been a time of discovery, a time of first love. But those days were gone.

"What's got you so distracted?'' Jake asked.

Nick shook his head. "The past haunts me,'' he said cryptically, then continued. "But let's stay on track here,'' he added, suddenly all business. "Do you, by any chance, know if Thomas has a job these days? If he's pressed for cash, then that would give him a motive for stealing the diary. He's always seen it as an easy way to make money."

"He's always pressed for cash," Jake answered. "What I'd like to do is search his house from top to bottom. If we do, I'd be willing to bet we'd find that diary."

"Forget it, Jake. Legally we can't do that. We have nothing to stand on since we have no actual evidence against him."

"Sure we do," Jake insisted. "His lousy track record counts for something. He admitted right in front of Captain Mora once that he'd broken into our home many times while our father was still alive. I should have pressed charges then, but I didn't. His past tells us exactly what he's capable of doing."

"Logical, but not legal. We need facts, not a history lesson."

"How about an unofficial search, then, like he did at our house? You keep him busy outside and I'll go in and look around. Even if he catches us, he won't do anything about it. He owes us and he knows it."

"*Think,* Jake. Don't tip your hand so easily. If we're careful, we can find out if Thomas has been sneaking into the ranch house again without ever letting him know anything's missing."

"All right," Jake said. "But I really like an in-your-face type of confrontation a lot better. It's more satisfying."

Nick grinned. Jake may have become a family man with responsibilities, but certain things never changed. Trying to divert some of Jake's compressed energy, he brought up the subject of the letter Eden's grandmother had written her.

"According to that, 'Tall Shadow' was connected to the

crime which resulted in her parents' death," Nick said. "As you know, Tall Shadow was Dad's nickname, and, if that's true, our father ruined an entire family. Eden's mom and dad are dead, but Eden is still paying for what happened, so our family could owe her big time."

"*If* it's true," Jake repeated. "And I really doubt that. Our father was many things, but no way I'm going to believe he was party to the theft of sacred items or the framing of an innocent woman. That just wasn't his style. He was like me, an in-your-face fighter."

"So you think I should let this drop?" Nick asked.

"Yeah, for now. Let's see how things develop. Unlike this matter of the diary, it doesn't require immediate action."

"Agreed."

A short time later they pulled up in front of their uncle's home. Thomas Ray had lived in the stucco and wood frame house for the past thirty years. There was a wire fence around the property and a sagging wooden gate that led to the backyard.

As the twin brothers stepped up onto the porch, a strong breeze blew the front door open a few inches. Nick stopped and glanced around, holding out his hand to signal Jake to remain still. "His truck's not here, so why's that door open? Our people generally don't use locks, but they do close doors." He peeked through the foot-wide opening into the house.

"Maybe he's still around. The fact that his truck's not here doesn't mean anything. His pickup's long past a stop at the junkyard. It could be over at Ralph's gas station getting its engine rebuilt, or broken down between here and Santa Fe."

"Point taken. Now hang back," Nick said, pushing the

door open completely. "If he's around, and this door's open, something's wrong."

Jake went inside first, despite Nick's warning. Cursing, Nick rushed in after him, hoping his brother wasn't about to confront a burglar.

"Jake, what the hell are you doing? You can't burst inside someone's home like this."

"Chill out. It isn't like we're breaking and entering." Jake bumped into a low table and a small clay pot fell to the floor, shattering into several pieces. "Well, okay, now it's entering and breaking. But we're here, so let's look around."

"This wouldn't be a legal search," Nick snapped. "It's a waste of time."

"Are you one hundred percent certain that our uncle isn't in trouble? The door swinging wide open by itself is enough to indicate suspicious circumstances. We're here, worried about a family member. You're not on duty now, are you?"

"Who do you expect to sell that load of garbage to? Captain Mora wouldn't swallow it."

"Fine, but let's look around anyway. We owe it to ourselves."

"You don't get it, do you? It's *illegal,* and I'm a cop. I don't want to arrest my own idiot brother."

"I'll tell you what. Go out back and see if our uncle is around the yard, maybe chopping wood or pulling weeds."

Nick's expression hardened. "I'm going to give you just the time it'll take me to go through the house and make sure there's no signs of trouble here," he snapped. "Then we both leave."

"That's the spirit. I'll work fast, and you work slowly. And if we happen to see the diary, we'll take it back."

"I didn't hear that," Nick said. Seeing the pot shards on

the floor, he stopped and picked them up. "No sense in advertising the fact that we were here," he said, then added, "At least this is something that was stolen from us originally. I remember seeing it at our house after Dad was killed, and I know neither of us gave it to Thomas."

Jake was already in the single bedroom searching by the time Nick threw all the ceramic fragments into the trash.

Several minutes later, Jake met his brother by the door. "He's only got a few pieces of furniture. I opened every drawer. The closets were full of clothes and cardboard boxes of stuff, but there was no diary. If it's here, it's too well hidden for us to find easily."

Nick looked around with a scowl. "Come on. We're wasting time." He led the way back to the truck.

Hearing his cell phone ring, Nick grabbed it from his pocket and flipped it open. He listened, then answered. "I'm on my way."

Nick glanced over at his brother. "There's trouble at the school. The principal reported someone watching the kids from inside a hedge behind the basketball court. There's a big cornfield just beyond the school grounds, so that's probably how he got in close. No one else is available so I'm responding to the call. Give me a ride over there, will you?"

"Sure thing." Jake pressed down on the accelerator. "Any ideas what that could be about?"

Nick nodded. "About two dozen pueblo kids will be initiated into the tribe soon. Anthropologists from area universities have been dying to find out what goes on during that ritual, so when they hear one's about to take place, they start nosing around."

Jake smiled. "Remember when it was our turn to be initiated? All the girls got off easy, but it was different for us."

"My knees were shaking by the time they turned to us and asked us if we *really* wanted to be finished," Nick answered.

"Then we had to promise never to reveal what went on because if all our ceremonies were made public, they'd lose their power, and our people wouldn't have the protection of our gods," Jake said.

"Most of the anthropologists have never respected that. They want to record and analyze everything. So they keep coming. Initiation rites aren't held every year, but the grad students working on a thesis or trying to make a name for themselves somehow always manage to find out when one's about due. That's quite a feat in itself, considering that even the kids don't know when it's supposed to happen."

"You know, I never thought I'd say this, but I can't wait until Noelle goes through the initiation rite. I like the feeling it gives me when I think that my daughter will continue the traditions that were important to me when I was growing up. It's a legacy that goes beyond a simple inheritance."

Nick said nothing. His brother had his family and, because of them, he'd always have a reason to look to the future.

But Nick had taken another road. He'd never wanted a family or kids. Yet now that he only had himself to worry about, he was starting to see that a man needed more in his life to feel complete.

Nick pushed those thoughts away. This wasn't the time to think about such things. He was a cop and there was work to do.

Chapter Four

Eden stopped by the wooden cubbyholes on the office wall that served as teachers' mailboxes, and pulled out all the envelopes, memos and student worksheets that had been crammed inside the small enclosure labeled with her name. She sorted everything on the way back to her classroom, then sat down at her oak teacher's desk and began to read through the paperwork.

A legal-size envelope with her name and the school address handwritten in pencil caught her eye. There was no return address on the letter, which had been postmarked yesterday.

Eden opened it, her hands shaking. As she read the short note contained inside, her stomach sank. It was getting all too familiar.

THIS PUEBLO IS ALL WE HAVE LEFT. YOU ARE HALF-WHITE AND SHOULDN'T BE LIVING HERE. THE POLICE CAN'T HELP YOU. LEAVE NOW BEFORE THINGS GET WORSE.

The unsigned note, in block letters, stunned her because a new dimension had been added to the note—a threat. She sat immobile, heart beating overtime, then stuffed the envelope into her pocket and rushed to the teachers' phone in the book room. Although the note hadn't mentioned her son, she had to make sure Christopher was safe. When Mrs. Chino, who ran a day-care center out of her home during the week, assured her that Christopher was fine, Eden finally relaxed.

Lost in thought, she returned to her classroom, wondering how to deal with the person who was trying to drive her off pueblo land. When she'd renewed her search for the truth, her main goal had been to clear her family's name so that her son would grow up feeling pride, not shame in their family. She'd never expected to have to fight another battle as well.

As her sixth-grade students came into the room, she focused on the class. She'd just started taking attendance when an office secretary appeared with a cryptic note from Mr. Puye, their principal.

Students are to be kept in the classrooms. A stranger has been seen on campus. Lock your doors as a precaution and stay alert. The police have been called.

Eden, who always kept her classroom doors locked anyway, walked to the window and tried to get a better look. A shadowy figure was partially visible behind the large hedge, but Mr. Puye was already walking in that direction.

Then a pickup pulled up, and two men jumped out of the cab. She recognized Nick and Jake. With Nick leading the way, they raced around the hedge and into the tall cornfield beyond the school grounds. The men disappeared quickly from sight and, as she looked back at the hedge, she noticed the shadow was gone.

Eden held her breath, waiting for another glimpse of Nick. He hadn't even thought to hesitate before entering the cornfield to track down the intruder. His dedication to duty was absolute. A man who possessed loyalty like his was just the kind of ally she and Christopher needed, but she wouldn't risk letting Nick have a hold on her life again.

An eternity later, or so it seemed, Nick and Jake emerged from the end of the cornfield. They were alone. The person hiding in the hedge had either escaped or been allowed to leave.

The principal gave them the "all clear" as the period ended. Eden dismissed her class for lunch and went to the office. After reading that last note, she knew the game had changed, and the possibility that the intruder may have actually been watching her was frightening. Of course it was also quite possible that this was an unrelated incident. What she needed now was enough information to settle the question, if only in her own mind.

As she entered the office, everyone was talking about what had happened. The consensus seemed to be that the upcoming initiation rite was attracting off-pueblo intruders. It seemed a reasonable assumption, but an unproven theory didn't quiet her fears as completely as she would have liked.

Hearing that Deputy Black Raven was still on campus, she lingered in the office, hoping to see him. She tried to tell herself that it was just because the intruder had rattled her and he was a cop, but deep down she knew it was more than that.

Moments later Nick strode into the office. His loose-legged stride was all masculine boldness and confidence. Women watched him out of the corners of their eyes, and exchanged wistful smiles when he wasn't looking.

Eden was pleased when Nick found her immediately

among all the staff and gave her a heart-stopping smile. Fires suddenly danced over her skin and an excitement as primitive as the desert itself lit up the air.

Nick walked over and placed a strong hand on her shoulder. "I was hoping to catch you." As he searched her face, Eden felt the full force of the black eyes that had always been able to see deep into her soul. "What's wrong?" he asked quietly.

She wanted to deny that anything was, but the words were all lodged in the back of her throat.

"Talk to me."

His voice caressed her, running down her jagged nerves like molten wax that both soothed and burned. Though several staff members remained in the room, as she looked into his eyes it was as if all the others had faded back into the dim recesses of another reality, and they were the only two people there.

"I'm okay," she said, her voice too shaky to pass as natural. "Really."

"No, you're not," he said firmly. "You can't fool a man who knows you in all the ways I have," he whispered discreetly.

Her breath caught. Images of another time and place filled her mind and she remembered the many layers of desire she'd discovered in his arms.

Hearing the school telephone ring, Eden quickly focused on the present. Many years ago she'd sworn she'd never lean on anyone like her mother had on her father. And yet, after hearing Nick's soft words she'd nearly turned her back on everything life had taught her. She'd have to be much more careful.

"I'm sorry, Nick. I have to go get my gradebook and some student papers before lunch is over," she said, taking a step away.

He was about to say something when Mr. Puye came out and caught his eye. As he excused himself and accompanied the principal into his office, Nick turned his head for one last look at her.

She knew then that he'd be coming around to her home later to finish the conversation. Nick never left any challenge unanswered.

EDEN REACHED into her pocket and clasped the note she'd received earlier today, wondering what she should do. If news that she'd been receiving warning notes got out, it was possible she'd be asked to resign until after the matter was settled.

Not that she would. She couldn't afford it, not with Christopher to support. But the last thing she needed was another complication.

Thoughts swirled like hungry buzzards in her head, colliding with each other, and undermining her courage. Back in her room a moment later, Eden collected her belongings and walked out of the building. She only taught half days, though if things went the way she hoped, next semester she'd be teaching full-time.

As she reached the fence at the end of the school grounds, Eden saw Nick parked farther down the road under the shade of an old cottonwood. Seeing her, he got out of his department vehicle and walked to meet her.

"We have to talk, Eden."

He stood proud and tall in his tan uniform, his eyes alert and focused, like a warrior of old. Nick was a living, breathing temptation on every imaginable level.

"I'm sorry, Nick, but I've got to stop by the post office to buy some postcards for a class project, then go pick up Christopher."

"No problem. I'll give you a ride and we'll talk on the way."

It hadn't been an invitation, but rather an order, and she bristled at his tone. "No thanks, officer. I'm walking."

Unexpectedly, Nick grinned. "Some things never change. You still hate having anyone tell you what to do."

His smile was infectious, but Eden didn't want to encourage him, so she forced her expression to remain stern. "That's right. Now please go away."

"You know I won't do that," he answered calmly. "You need my help and I need to maintain the peace here on the pueblo. That gives us common ground. Instead of fighting each other, we should work together."

Eden considered his offer then nodded. "I'm stuck in a difficult situation, Nick. I came here searching for answers about my family's past, but someone seems dead set on running me off this pueblo. If the school finds out that I'm being threatened, they can really make things difficult for me. Can you find the person harassing me and quietly get them off my back so I can finish what I came here to do?" She handed him the note she'd received earlier. "I found this in my mailbox this morning when I came in."

He scanned it quickly. "You mentioned getting notes before. When did you get the first one?"

"I began to feel uneasy, like I was being watched, just a few days after I moved in. The notes started right after that. I think it may be the work of someone my grandmother called 'Tall Shadow,' but I haven't been able to find out who he is yet." Eden told him about her grandmother's letter, but suspected from the look in his eyes that he'd already seen it. "This man may have been behind everything that happened to my family. It's possible that he's the one sending the notes now."

Nick remained silent for several long moments as they

got underway. "Eden, I understand all about family loyalties, believe me. And we'll get to the truth. But I have to tell you, no one by the nickname Tall Shadow lives here now. I'd know."

"I'm looking into a twenty-year-old case, and people come and go. I know that. But I can't back off and move away, Nick. My son deserves a mom who has the courage to do what's right."

"This is my fight, too, whether you believe it or not," he said, then as if unwilling to leave it up to interpretation, added, "We have the same goal and that makes us allies."

A swift, secret fire burned through Eden, but she fought to keep her thinking clear. They would be allies because she had no other recourse, but her only future, her only goal, was to give Christopher the kind of secure, loving home she'd always wanted but never had. Nick was her past, but Christopher's future was in her hands.

NICK DROVE AWAY from the Plaza, lost in thought and trying to ignore the sweet scent of the woman beside him. He had a real bad feeling about this business. The note Eden had received worried him far more than he'd let on. The implied threat was there, and could mean almost anything. To make things even worse, despite the fact that Eden had told him about the contents of her grandmother's letter, he was dead certain she was still holding back about something.

That wasn't surprising, of course. He was holding out on her, too. Neither of them had any reason to trust the other. The entire history of their relationship was one of crushed hopes and dreams. The past had left too many scars.

Nick tried to focus on his job. He needed to keep a sharp lookout for trespassers who might be trying to sneak onto the pueblo to document Tewa rites.

A few hundred yards from the rural post office, he caught a glimpse of several people gathered below in a small, brush-lined arroyo. It was deep enough to hide all but the tops of their heads.

"Eden, there's something going on down there I have to check out. Stay in the unit until I get back."

"What is it?"

"I don't know, maybe a fight. Lock the doors when I get out and stay inside, okay?"

Nick left the gravel road and parked the vehicle behind a line of junipers. After reporting his position to the dispatcher, he slipped out of the Jeep and crept forward noiselessly toward the scene of activity.

It wasn't long before he had a clear view. Two men were holding his uncle Thomas by the arms as the third punched him repeatedly. The broad-shouldered pueblo men had slicked-down hair, wore bolo ties, snake-skin boots, and had on fancy western-cut shirts. That was practically a uniform for the casino muscle he'd seen a few times. Ever since legal gambling establishments had opened on several nearby pueblos, crime had been on the rise.

Nick stepped out into the open, resting his hand on the butt of his pistol. "That's enough," he yelled out. "Let the man go."

The goon who'd been hitting Thomas spun around. Seeing Nick was a cop, he sucker-punched Thomas one more time in the gut, and then took off running with his pals.

The sound of a door slamming caused Nick to glance back. Eden was walking in his direction, pretending to talk to another officer just out of view. Nick realized she was trying to back him up by making it appear that he wasn't alone. He had to smile. That was the Eden he knew. She could always be counted on to help someone in trouble.

Nick went to his uncle's side and slowly helped him up.

Thomas seemed dazed, but he recognized Nick. Glancing across the arroyo, Nick saw that the men who'd assaulted Thomas had already reached an SUV parked on the other side. He'd never catch up to them now.

"Hey, nephew," Thomas managed, trying to crack a smile as he struggled to catch his breath. "And Eden. When did you join the force?"

Nick saw Eden approach, carrying his nightstick like a baseball bat. "I thought you were going to stay in the unit where you'd be safer," Nick said harshly.

Knowing she'd put herself at risk to help him made him realize that she still cared about him. But the undeniable fact that the knowledge pleased him, was disturbing in itself. If there were two people in the world who were better off without each other, it was Eden and him. "What if they'd been carrying guns? Did you think of that?" he added.

"Admit it, Nick. I helped out a lot," she said with a tiny smile and handed him the night stick. "Those thugs punching your uncle took off right away when they thought another officer or two were coming to help you."

"It could have backfired," Nick grumbled, then turned to his uncle. "Who sent the muscle? I want some names," he clipped. "What casino are they from?"

"I'm not pressing charges, so you're wasting your time."

"If I'm right, those aren't the kind of men who just fade away. They'll be back, and next time I may not be around to rescue your butt."

Thomas nodded slowly, shaking off Nick's helping hands. "I didn't think they'd come looking for me, that's all."

"You owe them money?"

Thomas shrugged. "When didn't I owe somebody

money? Don't worry about it. I'll find my own way out of this.''

''I don't think it'll be that easy. Once they've got their hooks into you, they don't like to let go.''

''True, true,'' Thomas said. ''But I'll come up with the cash somehow. I always have an ace up my sleeve, nephew. You must know that by now.''

He had a gut feeling his uncle was referring to the diary, but if that were the case, Thomas had a few surprises coming. Neither he nor Jake would ever pay a ransom for that diary, or allow themselves to be blackmailed like their father had been. And the pueblo residents whose secrets were in that journal were probably less able to pay blackmail than either him or Jake.

''A funny thing can happen when you have a card up your sleeve,'' Nick warned slowly. ''It can fall out onto the table anytime and, once people know you for what you are, you'll suddenly find that there's no place to hide. Trouble will find you no matter where you go.''

Chapter Five

Eden took a tissue from a small packet and began to dab a cut above Thomas's eyebrow.

Thomas seemed content to accept Eden's care, but Nick knew what was going through his mind. His uncle was weighing his options and looking for a way to avoid answering questions.

"Have you been by the ranch lately?" Nick asked. He took his uncle's arm as Eden finished, and led him toward the tribal vehicle.

Thomas slowed down imperceptibly, then matched Nick's pace again. "Why that particular question?" Thomas gave Nick a speculative glance and, as Nick opened the rear door of the tribal unit, got inside.

Thomas hadn't denied it. More than ever, Nick suspected that Thomas had the diary. Thomas wouldn't have been so cagey if he hadn't had something to hide.

"I owe you one, nephew, and Eden, too," he said as they got underway. "Things could have gone very badly for me in that arroyo if you hadn't come along. So tell me straight out what I can do to repay you."

As they reached the developed area of the pueblo, Nick glanced back at Thomas. His face had been bruised in several places and his left eye was starting to swell shut, but he'd be okay. "What I can always use from you, uncle, is information."

Thomas wiped his face clean with a handkerchief and straightened his shirt. When they entered the Plaza, he gestured toward the soda machine in front of the Cultural Center. "Let's stop there. You can buy your old uncle something cold to drink, and we'll talk."

Nick pulled into an empty parking space, parked, then led the way to the covered porch by the Center. Placing several quarters in the machine, he pulled out three cans of soda, tossed one to his uncle and handed another to Eden. "Tell me, Uncle, did you come to my niece's naming ritual last month? It was a big day for our family, but I don't remember running into you then."

Thomas smiled. "Yes, I was there with Theresa." He glanced over at Eden, then lapsed into a lengthy silence.

Eden stood. "I'm going to go to the trading post across the street and see if I can pick up the postcards for my class's project there."

Nick nodded, grateful that she'd sensed he and his uncle needed a few minutes alone.

As Eden walked away, Nick continued. "Tell me, did you get a chance to…look around the place now that Jake's family has taken it over? Curiosity and old habits can be a powerful incentive."

Thomas shook his head. "The past is over and done with. I'm not much interested in Black Raven Ranch these days."

"It still holds the things that defined your sister—our mother."

"If you're talking about her art, I agree. But if you mean the diary…" He shook his head. "That should have been destroyed a long time ago—burned to a crisp and the ashes strewn into the wind—if you ask me. But I guess you and

Jake couldn't bring yourselves to do that.'' He suddenly stopped speaking, studied Nick's face, then exhaled softly. "It's missing again, isn't it?'' The question was rhetorical. "You boys should have expected that to happen, you know. But don't come looking to me. I haven't got it. You two should keep better track of that thing.''

His response had seemed candid and not at all what Nick had expected. Now he wasn't so sure that his uncle had it. Then again, his uncle had survived for decades conning others. "That diary is our property. It's a record of our mother's past, and belongs with me and my brother.''

"Tell me something, nephew. Did you ever really read it?''

Nick hesitated, unwilling to lie but not wanting to give his uncle any more information. Instead, he glanced over at Eden who was crossing the street on her way back.

"Yeah, that's what I thought,'' he said, accurately interpreting Nick's silence. "Take my advice. Don't. Sometimes it's better not to disturb the past.''

Seeing the way Nick was watching Eden, Thomas smiled. "She's a real sharp lady, but she's another one who needs to learn that same lesson. Eden just came back, and already that old issue about half whites living on the pueblo is creating a stir. Then, there's the matter of those ceremonial objects that her parents are accused of taking. If she's come here looking for the truth about that crime, she's in for a few surprises. I doubt those things will ever turn up. And, to make things worse, she may not be able to live with what she uncovers, or the price it'll exact.''

"Just what do you know about Eden and her past?'' Nick asked.

Thomas slowly grinned. "So you're in love with her again after all these years. Or did you ever stop loving her in the first place?''

Nick's face became as neutral as he could manage. His uncle was an old poker player and could read every nuance in his expression. He'd have to be more careful. "There's nothing between Eden and me. We've just been trying to catch whoever has been harassing her."

Thomas shook his head. "Don't kid a kidder, nephew." He smiled at Eden as she came back and joined them.

Eden gave Thomas a worried look. "Are you going to be okay? You look like they punched you pretty hard."

"I've taken worse." Thomas looked at Nick, then back at Eden. "It's great to see you two together again. I remember when you'd both sneak off so you could be alone down by the river. Wasn't your favorite meeting place by that big old cottonwood?"

Eden's face turned crimson. "How did you know that? We were always so careful."

"I saw you two there a few times after school, but I never said anything because I thought you were good for each other." He looked directly at Eden and held her gaze. "I still do. You have a history together, and that binds you in its own way."

Eden froze, barely breathing.

Nick glanced at her, sensing her fear, but not understanding why she was afraid. There was so much he didn't know about her. And, right now, he just couldn't figure out why she felt so threatened by Thomas.

"Your mother, Isabel, and Nick's mother, Saya, were very good friends," Thomas said. "You two were just kids then, but I remember overhearing them making plans to fix you up someday."

"Did my father know about that?" Nick asked, surprised.

"No way. Saya's friendship with Isabel irritated him to no end because he seriously believed that no pueblo man or woman should ever marry outside the tribe. He really disapproved of Eden on principle, and that's why he tried to so hard to discourage you from dating her when you were both in high school. He changed a lot in his last few years, but back then he drew a hard line."

"I knew that Nick's dad didn't approve of my friendship with his son, but I never could blame him for wanting what he thought was the best for Nick," Eden said.

"But now you want to prove that you're as good as anyone else here," Thomas observed. "I can understand that, but consider everything carefully before you act. If you insist on digging up the past, you may uncover more than the secrets you were after."

"My parents were innocent. They didn't deserve what they got. I realize I can't change what happened to them, but I can affect the legacy I'll be leaving for my son. Because of him, I'm going to do whatever it takes to clear my family's name."

"If you're wrong about your parents' innocence, you'll lose far more than a reputation," Thomas said, shaking his head.

"What do you mean?" For the first time, Eden's voice held a trace of uncertainty.

"If you uncover proof that your parents did commit a crime against the tribe instead of proving them innocent, the house you're living in will be taken away from you immediately, and both you and your son will be banned from the pueblo forever. Remember that this has nothing to do with white man's laws. It's all about our way of doing things. You will be held accountable for what your parents did. The reason your father fought so hard to clear his wife was because he knew they would have lost their land and the right to live here if he didn't. He was fighting for more than justice. He was fighting for everything he held dear."

Eden paled. "My parents were framed and the truth needs to come out."

"Are you prepared to gamble that the ones who framed them won't also frame you?" Thomas took a final swallow of his soda, and set the empty can down on the table with a flourish.

Eden stared at the man's battered face, this time unable to reply.

Nick knew his uncle's words had rattled her badly, but he'd told her the truth. Although he wanted to help Eden, he didn't know how. Deep in thought, he looked at an indeterminate spot across the way and saw four people approaching, heading for the soda machine.

Thomas turned around and followed Nick's line of vision. "That's one Anglo family who has been among us as far back as I can remember. Marc Korman is now retired, but his wife, Rita, is the Cultural Center's buyer these days. Since she's Anglo, the tribe felt she could select pieces from local artisans without prejudice, or at least equal prejudice. The young one is Patrick, their son. He's the bookkeeper for the Cultural Center these days. The one who looks like an underweight pro-wrestler is Rita's brother, Wayne. He hangs around here a lot. If memory serves me right, the elder Kormans were working at the Cultural Center back when the artifacts were stolen. They were hired initially because their knowledge of art was very extensive and many thought that, back then, Anglo tourists would prefer to deal with other Anglos."

"I spoke to them last week and they made it clear to me that they believe my mother was the thief. But, for all I know, *they* were the thieves," Eden said quietly, still not turning around. "I made the mistake of talking to them together. If I had spoken to each one alone, I might have been able to learn if their stories didn't match up."

Nick looked at the four pensively. Except for Wayne Johnson, who was dressed in slacks and a tight-fitting knit shirt to show off his muscles, they were dressed like wealthy tourists, with colorful western shirts and denim pants. Rita wore a velveteen skirt and several pieces of turquoise and silver jewelry.

"Just walking advertisements for pueblo craftsmen, aren't they?" Thomas muttered. "My lady friend Theresa Redwing is a clerk at the Center. She says the Kormans are pretty good workers, for non-Indians." He laughed at his own joke.

A few minutes later, after the four had left, Eden finally relaxed. "The Kormans may have been the ones who killed my parents, or they may know who did, so I'm going to watch my step around them."

"Is it possible that my mother's diary could help Eden learn something about her own mother, something that could help her now?" Nick asked Thomas.

"Your mother kept a diary?" Eden asked.

"Yes, but it's missing. We're trying to find it now."

"The diary may help. But it's also likely she could end up finding out other things she would have been better off not knowing," Thomas answered cryptically. He picked up his soda can, crushed it in his grip, then tossed it into the nearby trash barrel. "We're even now, nephew. You saved my hide and, whether or not you realize it, I've just done the same for you and Eden."

As his uncle walked away, Nick muttered a curse. "I hate the games he plays. He knows a lot more, I'm sure of it. I just wish he'd come straight out with the truth."

"Don't be so hard on Thomas, Nick. Everyone has secrets. Even you."

Her words had cut close. He hadn't told her who Tall Shadow was. "Just remember one thing, Eden. I'm on the side of justice, and that's why I'll always be a good ally for you.''

Like her, he was now in a battle to clear his family and there was little he could promise her except that.

AFTER ARRIVING at Mrs. Chino's home, Eden walked through the always unlocked front door. Christopher, playing on a large blanket, let out a yell of excitement the second he saw her.

Eden smiled at Mrs. Chino, who was rocking another child in her arms, then walked over and picked up her son. ''I missed you, Christopher! Did you have a great day?''

The baby smiled, focusing on her face in a way that made all her cares instantly fade away.

Then Christopher looked at Nick. ''Da-da-da-da.''

Eden froze, her breath catching in her throat.

Nick winked at Eden, then scooped the baby from her arms and tickled him gently in the belly. Christopher laughed, enjoying the attention.

Eden watched, amazed at how Christopher had taken to Nick. Perhaps the baby knew instinctively what she'd never voiced to anyone. But Chris's paternity was one secret she intended to keep buried until everything was settled. If she and her child were barred from the pueblo, knowing Chris was his son would only add another level of heartache and confusion to Nick, who'd never wanted children at all.

Eventually he would have to know. She couldn't keep the truth from him forever. But the more time passed, the more complicated things got and the harder it became to envision the day when she'd finally tell him.

Saying goodbye to Mrs. Chino, they secured the baby's car seat in the back, then drove to her home.

''Tell me about Christopher's father,'' he said, his voice taut. ''Did you love him?''

Eden felt the words lodge at her throat. "Yes, I loved him. But in the ways that mattered most we were too different to make it work. Simply put, he didn't want anything to bind him and Christopher. The responsibility of a son was more than he could accept. We parted company," she said finally. "But that's a chapter of my life that's closed. My son and I are doing fine."

"Did you choose him over me because you wanted kids?" His eyes darkened and his hands clenched into fists around the steering wheel.

"I didn't plan Christopher, but I never saw myself as childless forever," Eden said, measuring her words carefully. She didn't want to lie, but she didn't want to give away her secret, either.

"So the answer is yes?" he pressed.

"Partly. I made a hard decision back then, Nick, based on what my heart was telling me. That's all I can say."

"I won't ask again."

She could feel his anger, and his sense of betrayal. She wanted to tell him the truth, but it wouldn't have helped anything. He still didn't want kids. That hadn't changed. It was one thing to play with a baby and quite another to take on the responsibility for one.

And the truth was that even if he knew and wanted to take part in her baby's life, she would do everything in her power to retain full custody of Christopher. She wanted more for her son than a father who was a cop. She knew first-hand all the insecurities that came from loving someone who courted danger for a living. A cop was the first on the scene, and with that knowledge came an agonizing daily uncertainty for his family. It was even harder on a child, more so than people ever suspected, and she would never put Christopher through that.

She brought her thoughts back to the present knowing

that it was what they both needed to concentrate on now. "Nick, there's something I need to ask you about the intruder at school," she said. "Everyone thought it was an Anglo spying to get the scoop on our upcoming rites. But is it possible the man was there to keep an eye on me instead?"

Nick considered it. "If the guy harassing you is out to make you feel unsafe on the pueblo, that would certainly be one way to do it. But that's the act of a stalker. If he continues to take chances, it won't be long before he's caught. He's lucky nobody was able to get a good look at him today."

"I just wish I knew where the artifacts were hidden. If I could prove my worth to the tribe by finding and returning those ritual objects, the ones who oppose having me live here might change their minds. Somehow I've got to make everyone see that I'm not here to take away the land or the culture. I'm here to give back what was lost, and bring the truth to light if I can."

Minutes later they reached Eden's home. Nick followed her in, then stood at the side window looking outside. "That trail may be overgrown with weeds right now, but it still leads to Black Raven Ranch. Don't ever forget that. If you ever need help, my family's not far."

Sadly she remembered the way it had been between them once. As kids they'd often sneaked out and met at the halfway point between their houses. She'd had her first taste of passion alone with him in that remote, peaceful spot.

As Christopher began to fuss, Eden quickly shifted her attention to him. "I think he's ready for dinner."

"I better go," Nick said. "I'll have to turn in a report on what happened with my uncle today."

"Thanks for the ride home."

Eden heard him leave and close the door behind him.

Nick had been her whole world once, but those days were gone forever. He had a new life here as a cop and his allegiance was to the pueblo he served. The three of them would never be a real family and the sooner she accepted that deep down in her heart, the better off they'd all be.

Chapter Six

The following afternoon, Eden was sitting alone at her usual picnic table near the Plaza when she saw Nick approaching. She waved, taking her hand off the stack of papers she was grading, when suddenly a gust of wind swirled around her. Her papers flew into the air, caught up by the miniature whirlwind.

Nick hurried to help her and snagged one sheet by leaning over and pinning it to the tree behind her.

Eden held her breath as they found themselves with their lips inches from each other's. In vain, she tried to suppress the shiver that coursed up her spine as she felt his warm, moist breath caress her mouth.

"Thanks for your help," she said unsteadily, ducking beneath his arm and moving away. Her hands were trembling as she gathered up the rest of the papers. "What brings you here in the middle of the day?" she asked, working hard to keep her voice smooth.

"We're working this case together, Eden, and that means staying in close touch."

His words teased her imagination, making her cheeks flush. "What we really need to come up with is a plan of action," she said, trying to regain her composure before he noticed.

"Agreed," Nick said crisply. "Here's the way I see it. We have two things to accomplish. I have to figure out who wants you off pueblo land badly enough to break the law. And your priority is to find the stolen artifacts and clear your parents' name. So you'll need to keep an eye on certain people, while I keep an eye on you." He paused, gathering his thoughts, then continued. "Over here you have a clear view of the Cultural Center, and from what I can see, they have lunch around the same time you do. It makes sense for you to do what you're doing and watch the people there. See who comes and goes, and who meets with whom."

"That's what I figured," she said. "Traditionally there have been so few job options around here that many of the Center's employees have been there practically forever. There's Theresa Redwing, sitting with your uncle under that tree," she said gesturing. "I'd say she's Thomas's girl-friend, from the looks of it. Daniel Hawk, who I believe works at your ranch in the mornings, is also here now," she said, pointing to a shady area filled with pines. "He's eating his lunch in his pickup. And, of course there are the Kormans—Marc, Rita and her brother Wayne Johnson, all of whom you must have walked past on the way over here. Wayne seems to be very close to his sister, because he's here almost every day around lunch, even though he doesn't work on the pueblo. Patrick was with them a little while ago, but I saw him get a call on his cell phone, then go back inside."

"What about Samuel Runningwater?" Nick asked. "Does he take a different lunch hour or have you seen him around?"

"I've been having my lunch here for close to two weeks now, and I can tell you that it's a lot harder keeping tabs on him. He comes and goes a lot and, despite being the director, doesn't seem to be involved that much with the Center. From what I hear, he's thinking of running for pueblo governor, and spends a lot of time walking around the pueblo, lobbying for votes."

Hearing footsteps behind her, she saw Bobby, one of her students, running after a football that had just bounced off his fingertips. Quickly she took a step back, widening the distance between her and Nick. Kids were very perceptive, and the last thing she needed was gossip to start up about Nick and her.

Eden deliberately returned to her chicken burrito and the papers she was grading. "I usually try to stick around here until all the Cultural Center employees go back to work. Then I'll walk or drive by from time to time to see if anything is happening."

Seeing another tribal unit pulling up at one of the parking barriers, Nick stood up. "There's Torres. Let's keep what we've discussed to ourselves," he warned as the young cop approached.

"Don't you trust him?" she asked, her tone whisper soft.

"He seems like an honest cop, but I think he wants to be captain so badly that he tries to take part in every investigation that concerns the PD. I've discussed this with him before. Our department is small, but that doesn't mean we should all be attached at the hip. He does have seniority, but I take my orders from Mora, not him." Nick didn't like Torres. There was just something about the guy that bugged him. He really wasn't sure if it was his imagination or not, but the man always seemed to be popping up no matter where Nick happened to be.

Torres was small in stature, but what he lacked for in size he made up for with intensity. His eyes had a predatory look, like a prairie hawk watching for a fat cottontail. There were hard lines around his face that gave him a stern, imposing countenance.

"Hey, Torres. What's up? You need me to back you up on something?"

Torres shook his head, looking almost bored as he glanced around. It was meant to look casual, but Nick knew that beneath the surface this man didn't do anything unless it was part of his master plan.

"I came to offer you two my help. I heard you're having problems here at the pueblo, Miss Maes, and as long as you're allowed to live here, you're under the protection of our department."

"I appreciate your concern, but I'm fine," Eden said, glancing over at Nick.

"Just keep your eyes and ears open, Torres. Let's see if we can find out who's been trying to run her off." Nick faced the other deputy squarely.

Torres stepped around Nick, and spoke to Eden. "I realize that you're in a very unpleasant situation," Torres said bluntly. "A lot of our parents disapproved of your father's marriage to a white woman, and as a half white, you haven't exactly been welcomed with open arms. Of course, your family's history makes you even less popular."

"If you're trying to cheer her up, you're failing," Nick growled, crossing his arms across his chest.

"I'm just stating the facts," Torres said. "You're going to need some protection, Miss Maes. Of course, the safest thing for you would be to find a place to live *off* pueblo land, but if you choose not to, then I can at least try to be around to put a stop to any harassment before it gets ugly." He paused then added, "Of course I'm not speaking as a citizen of this pueblo, I'm speaking as a member of the tribal police."

"Which includes me," Nick pointed out.

"Of course, Black Raven. I'm just trying to remind you, too, that we work as a team in our department. You don't have to tackle anything by yourself."

Nick stared at Torres, his eyes narrowed. "We both appreciate the reminder," he said coolly. "Thanks for taking the time from your shift to stop by."

As Torres walked away, Eden saw Nick scowling. "He really pushes your buttons, doesn't he?" she said.

"It started off as friendly competition on the firing range, and when we went on training exercises, but somewhere along the way it took a wrong turn. Torres wants to make sergeant and is convinced I'm out for the same thing. Since only one of us can make it, he sees me as an obstacle standing in the way of what he wants. I'm not, but he's got a chip on his shoulder."

"He was several grades behind us, but I remember stories about him...only I can't remember in reference to what."

"His features. His parents and grandparents are Tewa, but his skin color is very light and his features are somewhat different from those of most of our people. There's always been gossip that he's got white blood somewhere. His family has denied it, but..." He shrugged.

"That may be why Torres offered to help me. If you've ever been set apart because of things you can't do anything about, you would understand how difficult it can be."

"Maybe," he said, unconvinced. "But, to me, his offer just doesn't come across as sincere." Nick glanced at his watch. "I better go grab something to eat before I run out of time."

"Where do you go, out of curiosity? There aren't any restaurants here on the pueblo, just candy and soda machines."

"Do you remember Miss Consuelo? She worked in the high school cafeteria for years."

Her eyes widened. "My goodness! She's got to be close to one hundred now!"

"She is, but she's sharp as a tack. She cooks up the best enchiladas and burritos around and sells them to our department. It works well all around. She makes extra money, and even Captain Mora looks well fed these days, though he's a bachelor like me."

The smile he gave her was so utterly masculine it made her breath catch. She looked away, wondering if she'd ever have a moment's peace again. Being around Nick was like standing in the middle of a storm. It challenged her, and tore at her, demanding a surrender she wasn't capable of—not anymore.

Bobby and two other boys from Eden's sixth grade class approached. "Yes, gentlemen?" Eden asked, looking at her watch and noting the school lunch period was nearly over. "Can I help you?"

"Actually, we were hoping that Deputy Black Raven could help us…"

There was uncertainty in the boys' eyes—something she usually didn't associate with Bobby or his two companions. She looked at them, intrigued.

"Okay. What can I do for you guys?" Nick asked.

"Well, we were wondering about something…" Bobby stared at the sandy ground. "Well, what I mean, is we were hoping that you could give us some pointers about the finishing rite? We'll be going through that soon, you know."

"Yes, I do," Nick said, "but you guys know the rules. You'll find out everything you need to know when the time comes, and not before."

Eden watched the boys exchanging uneasy glances, once again feeling like an outsider. Out of deference to her mother's wishes, she hadn't gone through the finishing. She'd heard stories about it, of course, but she'd never actually experienced it. Of course, even if she'd gone through the rite, the boys' portion of it was supposed to be vastly different from that of the girls.

"It's something that you'll never forget, boys," Nick said with a knowing smile.

"But can't you even give us a tiny hint?"

"Nope, and when you get asked that question many years from now, you'll have to say the same thing."

As they walked away, disappointed, Eden glanced at Nick. That continuity of blood and heritage was what she wanted to claim for her son. But unless she, as a half Tewa, could claim the right to live among the tribe, her son would never grow up knowing the richness of his father's Tewa world. For her son's sake, it was a fight she had to win.

THE DAY PASSED slowly. After finishing his patrol, Nick headed back to the Plaza. Captain Mora's instructions had been clear. He was to find whoever was trying to run Eden off the pueblo, but nothing more. The note, written by Eden's grandmother, was speculative at best.

Yet, the implication against Tall Shadow, his father, continued to bother him. He couldn't just let it go. It was a matter of honor to him to clear his father's name.

Of course it was also conceivable that he'd find damning evidence instead. He didn't think that would happen, but there was a chance, and he had to face it squarely. If his father had had anything to do with the theft of the artifacts, if he'd somehow framed Isabel Maes, he'd clear Eden's family—but he and Jake would pay dearly. They'd almost certainly lose Black Raven Ranch, their livelihoods and their right to remain on pueblo land.

Maybe he should have let the matter drop and not take

the risk, but he wasn't the kind of man to play it safe. His gut instinct told him that someone had deliberately used his father's name to keep others in line, dishonoring all of them in the process. That was not something he could shrug off or ignore. Everything in him demanded he preserve his father's good name.

Nick parked next to the Cultural Center, then went to the soda machine in the covered *portal* and bought himself a soda. Looking around casually, he saw Patrick Korman taking a break at one of the tables. Rita came out and joined him a moment later.

He sat down on a bench and listened in, but their conversation was too general to be of much use to him. As his gaze wandered over to the school yard, he saw two of the boys he'd met earlier throwing a football back and forth.

The finishing ceremony would be taking place soon. He hadn't been told which day it would be, but he could sense it drawing close from the intensity of the preparations all over the pueblo. He watched the kids, wondering what it would have been like to have a son getting ready for the rituals. He envied the excitement within the pueblo families now, and the sense of tradition as they prepared for the rite of passage.

Taking the final swallow of his soda, he crushed the can with one hand and threw it into the trash. He wouldn't drive himself crazy with thoughts like this, that maybe he was missing out on something by insisting on bachelorhood. The plain fact was that he wasn't cut out for relationships. Life had proven that to him enough times.

As he drove past the Kiva, he saw Captain Mora standing by the door to the *Sipofene,* the antechamber used for the finishing ceremony. Juan Ortiz stood beside him. Ortiz was a *Towa é,* a War Captain, a title that these days only meant a guardian of the tribe.

Captain Mora waved and Nick slowed down, parked, and went to meet him.

"We have a problem," Juan said. "As you know, we're responsible for insuring the secrecy of the pueblo rites. It's our duty, and one we do as well as we're able, but this year we don't have any young people to help us. Our youngest member is sixty-two and we can't cover as much ground as quickly as we could in the past. We're going to have to rely on our police department much more than we ever have."

"I've assured them that we're up to the challenge," Mora said. "But since you'll be out in the field more than I will, I wanted you to be aware of what's going on."

"We can handle it," Nick nodded. "If the *Towa é* and the police work together, no one will slip past us. Outsiders really stick out around here."

Juan relaxed visibly. "As *Towa é,* that's what I was hoping to hear. We have the option of closing off the pueblo to outsiders, but the Summer Chief, who will be in charge until the Winter Chief takes over during the second half of the year, is very reluctant to do that. The harvest season is the best time for our craftsmen and farmers to sell their goods. No one likes to interfere with that. We all realize how much our people depend on tourist dollars to see them through the long months of winter."

"May I make a recommendation, Captain?" Nick asked. Mora nodded. "Speak freely."

"I think the Summer Chief is right not to close off the pueblo. But we do need to take extra precautions. I recommend that we carefully scrutinize anyone in a vehicle with a university parking sticker. If they bring out a camera or if we suspect that they have recording devices, we'll take them to the station. Then, they can either consent to a search, or be escorted off our land."

"That's going to create some hard feelings, particularly in those instances when we're wrong and find nothing," Mora warned.

"Yes, but what we're trying to protect is worth that price," Nick said flatly.

"I like the way you think, Black Raven," Ortiz said with an approving look. "You've done your father proud."

Nick had never gotten along with his father, but now the words meant the world to him. Wondering when he'd grown so soft, Nick walked back to his Jeep feeling like a stranger to himself.

THAT NIGHT, after putting Christopher to bed, Eden walked outside and sat down in the *banco* beneath the old cottonwood in her backyard. The stillness outside was so total that it soothed her jagged nerves.

She took several deep breaths, enjoying the evening. She'd missed this house, her childhood home, all these years away, but it wasn't until that very moment that she realized how much.

The faint sounds of a car reached out to her through the silence. Walking to the back gate, she looked down the road. From where she stood, she could see a tribal police unit on its patrol. She was too far away to know if it was Nick, but an instinct she couldn't define assured her he was keeping watch over her.

The magic between them was still alive and it was drawing them together no matter how hard they resisted. She and Nick had found something in each other's arms that had touched their souls and changed them forever. On that fateful night so many months ago, she'd loved him as only a woman in love could love a man. But by giving him everything, she'd lost a piece of her heart forever.

Chapter Seven

As the day of the finishing rite drew closer, the mood around the pueblo shifted to a more serious note. The finishing rite was held before another ritual, the Coming of the Gods, which would also take place in the Kiva and was one of the most holy ceremonies conducted at the pueblo.

Although Eden knew Nick was putting in very long hours, she missed seeing him. And that was a very bad sign. His presence in her life had suddenly made her remember what is was like to feel vibrantly feminine and desired. Every time he was around, it was as if the air itself became supercharged with electricity. Colors were brighter and the sun was warmer.

She stopped those thoughts abruptly. She was sounding like a woman in love and that was just plain crazy. Promising herself not to give in to fantasies and stupid dreams, she sat down across from the Cultural Center, enjoying the coolness of the morning air.

The full-time teaching staff was in Santa Fe this morning for a workshop, and the students were off. All the sixth grade students, including her own, were supposed to be using the time to write an essay on the harvest season. Everyone was scheduled to return for afternoon classes in another forty minutes, but right now the school grounds were virtually empty.

Ineligible for the workshop as a part-time teacher, she'd stayed here, hoping to catch some activity at the Center, but everything seemed painfully routine today. Wayne and Rita had shared a snack, then he'd driven off and Rita had returned to her office. Eden could see her working just on the other side of the glass window.

"Good morning," Deputy Torres greeted.

Eden jumped, then turned her head. She hadn't heard him approaching.

"Did I startle you?"

"A bit," she admitted. "My mind was a million miles away, I guess."

Torres sat on the *banco* beside her. "You seem very interested in our Cultural Center."

Although it had come out sounding like an offhand comment, there was an intensity in his eyes that told her it had been far from that. She forced herself not to react. "I'm still very curious about the place," she admitted. "Most of the trouble that has plagued my family has its roots within those walls."

"Do you ever wonder what happened to those artifacts your mother was accused of stealing?"

"I do," she conceded. "I wish I could find them and clear up that part of the past at least, for my son's sake."

"Is that it? You want him to grow up and live here? Is his father Tewa?"

She stared at him coolly. "What his father is, or isn't, makes no difference. I am part of the tribe, and so is he."

"You're *half*-Tewa," he said. "And the hard fact is that as long as you live on our land, some people will try to make things unpleasant."

"I have my rights. I was born in this village, and I belong here. This is my home and my son's as well."

"Your case would be stronger if your son's father was a member of our tribe, but, although I could be mistaken, that isn't the case. No one has claimed him—that I know of. Isn't that true?"

"I claim him," Eden said, unable to keep the anger from her voice. "That's all he needs."

Torres shrugged. "Tell me. Do you know if Paul Black Raven ever spoke out publicly against your family?"

She wasn't sure where this was leading, but his questions were making her skin crawl. "It was no secret that he didn't believe my father should have remained at the pueblo after he married my mother. Paul Black Raven, like many others, felt that no Anglo should live on this land that was paid for by Tewa blood."

Torres nodded slowly. "The Spanish and the Anglos tried for hundreds of years to drive us off or destroy us. They embarked on a campaign meant to kill our spirit as well. As a half-white woman, you have the blood of those who wanted to obliterate our people flowing through your veins. Many say that your heart will always be torn in two and for that reason alone no one here should trust you."

"I can't change the way others see me. All I can do is follow what I know is right."

"And that is?"

Hearing footsteps behind her, she turned, and saw Nick walking up.

"Eden's doing what any other citizen should be doing," Nick said, his tone harsh. "She's standing her ground against people who are trying to force her into doing something she's not willing to do."

"Leave?" Torres said with a derisive grin.

"That, and other things," Nick sat down. "The next

patrol of the access roads is yours. I'm on break as of two minutes ago.''

Torres stood up. ''Be very careful, Miss Maes. You have many enemies here, and the police can only do so much.''

Eden watched him walk away. ''That sure sounded like a threat,'' she whispered.

Nick shook his head. ''It was an honest warning. It's just the way he said it that makes it sound bad.'' He glanced at her. ''Did he rattle your nerves?''

''A bit. I don't like his attitude, and I don't understand what he's really after.''

As she met Nick's eyes and she saw the gentle concern mirrored there, her pulse automatically quickened. A powerful yearning for something she didn't dare name wound through her, leaving her feeling empty inside. Frightened by that inexplicable sense of vulnerability, she forced herself to look away. ''He's not as intimidating as he is irritating.''

''Actually, he's a lot more than irritating. If he gets on your nerves, let me know and I'll handle it for you.'' He paused for a long time. ''So, have you missed me?''

Her breath caught in her throat, and her heartbeat thundered in her ears.

''I see that you have,'' he murmured, his voice a husky whisper. ''Good. I never thought I'd say this but...I'm getting used to having you around.''

Something twisted inside her. Even that small admission, in the face of what he saw as her betrayal, had cost him and, because of that, had touched her soul.

More than anything else in the world, she wanted to say something witty to lighten the mood, but the words were all lodged behind the lump at the back of her throat.

She stood up, trying to look completely in control, but her legs felt like wet noodles. ''I have to get back to work.''

"But there's no school."

"Classes start again in a half hour." She held her head high and walked away, but her hands were shaking. As she headed back to the school, she heard his throaty chuckle and felt her skin prickle. She had to stay away from Nick. No matter how hard she fought it, he made her want things she had no business even thinking about.

As she entered her classroom through the outside door, she finally relaxed. Here at last was a world she understood.

NICK DROVE AROUND the perimeter of pueblo land, alert for intruders hiding in less-populated spots. They were here. He couldn't *see* them, but he could *feel* their presence. It was part of the instincts he'd developed as a cop.

He stayed sharp, knowing what he had to look for— tourists who appeared perfectly ordinary except for that certain look in their eyes. The intensity mirrored there always gave them away.

Occasionally, he saw practice ceremonies taking place in solitary desert canyons, but he continued driving, keeping his distance, not wanting to disturb them.

Then, getting a call to report to Mora's office, he cut his patrol short and headed back.

Twenty minutes later, he sat in Mora's office while Deputy Torres took over patrolling.

"I hear that there may be some tension between you and Torres. Is there any truth to that?" Mora asked.

"We're not each other's favorite people, but we're professionals and we'll back each other up without question."

Captain Mora's eyes narrowed. "Funny. He said pretty much the same thing."

Nick looked up. So the captain was keeping a closer watch on them than he'd let on. He wondered how much of this had to do with Eden. "Anything else on your mind, Captain?"

"Yeah, as a matter of fact there is. I've overheard some of our people talking. The Maes woman is stirring up more gossip. Some have claimed that she's trying to get an 'in' with our department."

"I hadn't heard that one yet," Nick said without expression. He had little doubt about where this bit had come from. Torres had probably dropped it in the captain's lap for effect. "Do you also think that's what she's doing?"

The captain leaned back in his chair. "Except for when she came to me with that letter, I've barely spoken to her. You'd have a better feel for this. What do you think?"

"Eden knows she'll need support from the police because someone clearly wants her off our land. She also wants to know about her past and may need our cooperation there, too. But she's made no secret about either."

"Don't let this case become any more personal than it already is."

Nick nodded, wondering if Mora had found out who Tall Shadow was. "But it's important that we uncover the truth."

"To whom? You or Eden?" Mora held up his hand. "Don't answer that. Just remember that you work for this department, not Eden Maes or yourself."

"That was never in question," Nick answered flatly, wondering how much gossip Torres had actually passed on.

As he started toward the door, the dispatcher came in and handed the chief a note.

"Nick," Mora said, calling him back. "Get over to the Cultural Center. Theresa Redwing called and asked that we send a deputy. Someone's been casing the joint. I'll be standing by if you need backup."

"On my way," Nick said, and hurried out.

Nick drove directly to the Center, eyes open for strangers or anything out of the ordinary. Noting that there were no other vehicles parked next to the Center, he climbed out of his Jeep. Suddenly Rita Korman came charging out the front door and the skin at the back of his neck began to prickle.

Nick looked around the area again, wondering what he'd missed. "Is there an emergency?" His eyes narrowed, and his hand rested on the butt of his pistol.

"Not at the moment, but it's about time one of you officers got here."

Patrick, a tall Anglo man in his early thirties, came out and greeted him calmly. "Please come in. We'll talk in my office," he said, giving his stepmother a warning look that stopped her in her tracks as she started to follow.

Nick followed the younger male Korman in, then waited for Patrick to close the door. "Sit down, Deputy Black Raven," he said, then walked to his desk. "We have a serious problem. Lately, we've noticed that Eden Maes, the daughter of the woman who stole some artifacts from this center many years ago, has been casing us out. It's making all of us very nervous."

Nick stared at Patrick for a moment. He knew why Eden was keeping an eye on them, but that wasn't information he cared to share. "What exactly has she been doing that has you worried?"

"She's out there every day at lunch, and usually part of the afternoon as well. She watches everything, and seems to be taking notes. I think she may be planning a robbery. Can you arrest her, or at least take her in for questioning?"

"She has a right to sit wherever she wishes in the Plaza. She's a teacher who works mornings, eats lunch, and is probably just grading papers. You have lunch outside some times, don't you?"

Rita suddenly came into the room. "I'm sorry to burst in on you two, but the doors here are paper thin and I don't think Patrick is explaining this very well. This Maes woman poses a threat to us, and we need to have this resolved once and for all. Years ago, when you two were just kids, the tribe entrusted us with religious artifacts that we kept under lock and key. But we failed to live up to the pueblo's trust. Items were stolen right from under our noses by her mother. I won't have this happen again. You have to find out what she's up to and put a stop to it before it's too late."

"The woman is perfectly within her rights to sit there and work or eat," Nick said flatly.

"Don't you see what's really going on? Since she hasn't lived here for many years, she probably doesn't know that we no longer store ceremonial items for pueblo societies. She's using the excuse of working at that table to get to know our employees' schedules and daily routines. She's undoubtedly planning to rob us."

"A robbery," Nick said, trying not to smile. Recalling the way Eden had handled his police baton, like a pseudo-baseball bat, he couldn't quite make the mental leap to picturing Eden with a mask and a gun.

"You think we're just being paranoid?" Rita groaned, shaking her head. "You're making a big mistake. I won't have you dismissing our concerns like this. I'll take our complaint all the way to the pueblo governor if I have to."

Rita walked to the wrought-iron-barred window and pointed Eden out to Nick. "There she is again, sitting at that same picnic table. She's watching the doors, and us inside."

Nick looked out. Looking at Eden was like having a ray of sunlight touch his cold heart. He felt compelled to protect her from even this vague form of harassment. "See that burrito in her hands? I'd say she's having lunch. That also probably explains why she's sitting at a picnic table.''

"You aren't going to take any of this seriously, are you?" Rita's voice rose in anger.

Patrick took Rita's arm, and giving Nick a sign to wait, led her out of his office. He returned a moment later. "I have to apologize for my stepmother's outburst. She's usually not like that, but she's genuinely worried that something else will happen here at the Center. Last time, when the mask and fetish were stolen, she blamed herself, and took it very hard.''

"I'll increase my patrols," he assured Patrick, standing. Suddenly a gunshot reverberated inside the building. Nick immediately ran down the hall toward the sound, thumbing loose the safety strap and reaching for his pistol. Standing just outside the open doorway, he glanced inside the room. Rita was standing by a large floor safe, her face the color of chalk. A small, semiautomatic pistol was in her hand, and a shell casing lay on the floor.

Instinct and training made him glance out the window, trying to determine the trajectory of the bullet. That's when he saw Eden across the way, looking around frantically, trying to figure out what had happened. Fear was etched clearly on her face. Waves of anger swept over him as he realized that he could have lost her to one stray bullet.

Nick traversed the room in three steps, and took the pistol from Rita's shaking hand. Checking the handgun, he noted the clip was missing, then saw it still clutched in Rita's other hand.

"What happened?" he demanded, taking it from her. Looking around, he finally found the small bullet hole in the adobe wall beneath the window. The bullet had not penetrated the compacted earth.

"I thought I'd get my brother's .22 caliber pistol out of

the safe,'' Rita said, her voice unsteady. ''I borrowed it a few days ago, because for the next week or two we're going to be keeping late hours here. I'd taken the clip out. What was that round doing in the chamber? Wayne should have seen to it that it was unloaded properly.''

''We're just glad you're all right.'' Patrick, who'd come into the office just behind Nick, put one hand on Rita's shoulder. ''Take the pistol with you, Deputy. I don't want that thing hanging around here. I hate guns. Wayne can pick it up at the police station when he wants it back.''

''You can't just hand it over,'' Rita argued. ''We need to protect ourselves, Patrick. You can't go on pretending that everything's okay. We're going to be robbed. You'll see.''

''Perhaps you should listen to your stepson,'' Nick said. ''Had the bullet passed through a window or out the doorway and killed someone, you would have been charged with manslaughter.'' His fist clenched and his blood went cold as the full extent of the danger Eden had been in really hit home. ''You would have faced prison time, not to mention having to live with the knowledge that you killed or maimed someone,'' he said, trying to keep his tone steady and free of the anger that tore at him. ''We don't require gun licenses in New Mexico unless it's for someone who carries a concealed weapon. But owning a gun carries responsibilities.''

Thinking of what just happened sobered her. ''I just don't want people to think I take my responsibility to this Center lightly. Many still believe that part of the reason the sacred artifacts were stolen was because Marc and I neglected to have proper security measures in place. That's not true, but people continue to blame us.'' She paused and in a shaky voice added, ''I can't go through something like that again.''

Patrick led Nick out into the hall. "Don't worry. There'll be no more guns brought into this Center unless they're being carried by a qualified security guard or a police officer."

"Keep an eye on your stepmother," he said firmly. "She seems to be really stressed out."

He nodded. "She wasn't always so nervous about this Center. Her attitude really changed after the theft. I was just a kid back then, but even I noticed it. There was a lot of blame being passed around, but Rita was her own worst enemy. She just couldn't seem to let it go. She kept turning things over in her mind, wondering if she should have done this or that."

Nick nodded and wondered if Patrick realized that what he was really saying was that Rita was a loose cannon when it came to Eden.

"I know what you're thinking, Deputy," Patrick said, "but you're wrong. My stepmother didn't take that pistol so she could shoot Eden, or even threaten her. She's into health, exercise, and environmental issues. Rita won't even go dove hunting with my dad and me. She's not a killer."

Nick nodded, but remained unconvinced. All he really knew was that now he had even more reason for keeping a close eye on the Cultural Center. Rita didn't want Eden on the pueblo, but he wasn't certain how far she'd be willing to go to insure her departure.

Nick walked outside and climbed into his unit, glancing back one last time to look at Eden. She was still sitting at the picnic table, her attention focused on some papers.

As the sun danced on her silky, chestnut hair, he suddenly remembered how it had felt cascading over his naked chest one night so long ago. Nick groaned softly as his body became impossibly hard. The woman was driving him crazy. He had to find a way to keep her out of his every waking thought before she staked a new claim on his heart.

Chapter Eight

Nick was ready to drive off when Rita waved at him, calling him back. Parking, he went to meet her.

"Deputy, I'm sorry to keep you, but I'd like another moment to speak to you before you leave."

"No problem." Nick studied Rita Korman, a lean, fit-looking woman in her mid- to late fifties. She seemed composed, but what he read in her eyes was fear and frustration, a bad combination by anyone's standards.

"I want you to understand where I'm coming from. I've spent the last twenty-five years working for your tribe, and I really do care about this place. That's why having that particular woman watching us unnerves me so much."

He nodded thoughtfully. Rita sounded sincere and had held his gaze steadily. "I can understand that. We all want to protect what we care about."

"I've done my best to safeguard the Center, believe me. Our security layout here is second to none. The only thing missing is an armed guard, but the tribe's funding isn't sufficient to cover it."

"What kind of antitheft devices do you have in place? For instance, are the video cameras tamper-proof?"

"They certainly are. And that's not all. Would you like to take a look? I'd be glad to show you."

Rita escorted him through the entire building, including the loading dock, then led him to her office.

"The old safe over there is just for petty cash and overflow, but the large safe built into the closet is state-of-the-art. It would take several hours and a professional safe-cracker to even make a dent in it."

Rita was paranoid, but at least the Center was better off for it, Nick mused. "Tell me something. Theft isn't something normally associated with our pueblo. How do you explain what happened twenty years ago?"

She considered it for a long time before speaking. "We all know that Isabel Maes took the artifacts. My guess is she did it to get back at the tribe. She must have harbored some pretty deep resentments since no matter what she did, she was never really accepted on the pueblo."

"Do you have any theories about where the artifacts really went? Or where they might be now?"

She shook her head. "I've been over and over that. I think we're still missing a piece of the puzzle. I figure that Isabel took the artifacts to her husband. As a veteran cop with the Bureau of Indian Affairs, he would have certainly known the right fences. Is that the correct term? I've heard it on T.V. cop shows," she said, then seeing him nod, continued. "But if what I suspect is true, and the artifacts were passed to a fence, they're long gone and this pueblo will never see them again. They're probably in a private collection back east, or in California."

"Hey, sis. What's this I hear about an accident with my gun?"

Rita turned her head and saw her brother, Wayne, coming down the hall. "Hi, Wayne. I'll fill you in on the way to the fitness center, okay?" She turned back to Nick. "You'll have to excuse me, Deputy. I teach an aerobics class twice a week at my brother's gym."

Rita tried to escort Nick back to the door, but he remained where he was. "Can you get me a detailed description of the stolen items before you leave? Maybe a copy of what was given to the insurance company, if you still have it around."

"No problem. I know where that's kept. We never did box those records up because, as far as I'm concerned, that matter's still pending."

Rita walked to the reception area, went to Theresa Redwing's workstation, and reached into the bottom drawer of the file cabinet behind her desk. A moment later, Rita handed Nick a copy of an old insurance form.

Nick studied it. The descriptions were there, but no photographs. "I don't suppose there are photos anywhere?" he asked, suspecting the answer.

"You know the tribe prohibits having photographs taken of ritual objects. Believe me, the insurance company and I have both tried to get the Summer and Winter Chief to make an exception, but they've never budged."

A few minutes later, Nick resumed his patrol. He hadn't really planned it but, somehow, he found himself driving past Eden's house. A twinge of disappointment bit into him when he saw that the curtains were drawn and no one appeared to be there. Cursing himself for acting like a lovesick idiot, he headed back out on patrol.

IT WAS MIDAFTERNOON by the time Eden headed home. Today she'd given the kids an assignment that would also help her out. She'd asked her class to gather information and draw historical maps showcasing the layout of the pueblo twenty years ago, and explain how things had changed. The kids would learn a lot about the pueblo's recent history and, hopefully, it would give Nick and her some idea of where to search for the artifacts.

Following a spur of the moment impulse, she stopped by the tribal newspaper and set another plan in motion. Nick would disapprove, hating the fact that she hadn't consulted with him first. But she had to do this for him. She'd overheard some of the teachers at school talking. Too many people thought that she was using Nick and getting him involved in a fight that would make him lifelong enemies at the pueblo. Her plan would point out to everyone that the fight was strictly her own. And, with luck, she might get a lead or two out of it.

After leaving the newspaper, Eden stopped at Mrs. Chino's and picked up Christopher. "Hey, little love," she said, shifting her squirming baby to get better hold of him.

Every time Christopher smiled, she could see a part of Nick mirrored there. Her heart did a funny little twist inside her as she realized that the three of them shared a blood bond that could never be broken.

By the time she reached her home, she saw Nick leaning against his department's vehicle, waiting. Her heart began to pound. The flash of his eyes on her made her feel a simmering in her blood and a fire growing deep in her center. She met his gaze and seeing the anger that glittered in his dark eyes, knew that he'd learned of her visit to the paper in record time. Her guess was that they'd called him the minute she'd left. The young woman behind the desk had been very apprehensive about the ad Eden had wanted to place, and had even called the editor-in-chief before taking her money.

"We have to talk," Nick clipped. "I just came from a meeting with Jerry Chevarria."

"I didn't know you had any interest in the pueblo's weekly newspaper," she said, unlocking the door and going inside.

"Don't try to sidetrack me," he said roughly. "Jerry told

me that you visited him up shortly after noon and placed an ad. Why the hell didn't you talk to me before you did something like that?''

She set Chris down in the playpen with his toys. "I don't need your permission to conduct my life and my business." She avoided looking directly at him, realizing the danger. The challenge in his voice was igniting her own anger and a reckless excitement that sparked the very air between them.

"You don't get it? This is a *police matter.* You can't do whatever you please. Jerry told me that you were offering a five hundred dollar reward to anyone who could lead you to the cache of stolen goods or information leading to an indictment of the real criminals.''

"It's no different than what those crime-stopper programs do," she said. "For twenty years the police have made no progress at all, and there's nobody even investigating this case anymore except me. Why do you have a problem with the fact that I'm doing something to get this case solved?''

"People are already trying to drive you out of here. By doing this, you're turning yourself into an even bigger target." His voice boomed in the room, but hearing Christopher's whimper, he suddenly grew still.

Nick walked over to where the little boy was, then brushed his knuckles across his cheek. "Sorry about that, little guy. I didn't mean to scare you. I was only hoping to scare some sense into your mom.''

Eden saw the tenderness in his eyes as he looked at Chris, and it tore a piece of her heart away. Yet when Nick looked away from the baby and back at her, the cop he was overshadowed everything again. It was then that she remembered the many arguments between her mom and dad. Even in the midst of their anger, her parents had always been careful around her. Eden's dad, in particular, had always gone out of his way to speak gently to Eden and reassure her, though it really hadn't helped much. It was unbearable for a child to have to witness her parents trying to hurt each other.

"Don't push this, Eden." His face was hard, and there was an unmistakable tension about his jaw.

He looked formidable, anger and determination glittering in the darkness of his eyes. If the stakes hadn't been as high as they were, she might have backed off. "We need to stir up the waters a bit and see what comes up. It's the only way to find leads at this point."

"A plan like this is going to bring out every lowlife for miles. You'll get scam artists playing games with you, trying to get you to hand over cash any way they can. And, if the criminals you're hoping to unmask are still around, and let me remind you that so far there's been no evidence of that whatsoever, you'll be presenting yourself as a target."

"I'm not going to back off." As she stood in front of him, she could feel the raw power emanating from him. His face was granite, his eyes lit up with anger.

"I *will* stop you, Eden. I'll get that ad pulled no matter how high I have to go in the tribal government."

Eden knew it was no idle threat. Nick could do that easily and there'd be nothing she could do about it. His word would carry far more clout than hers ever would with the council.

"All right, Nick. You win this round. But don't get used to it," she warned. "I call my own shots."

"Not while I'm around." He turned and walked away.

Defiance coiled inside her as she saw the smug look of satisfaction on his face. She picked up Christopher's toy dinosaur from the floor and as her hand curled around it, it was all she could do not to throw it at him.

Almost as if reading her mind, he stopped and turned to face her. "If you throw that, I'll do more than duck," he growled, daring her with one level gaze. "Don't start what you can't finish."

It was a challenge, clear and simple. She hurled the toy at him.

He caught it in midair with one hand, then, with a dark smile, narrowed the gap between them. As he came toward her, Eden could feel the tension inside him. Every tiny fiber in her body quivered to life as a mixture of expectation and excitement coursed through her.

The moment screamed with danger. She knew she had to move away, now, before it was too late, but something held her to the spot.

Nick laced his fingers through her hair, holding her face in his hands. "You make me crazy," he growled, the words both an angry protest and a surrender.

He took her mouth, his lips opening over hers, demanding everything. She responded to him—fire matching fire. Her tongue came forward to meet his, circling, and tasting him. He groaned as if she were stealing the dearest part of his soul.

Nick shuddered from the force of wanting her. Pleasure sizzled down his body as he rubbed his maleness against the softness at the apex of her thighs.

She wanted to be taken—to feel him moving within her. Desperate for a warmth only they could give each other, their caresses grew hotter. Everything female in her responded to him as naturally as a flower to the desert sun. But, in a matter of heartbeats, they'd cross a threshold neither was prepared for.

Suddenly, as if they'd shared the same thought, he released her and stepped back. His black eyes glowed with passion as they burned into hers. "I *will* protect you, Eden. Even from me."

He strode out of her home without even glancing back.

AN HOUR LATER, Eden answered a knock at her door and found two of her students there, waiting. "Berta, Terri. What brings you two here?"

The girls came inside and, at Eden's invitation, sat down on the sofa.

"Today, I went to my grandma's looking for photos that could help me with our assignment," Berta said, "and I found out that Mrs. Black Raven, the deputy's mom that is, used to show everyone at the women's society photo albums that went all the way back to the time when cameras were first invented. My grandma said that theirs is the best record around of the pueblo. I was going to ask Deputy Black Raven if we could look through those albums, but a few hours ago we saw him driving away from here in a real hurry. Later we found him by the soda machine, but he still looked pretty ticked off. Did you two guys have a fight?"

She gave the kids a hard look. "That's between the deputy and me," she said in a no-nonsense tone. "And as far as the school assignment goes, you'll have to use your own family's albums or library resources."

The girls exchanged quick looks. "You *did* have a fight," Berta said flatly.

Eden glared at them. "Is that all, girls?"

Berta and Terri quickly stood up and headed to the door. As they stepped out onto the porch, a flicker of light caught Eden's eye and she turned her head. Somewhere near the top of the mesa north of her house, a figure sat, watching through binoculars. As Eden squinted, trying to see who it was, the person walked off.

"Who's that?" Terri asked.

"Probably a hiker," she said, working hard to keep her tone casual. "Maybe he's gathering native herbs. It's nothing to worry about."

"But he had binoculars. I saw them. And he was looking down on your house. Are you sure you'll be all right?" Berta asked.

"I wish Deputy Black Raven and you hadn't broken up," Terri added.

"We didn't break up. We were never involved in that way," Eden said firmly.

"Something must have happened between you two. He looked really mad and you look sad."

"You both have an overactive imagination," she said sternly, hoping to put an end to their speculation. One look at Berta's worried expression, however, told her what a vain hope that was. "Stop making something out of nothing, okay, girls?"

"If you say so, Miss Maes," Terri said.

As they walked away talking in low tones, Eden had a funny feeling that she hadn't heard the last of this yet.

NICK WAS patrolling down the Plaza when he saw two girls trying to flag him down. Curious, and recognizing them from earlier when they'd begun to approach him then changed their minds, he slowed and pulled up next to the kids.

"What's going on, ladies?"

"We're worried about Mrs. Maes. We just came from her house, but I think we shouldn't have left her there alone," Berta said.

"Why's that?" Nick asked, the skin at the back of his neck prickling.

"She was really upset about something—or maybe scared," Terri said. "It's hard to tell what she's thinking, but she sure wanted to get us away from her house."

"Maybe it had something to do with the hiker," Berta added.

"What hiker?" Nick asked quickly.

They told him about the figure they'd seen up on the mesa. "She said he was probably someone looking at native plants, but with binoculars? I don't think so."

"And you say he just disappeared?" Nick asked, his gut knotting. Eden was a proud woman, not used to asking for help unless it was absolutely necessary. But, in a case like this, waiting until the last second could lead to major trouble.

"Well, the guy walked off, then we couldn't see him anymore. After that, Mrs. Maes hurried us out the door. Maybe she just wanted to get us safely away in case of trouble."

Nick's heart pounded against his ribs. Every instinct he possessed was telling him to get to Eden's house fast. "I should check this out. Step away from the vehicle, girls. I've got to get going."

Turning the patrol unit around, he headed back to Eden's home using a silent approach. If he caught the guy harassing her, he'd haul him in, even if he had to do it one body part at a time.

A few minutes later, he arrived at her house. The front door was closed and the curtains were drawn. But when Eden was at home, the curtains were always parted and he knew she was there now. There was a light on inside the house.

Heeding his instinct for caution, he drew his weapon and

moved in on foot. He stood silently by the windows, listening, but there were no sounds inside. Fear pounded through him, but he pushed it back, knowing he needed to keep his thinking clear.

Moving to one side, he peered inside the house through a slit in the curtains. His blood nearly froze when he saw the condition of the room on the other side. A shattered flowerpot lay on the carpet along with several photo frames and books. Loose papers were scattered everywhere. But there was no sign of Eden or Chris.

Seeing an open window farther down, he crept toward it and noiselessly crawled inside. The unnatural stillness in the house unnerved him. He was moving slowly down the hall, when he heard muffled sounds coming from inside the bedroom ahead.

The thought of someone in the bedroom with Eden, someone who might harm her, filled him with a deadly combination of fear and the determination to help her. Kicking the closed door open, he moved in at a crouch, ready for action.

Eden stood before him, hair still wet from the shower, wearing nothing but a towel and trembling. Her eyes were wide and her face pale as she stared at the gun he was pointing at her.

The fear in her eyes felt like a cold blade to his heart. "Sweetheart, I'm so sorry," he said, immediately putting away his gun. "I thought you were in danger. Don't be frightened." He tried to draw her into his arms, but she pulled back suddenly.

"What the hell do you think you're doing?" she demanded. "Have you lost your mind?"

"I was trying to save you," he said.

"Oh really? And who's going to save *you?*" she said, then socked him in the jaw.

Chapter Nine

"Ow!" Eden staggered back, holding her hand. "You clod! Your jaw's made of granite."

"I've been told that before—and been called worse." He tried to reach for her hand, but she pulled away.

"Get out of my house! Now!"

"Eden, let me explain," he said. He ran a hand through his hair, scowled, then jammed his hands into his pockets. "The kids...two girls...well they made it sound like you were in serious trouble."

"The kids?" she repeated, then slowly her expression changed from confusion to understanding. "Berta and Terri," she said. "What did they have to do with this?"

As she looked up at him, and saw his gaze sweeping over her intimately, Eden was suddenly and searingly aware that she was wearing nothing but a towel. Memories of another time, of pleasures that had lasted long into the night, flooded into her mind. He'd reached for the towel she'd been wearing that afternoon, pulling it off her and had made love to her. That night he'd taught her about the wild side of desire.

"Don't look at me like that," he said, his voice husky.

"Like what?" she managed, her voice trembling.

"Like you'd welcome the pleasures you know I can give you," he growled.

Hearing Christopher crying, she stepped back quickly, her sanity returning. How could she have allowed herself to become so vulnerable? "The only man in my life is Chris, Nick, and that's the way I'm going to keep it. Now go wait for me in the living room. I'm going to get dressed, then I'll go get my son."

As soon as Nick left the room, Eden slipped into her rattiest jeans and an old, threadbare sweatshirt. She wanted to look as unappealing as possible. With luck, that would cut down the tension between them.

By the time she stepped out of her room, she saw that Nick had picked up Christopher and already had him in the living room.

Nick smiled as she walked down the hall to join him. "I hope you don't mind. Christopher seemed impatient, so I thought I'd give you a hand with him." His gaze coursed over her as intimately as a lover's caress. "You look beautiful."

"Oh please. This old sweatshirt has more holes in it than swiss cheese."

"I know," he answered with a slow grin.

She glanced down quickly, verifying that none of the holes were in any strategic places. As she looked back up, the smoldering look he gave her made her tingle all over. Needing a distraction, she reached out for her son, but Christopher ignored her, and continued to cling to Nick.

"I guess you win today's popularity contest," Eden said curtly, flexing her hand and trying to work out its stiffness.

"How are your knuckles?" he asked gently.

"They smart," she said, then quickly added, "But it was worth it." Seeing that she hadn't even left a mark on his jaw, her annoyance grew. "Now tell me, what on earth did those two girls say to you?"

"They told me there was a man watching you. I came over right away, but your curtains were drawn. You never do that when you're home. Then I saw the mess in here," he said, gesturing to the books and papers on the floor. "I thought you had an intruder in the house. I came in, heard a noise in the bedroom and thought you were in serious trouble."

Afraid that he'd sense the gentle warmth that had begun to replace her anger, she knelt by the coffee table and began to pick up the pot shards. "This was Christopher's doing. He tried to pull himself up and yanked on the table runner. I cleaned him up first, then decided to take a shower myself before coming back to pick up the mess. I closed the curtains because I didn't want any unexpected company and my students sometimes drop by when they know I'm here."

"What happened to the guy watching the house?"

"I don't think he *was* watching the house. I think it was a hiker. He certainly made no threatening moves, and didn't come any closer. He had binoculars, but he could have been bird watching for all I know."

"At dusk? Not likely. If you see him again, let me know right away."

"You've got it. But I think we've got another problem. The girls were playing matchmaker. They felt you and I were on the outs and they wanted to help us patch things up. If they mention any of this to anyone else, the gossip will be rampant."

"There's nothing we can do about that, so my advice is let it go. If you say anything, you'll just make it worse."

She nodded. "You're right. Some things shouldn't be dignified with a response." Remembering what the girls had said, she added, ''By the way, is it true that the Black Ravens have an extensive photo archive?''

He nodded. ''We had quite a few shutterbugs in the family. My mother, for example, was always taking photos of everything. She'd use them as frames of reference when she worked on her paintings. We have shelves full of photo albums filled with only her pictures. Come to think of it, those would give us a good idea of how the pueblo's changed over the years and may suggest places we should look for the artifacts. We may not remember someone's barn being torn down or erected, but the photos would catalog everything.''

''I'd love a chance to look through them.''

''Why don't we go over to Black Raven Ranch now?'' He looked down at the infant still in his arms. ''On second thought, maybe that's not such a good idea. Christopher is sound asleep.''

Eden touched the baby's cheek lightly and smiled. ''He'll sleep until close to daybreak. He won't be any trouble, if you don't mind my bringing him along.''

''You two are always welcome at the ranch,'' he said, in a low clear voice.

She suppressed the shiver that touched her spine. ''Let's get going then. I'm eager to get started.''

NICK LED HER into the den at Black Raven Ranch. The place had become a real home these days with Annie and the baby here. The sadness and coldness that had been a part of the house for as far back as he could remember were now gone. Yet the truth was that, these days, he was always finding excuses not to stop by. It was hard for him to see how complete his brother's life had become. In comparison, his own life felt empty, almost as if a vital piece were missing.

Tonight, with all the family gathered together, and Chris and Eden beside him, those feelings didn't seem quite so strong. He found himself relaxing as Annie and Jake sat across from them with Noelle, who'd refused to go to sleep. Martin was also there, sipping a glass of iced tea.

"I don't understand what you're trying to do," Annie said to Eden. "Even if you found the artifacts, people would only assume that you were finally able to figure out where your mother hid them. It certainly wouldn't clear your family's name."

"I know, but if I find and return them, I'll earn a bit of goodwill for myself. Maybe I can even change the minds of some of these people who believe I'm getting something for nothing by claiming land here, though I'm half-Tewa. Of course, I'm also hoping that I'll be able to find a solid lead to the real criminals, either hidden with the artifacts, or during my search. There's no guarantee that'll happen, I know, but it's all I've got to hang on to right now."

"Returning the artifacts would certainly do a lot for you in the eyes of the tribe," Jake agreed.

As they talked, Nick saw the way Eden would look at Jake, then back at him. His brother's face was identical to his own, yet, like Annie, Eden had never had any problems telling them apart. He'd asked her about it once when they'd both been teenagers, and she'd told him that it was who they were inside that defined each of them. The light in their eyes, their feelings, and their reactions made them each very different from each other, despite their outward appearances.

Nick wondered if she still believed that. Jake and he were physically more alike these days than they'd ever been. Yet, more than ever, it was important to him to know that she saw him as a man, distinct from his brother, though they shared the same face.

"I have the albums upstairs in my office," Annie said. "If Jake and Martin will help me carry them, I can bring them down here so we can all have a look."

Jake and Martin stood. "Whenever you're ready," Jake said.

Annie handed Noelle to Eden. "Can you take care of her for a few minutes?"

"No problem," Eden said, taking the squirming baby into her arms. Noelle was reaching out for everything in sight, and Eden laughed when she grabbed Nick's shirt.

Eden pulled Noelle back onto her own lap. "She's a lot more active than Chris is at this time of night. I wonder if Chris will get that way at her age." She glanced at her son, asleep in Noelle's playpen.

"Chris has a totally different personality. I think that'll hold true no matter how old he is."

"You're probably right." Eden glanced up at Nick. "You know what's really surprising to me is how much you and Jake have grown alike as the years have gone by. You even wear the same style clothing."

He shrugged. "Jeans, boots and Western shirts are practically a uniform around here," he said. "Does that mean you're starting to have trouble telling us apart?"

She shook her head. "No. I always know it's you once I see your face. The telltale difference is there in your eyes," she explained, then grew quiet, trying to find the right words. "Yours are gentler, softer somehow than Jake's are. Well, except for when he looks at Noelle and Annie. But, even then, that gentleness stays there only for an instant, then it's gone."

Her answer warmed him, but suddenly uncomfortable with how deeply she'd touched him, he gave her a playful grin. "Wait a second," he said, feigning horror. "Are you saying I'm a wuss compared to my brother?"

Jake came in then. "Of course you are. You always have been. That's why the prettiest girls always picked me."

Eden laughed but came to Nick's rescue. "If I remember right, neither one of the Black Raven brothers ever lacked female company."

Jake reached for Annie's hand and kissed it. "A Black Raven man never gives his heart away easily—until that one special woman comes along."

Nick looked at Eden, fighting the impulse to draw her closer to him. What his brother hadn't said because Annie already knew it, was that once a Black Raven man surrendered his heart, it was for a lifetime.

Nick's gaze stayed on Eden, and when she smiled at him, he felt the familiar sweet fire she always created in him. Even betrayal hadn't completely destroyed his feelings for her. Sensing Jake was watching them, he glanced away from her. Jake could read him too well, and there was no way he wanted his brother to know how much he still cared for Eden.

They began to study the old photo albums, Jake and Annie working together because she was the only one who hadn't grown up at the pueblo. Together, they made notes of homes and storage places used by friends of Saya Black Raven and/or Isabel, marking down places that may have doubled as a hiding place for the artifacts.

Martin grew quiet and pensive as he leafed through the album he was holding. "I just remembered that one of my nephews was allowed to take hundreds of photos for an anthropologist several years back. Those photos are in a restricted section of the university library, their special collections room."

"That's a good lead, Martin," Nick said. "Thanks."

"Here's another," Eden added quietly. "The barn pictured in the background of this particular photo is one I remember well. It belonged to Grams. She moved in with me after Mom and Dad died. I stored their furniture to make room for her own.''

"When's the last time you were there?" Nick asked.

"Ages ago. And I never searched through those pieces of furniture, though I'm sure the police did at the time."

"Undoubtedly," Nick conceded, "but it can't hurt for us to take a look. How about if we go over there early tomorrow morning?"

"It'll have to be before eight in the morning. I have school," Eden answered.

"I'll be there at a quarter to seven." Nick glanced over at his brother and noticed that Annie was leaning against him, her eyes nearly closed. Jake's arm was draped protectively over her and Noelle.

"You look as if you've had a long day, Annie," Nick said gently.

She nodded, her eyes heavy. "Noelle doesn't sleep on my schedule. She'll be up again at around four in the morning."

Eden gave her a sympathetic look. "Let's call it a night, then. These albums will still be here tomorrow."

Annie gave her a grateful smile. "I really appreciate that. I'll be up early," she said, glancing at Noelle, then letting out a soft sigh. "I'll start looking through everything again then and make a list of any areas that look promising."

Thanking Jake and Annie, Eden picked up Christopher and placed him in his carrier. Her little boy never woke up. Eden smiled. "As I said, he's out for the count now."

As they drove back in Nick's vehicle, they passed by the old barn, the one they were going to visit tomorrow. Eden called his attention to it. "That's the place. I don't know if anything's still there. Although Grams relinquished her old home to the tribe when she moved into my parents' house, I believe she kept the barn because she needed storage space. Why don't we stop by now and see what's there?''

"It's too dark. We won't be able to see much of anything."

"That old barn was wired with electricity ages ago," she said. "Dad came here at night a lot to practice his guitar and sing. He was such a lousy musician, Mom insisted he do it somewhere where people couldn't hear," she said, chuckling.

He smiled. "I remember hearing others talk about that. No one could figure out why he kept practicing when he obviously didn't have much of a gift for it."

She laughed. "That was my dad. Nothing anyone ever said stopped him from doing what he wanted. He used to say he didn't play for anyone else's entertainment—just his own. Mom agreed wholeheartedly."

Nick drove down the fence line, then parked in front of the old barn.

Eden looked at the tall wooden doors, carefully scrutinizing them in the beams of the Jeep's headlights. "Those doors have been damaged. Look at the splintered wood where they come together in the middle. Someone must have used a wrecking bar to force them open, ripping the lock right off."

"Not necessarily. That wood could have dried out on its own. The sides of the barn aren't in any better shape. The desert sun can tear apart almost anything, given enough time."

He grabbed a flashlight, flipped off the safety strap from his holster, and kept his hand within reach of his pistol as he climbed out of the vehicle. "Let me check things out before you turn off the lights and engine and follow me in.

If there's trouble, put the car in reverse and get out of here.''

She watched him for a moment. Was he kidding? She was capable of many things, but not abandoning someone when the going got rough. Yet, as she looked at Chris sleeping in the back, she realized she'd have no other choice if something did go wrong. Her stomach twisted into a knot. "I'll make sure you're safe no matter what, sweetheart. But I'll have to come right back. Nick deserves that much from both of us."

Hoping that she wouldn't have to make any drastic choices, she waited, but Nick soon returned. "Someone's been here recently, all right, but whoever it was is long gone now," he said. "Come in with me and tell me if you notice anything missing."

"I'll try, but it's been a *very* long time since I was here." She unfastened the car seat and carried Chris inside the barn with her. Nick joined her after turning off the engine and grabbing the ignition key.

With the help of Nick's flashlight, Eden located the wall switch that turned on the single lightbulb dangling from a cord near the center of the interior. A clear brightness illuminated the small wooden building, which was crowded with old furniture and boxes resting on wooden pallets.

Eden glanced around, recognizing pieces such as her parents' bed and dresser. Memories came flooding back and, with them, a sadness that was hard to shake off. Her whole family had been ripped from her, victims of a web of deceit that followed her to this day.

"Are you okay?" Nick asked quietly.

She nodded. "Sometimes it gets to me, that's all. I loved my parents, but their love for each other was more like a curse than a blessing. My dad's job as a BIA cop nearly destroyed my mother because she loved him so much. In the end, when they finally stood together, it cost them their lives. The way I see it, all their love ever really did for them was define their version of Hell.''

''My parents were like that, too,'' he said, his voice taut. ''And he was a rancher, not a cop. The only thing worse for them than being together was when they were apart. I don't think love comes with any guarantees of perfection.''

She held his gaze. ''And look at you and me… We've hurt each other time and time again.''

He spoke slowly, and with effort, as if the words he really wanted to say stayed just beyond his reach. ''But something—something right—brings us back together.''

''And eventually pulls us apart. We just aren't good for each other.''

''I have to disagree,'' he said. His smile, so full of male confidence, tore her breath away. ''There are times when we are *very* good for each other.''

Feeling herself responding to him, she moved back, focusing on the furnishings that represented a piece of her past. ''Let's get to work,'' she mumbled quickly.

They went through each piece together. Nick checked the drawers and compartments, searching bottoms and sides as well, looking for anything that might have been overlooked. When they reached the last piece, a nightstand that had been damaged by a leaky roof, Eden opened the drawer and found a small snapshot inside.

Her eyes misted as she saw the photo of her and her mother taken their last Christmas together. ''I was happy then,'' she managed. ''We weren't the ideal family, but we had each other. Then, after they were gone, there was nothing for me—just recriminations and the distrust of an entire pueblo. I was so terribly alone and unhappy.''

''Those days are gone, Eden. You'll never be able to

recapture what you lost, but you have other things in your life now. Open your eyes and really see what's there.''

Her gaze gentled as it settled over her son, who was still asleep in the carrier now resting on the dining table. ''My son is the biggest blessing in my life.''

''There are other things, too. But you have to reach out and take them,'' he said, grasping her shoulders and turning her around to face him.

As they stood face to face, she held her breath. There was a world of wanting in his eyes, but it was far more than passion. She could see the reflection of love in his eyes. Something melted inside her, taking away every reason for resisting.

He cupped her face in his hands, then traced her lips with the tip of his tongue.

Eden wrapped her arms around him, trembling. Feeling his breath on her mouth, she waited for his kiss, needing to taste him and feel the heat of his passion, but he didn't move.

''What happens next is up to you, Eden,'' he said, his voice a throaty whisper. ''You have to need me as much as I need you, or it's no good.''

She kissed him then, putting her heart into it in a way she hadn't done since that one fateful night so long ago. Eden pushed the folds of his shirt aside, and pressed her palms against his chest, caressing his smooth muscles. ''You tempt me every time you come close, Nick, and when you touch me all I want is more.''

Nick's body felt as hot as a furnace. He'd loved her once, but she'd walked out on him. This time she would remember every kiss, every touch. Tonight, he would burn a path to her soul.

''I want to kiss you in all those secret places that drive you wild. I want you to remember the fire…''

Nick pulled her blouse open, pushing her bra aside and pressed her against his own naked chest. "I like the way you tremble in my arms," he said in a raw voice, then covered her mouth with his, swallowing the little cries that came from the depths of her being.

His kiss was hot and hungry, and the slide of his lips against hers made her wild.

"This is the way it should be," he said, his voice seductively rough and masculine.

Nick lowered his head and took her breast into his mouth. The sensations that ripped through her made her arch against him, craving more.

Her soft cries tore through him. Nick slid his hands down her back to the curve of her buttocks, then lifted her against him, letting her feel his hardness. Her body softened, yielding to him in a way he remembered well.

"Nick." His name was a whispered plea on her lips. She moved instinctively against him, fitting herself against his heat in a way that made everything male in him respond.

He kissed her again, not knowing or caring who was possessing and who was being possessed. Her body told him that she was his, and the time was now. Blood thundered through his veins, driving him to take everything she offered him.

Suddenly a car horn blasted, rattling the windows. Chris awoke and immediately began crying. As tiny rays of light from a pair of headlights forced their way through the cracks in the outside walls, Nick moved away from Eden, cursing under his breath.

Nick walked to the barn doors and looked outside. A tribal vehicle continued down the road, slowly. "It's Deputy Torres. But what he's doing here is beyond me."

"He may have seen your tribal unit and came by to make sure everything was okay."

Nick crouched by the ground, and saw footprints that weren't his or Eden's just outside the entrance. Anger filled him. Torres's insistence on knowing everything that was happening was getting old in a hurry and, tonight, he'd learned far more than Nick had ever meant for him to discover. The car horn and headlights as he was leaving had only been his way of announcing he'd been there.

As he turned around to look at Eden, he saw her cradling Christopher in her arms, her blouse still open. The fire in him burned unabated. Yet, as their eyes met, he knew their moment had come and gone. Desire no longer shined in her eyes. All he could see now was bewilderment, and a trace of fear.

The knowledge nearly destroyed him. He didn't want the love he could give her to be tainted by regret or fear. If that's what was left in her heart when he no longer held her, then it was no good.

"You better take us home, Nick," she said, now that the baby had calmed down.

He nodded, devastated by what he'd discovered.

"This can't happen again," she said quietly as they got underway. "We'll only destroy each other if we keep going down this path. You don't want a family, and, like me, your life is set up the way you want it. You've got your career. I've got my son and he'll always come first. You and I had our chance and it slipped away from us. We have to accept it. Trust is not something that will ever come naturally between us and, without it, we have nothing."

"Time changes everything, Eden. You know that. I'm not the same man I was a few years ago before my father's death brought me back home. I wouldn't have ever risked a relationship back then with a woman who had a child. But life has a way of tearing us down and reshaping us. I don't see having a family in the same light as I used to. A man needs something more than himself. But trust is another thing. It isn't something I can do anymore and I'm not sure that'll ever change.

''That's why we have to back away from each other. A relationship where trust doesn't exist can't survive. If we allow emotions to draw us together, we'll rip each other apart. I don't want that to happen. We already carry too many scars from the past. It's time we both realized that some things are just not meant to be.''

She saw the hesitancy in his eyes and understood exactly what he was feeling. It was hard to walk away from what their hearts so desperately wanted, but they had no choice. Destiny had left them with no other options.

Chapter Ten

It was just past noon, and Eden was walking back from school. Today Mrs. Chino would keep Christopher until mid afternoon so Eden could run some errands. Although she loved her little son, it was incredible how much more time even the simplest things took when he was around.

Hearing a vehicle approaching from behind her, Eden turned her head. Her pulse began to race as she saw Nick turning toward her in his old Jeep. They'd canceled their early morning trip after last night's adventure, so she hadn't expected to see him.

He pulled to a stop beside her. "I got a phone call from Annie this morning. Noelle got them up even earlier than they'd expected, and both she and Jake took advantage of the extra time to study the photo albums. It turns out that they found a snapshot of your mother and mine by an old farmhouse near the Rio Grande. Jake and I both remember that place because Mom used to love to pack a picnic basket and spend the day out there when we were kids."

"You think my mother might have used the farmhouse as a hiding place instead of my grandmother's barn?" she asked.

Nick looked relaxed out of uniform, wearing a chambray shirt unbuttoned nearly halfway down with the sleeves rolled up. There was a radiant male vitality about him that wrapped itself around her, making it difficult to keep her thinking clear.

"I don't know if we'll find anything out there, but it's worth checking out, don't you think?"

"You bet. I assume you're off duty at the moment." The really frightening thing was how badly she wanted to be with him right now. Finding the artifacts meant the world to her, yet what she wanted most was time to spend with him.

"I'm off and I won't be reporting to work until late this evening. I'm working graveyard tonight. So I'm heading out to the farmhouse now. Do you want to come?"

As she saw herself reflected in his eyes, she understood how easy it would be to lose herself in that dark gaze, and never want to find herself again except through him.

Her own vulnerability frightened her and she forced herself to focus on the task at hand. "I don't have to pick up Chris until this evening, so this is a good time for me," she said.

Eden slipped into the passenger's seat. "By the way, I had a long talk with the two girls, Berta and Terri, this morning. I don't believe they'll be playing matchmaker again for a long time. But kids do have short memories, so stay on your guard," she warned.

He laughed. "A part of me tends to see what they did as a good deed. I can't honestly say that I regret having seen you wearing only a towel."

Eden shot him The Look, something she'd already begun to perfect as a teacher. Not surprisingly, it worked.

The ride across the country road was rough, but she'd expected that. After thirty minutes of driving, however, she began to suspect that they were going in circles.

"Nick, far be it from me to criticize, but I recognize that canyon. We've been here before."

"I know," he answered, looking in his rearview mirror.

She turned her head. No one was behind them. The muddy dirt track was completely deserted. "Why are you going in circles, then? No one's following us."

"There's someone back there, all right. I saw the flash of chrome twice. He's just being cautious."

"Do you think he's hoping we'll take him right to the stolen goods?"

"No." His gaze kept darting to the rearview mirror. "No one knew where we were going and why except Jake and Annie. My guess is we're about to be paid an impromptu visit by whoever's been trying to run you off the pueblo."

"Can you lose him?"

"Probably. But I don't know how long it'll be before we get another shot at him and, as long as he's not in custody, he's a danger to you." His jaw was clenched and his hands were wrapped so tightly around the wheel that his knuckles were pearly white. "What I would like to do is reel him in, then spring a trap," Nick said, his voice low and lethal. "But there's risk in what I'm proposing, just as there's risk in letting him go. This has to be your call. Just remember that I know this area like the back of my hand."

"And if he does too?"

"That's a possibility," he conceded, then in a firm voice added, "But I'll guard you with my own life, Eden. Don't doubt that for one second."

"I don't," she said. "And you're right. It's time to fight back. He's had me on the run for too long. Let's go for it."

With a nod, Nick accelerated down a bumpy road bordered on both sides by salt cedars and tall willows. From the direction they were taking, and the type of vegetation, Eden knew they were headed toward the river.

"I think I recognize this spot. Weren't there some old wells around here that we were always warned to avoid? Some were covered by boards to keep animals from falling in."

"That's part of my plan. Just hang on, I'm trying to get far enough ahead of him so I'll have time to set the trap," Nick said, keeping a sharp eye on the trail.

Just as they were nearing a low ridge she recognized as a flood-control levee, Nick left the trail and drove into some brush, coming to an abrupt stop. "Quickly now, follow me." He grabbed the keys, and reached over and took her hand, pulling her out of the driver's side with him.

Her hand was small, but it fit inside his as if they'd been made for each other.

Nick led her quickly over the levee and into the low, marshy terrain on the other side. The ground was damp in places where moisture had seeped up from the water table only a few feet below.

"The place I'm looking for should be just about... whoa!"

Nick stopped suddenly, and pointed at the ground in front of him. Barely visible below the thick, overgrown marsh grass was a board. "That's one of those wells. I remember almost falling through one of those." He placed a foot upon the board, and it began to bend under the pressure. "Perfect. Now, one more print. Could you take off your left shoe? Leave the mud on if you can. And do it quickly, please?"

Now she knew what Nick had in mind. Pulling off her shoe, she handed it to him. She stood balanced on one foot, trying to avoid sticking her bare foot into the mud.

Nick leaned over and made a left shoe impression farther

out, as if someone had walked over the board. He then pushed some of the grass aside, as if it had been parted by someone passing through.

"Here." He handed her shoe back to her. "Now, stepping in my prints, follow me. And let's move fast. I think I hear him coming."

Slipping on her shoe hastily, Eden followed literally in his footsteps. As they passed through a thicket of tall willows, she followed his example and ducked low, moving at a ninety-degree angle another ten feet before stopping. Here, they'd be out of sight from anyone approaching on the same path they'd followed.

They'd only waited a minute or two before Eden heard someone drawing near. The steps got closer then stopped. Everything became silent except for the high-pitched whine of mosquitoes buzzing near her head.

Then she heard the crunch of wood splitting and a startled cry. Nick leaped up from his crouched position and ran toward the sound. She followed, eager to find out the identity of her enemy.

They arrived at the old well and found a large hole where their adversary had fallen through. Inching closer to the edge, they peered down. Tewa curses Eden hadn't heard in years erupted from the mouth of their trapped prey. But it was the face of her enemy that surprised her most.

"Deputy Torres! You're the one who's been trying to run me off the pueblo? I don't understand. Why would you of all people turn your back on your oath? I'm not your enemy."

Nick's expression was cold as he looked down on his adversary. "Let's just leave him here. Next rain, he'll probably rise to the surface and somebody will find the body."

There was another string of curses from Torres, then he grew quiet for a moment. All they could hear was grunting and the sloshing of his feet and hands against the muddy sides of the well. "I can't get out of here without your help," Torres said finally. "I'm hanging on to a tree root, but if I try to pull myself up, it could break. And there's nothing to hold on to beneath me. If I slide down, I'll hit the water and I won't be able to climb out. So how about it, Nick? Give me a hand up? I'm a cop, too."

"You were—until you started harassing Eden. Now you're just another criminal who has run out of luck. Give me one good reason why we shouldn't just walk away, rub out our tracks, and pretend we never saw you today."

Eden looked at Nick. He was after something. She knew Nick too well to believe that he'd actually leave the man there to die.

"Give me a good reason to save your butt, Torres. Otherwise, I'm going to look very cruel to Eden here when I grab her arm and we leave without you," Nick snarled.

"Do you want a confession? Is that it? Okay, I'll give you one. I've been trying to run her off. I don't think a half white should get Tewa land or a house. I was chasing her across the desert that night when you interfered. And the notes are my work too. I admit it. But I didn't want to hurt her or her kid, I just wanted to scare her into leaving. Hell, I'm not the only one who feels this way about half whites. Even your own father was against her family living here. Didn't you know that?"

"Leave my father out of this," Nick snapped. "He'd have never terrorized a woman. What you did was beneath contempt."

"All right. You've got me. I'll stop bothering Eden from now on. Just get me out of here."

Nick looked up at Eden, and moved her away from the hole. "Once he gets out, it'll be his word against ours. We don't have anything that'll stand up in court. We could call

Mora for backup and let him hear his confession, but Torres may not be able to hold on that long. And it's a long drop, not to mention he probably can't swim.''

She suddenly understood what he'd been trying to do. ''Give me a second.'' Eden went back and looked down into the hole. Torres was clutching the side of the opening with both hands. He was looking up, his face muddy, his eyes wide with fear.

''That night you chased me across the desert, when you were supposed to be on duty, you weren't driving your truck or a tribal unit. Whose pickup did you use?''

''My cousin's. He lives in Santa Fe. I told him it was to help a friend move furniture. If it's proof against me that you want before you'll help me, you can ask him. His truck got banged up out here, and it was easy to see that I hadn't used it for what I said.''

''Okay. Now let's see about getting you out of there,'' she nodded to Nick.

''I'm going to have to go back to the Jeep and get some towrope I keep behind the seat. You might want to find out everything you can while I'm gone,'' Nick told her loud enough for Torres to hear. ''If he refuses to keep talking, I don't have to find the rope.'' Nick said. ''And if he manages to climb up before I get back, knock him back down with one of those boards.''

Before she could answer, Nick turned and took off at a jog toward where they'd parked.

Eden turned back toward the hole, got down on her hands and knees, and smiled at the deputy straining to stay above the water. ''Let's talk to pass the time until Nick gets back with a rope, Deputy. Okay with you?''

AN HOUR LATER they were standing by the Jeep, scraping mud off their shoes. Torres was muddy all over, and he was using bottled water and a handkerchief to try and get as much as he could off his face and uniform before he went back to the station.

"We'd better get going, Eden. We still have a few things to do today. I think Torres can find his own way back." Nick noted the handheld radio resting on the hood of Torres's vehicle, drying out. It had fallen into the water, and Torres had insisted on plucking it out of the well before coming up, though it would probably never work again.

"Are you planning to turn me in?" Torres asked, a lot surer of himself now that he was no longer in danger.

Nick looked at Eden. "It's your call."

Eden looked at the deputy. He'd done his best to frighten her, but nothing more. She met his gaze with a steady one. "The tribe needs you and, as far as I know, you've done a good job until now. If I file a complaint and press charges, it'll ruin everything you've ever worked for and create a hardship for the tribe. I'd rather not take this any further, but I want your word that you'll leave me alone."

"You have it. My job means a lot to me. And, for the record, I really wouldn't have hurt you," he answered honestly. "You'll never have any more problems from me. And you can count on my help, should you ever need it."

Eden believed him, but she looked at Nick, wondering if she was being naive.

"He *will* leave you alone," Nick said, his voice hard, "because if he doesn't, *I'll* come after him."

"All right," Eden said at last. "As long as you stay out of my way, we'll have nothing to fear from each other."

Nick took her hand as they walked back to his vehicle. "You did the right thing, Eden. He made a mistake—a big one, but he'll never be a threat to you again. He owes you one now, too, and he knows it."

"I still don't get it. He's the last person I expected to come after me."

"Torres has always wanted to be accepted by the tribe, some didn't believe he was a full-blood Tewa, and gave him a hard time. I think that by coming after you, he was trying to prove his Tewa heritage. Or more to the point, his allegiance to our tribe."

"I know what that's like. Despite what he's done, I can't quite bring myself to hate him."

As they headed back to the Jeep, Nick glanced down at his clothes and then looked at her. "We need to be hosed down."

Eden grimaced. "This mud really sticks to you and it smells like a swamp." She wiped the face of her watch, leaving a muddy smear, but managed to check the time. "Oh-oh. I've got to go pick up my son," Eden said. "Can you drop me off at Mrs. Chino's?"

"If we show up at Mrs. Chino's looking like this, she'll refuse to give Christopher to you," he said. "Let's go to Black Raven Ranch. We can hose down outside, dry off just enough to go inside the house, then shower."

"I don't think Annie's going to be thrilled with that idea."

"She won't mind," he assured her. "She thinks of you like family, Eden. She told me so herself." Nick was certain it was because Annie had sensed his feelings for Eden, but some things had to remain unsaid. "It's probably because she and you have babies so close to the same age," he added instead.

Eden nodded, but didn't respond.

"Plus I think it's important we fill someone else in on what happened to us out here today. I want my brother and Annie to see us looking like we do now, then I want to write down every detail, especially what Torres said about the tan truck and his cousin. I also want to have a record of the time he was out of touch with the dispatcher today. We want all this documented and witnessed just in case he ever gives either of us any trouble.''

They arrived at Black Raven Ranch a short time later, and were about to clean up when Annie came outside.

Annie looked at Eden's clothes and grimaced. ''Those are going to need a lot more than a hose can do. Come on. You can use my shower and borrow some of my clothes. We're the same size. But what on earth happened?''

''It's a long story,'' Eden said with a sigh. ''But I've got to hurry. I've got to get to Mrs. Chino's and pick up Christopher.''

''Don't give it another thought. Mrs. Chino was supposed to baby-sit for us tonight. She can bring your baby here, and take care of both our kids while the four of us have a long, relaxing dinner. What do you say?''

''It sounds wonderful. Are you sure you don't mind going through all that trouble?''

''Are you kidding? I want to hear everything that happened to you two! Curiosity is killing me.''

As Eden started to go inside, Nick came up. ''I'll go to the bunkhouse to clean up, but I'll be back. See you in a little bit.''

''Nick?'' she said before he strode off. As he turned around, she suddenly paused. ''I don't know what to say. Thanks doesn't seem enough after what you did. For the first time since I returned, I don't have to watch my back.''

He wanted to tell her that he'd always stand between her and anything that threatened her. But, as usual, what came out was totally different.

''I'm a cop, Eden. It's all part of what I do.'' Particularly for the only woman I've ever loved, he added mutely and walked away.

Chapter Eleven

Hours later, they sat downstairs, having dinner. Tonight was Annie's once a week break from the demands of motherhood and her gift to Jake and herself. Christopher was with Noelle upstairs in the nursery and Mrs. Chino was looking after them. A sense of family pervaded their gathering.

Eden found herself relaxing in the warmth and comfort of the Black Raven home. After the dinner dishes were done, they all adjourned to the den and Jake poured them each a brandy.

The warmth of the smooth drink felt wonderful. Nick sat on the sofa next to Eden, while Annie and Jake sat on a Navajo rug, going through the contents of a trunk filled with mementos that Annie had found in one of the empty bedrooms.

Eden couldn't help but notice the way that Jake always seemed to reach out for Annie, gently touching her hand, or brushing a strand of hair from her face. Filled with longing, Eden glanced at Nick, scarcely aware of the instinct that had compelled her to do so. As her eyes met his, the tenderness reflected there took her breath away. The yearning to touch him, to feel his warmth, ribboned around her.

"Hey, Nick. Stop being the macho cop, will you?" Annie teased, oblivious to the awareness shimmering between them. "You've said what, about four words this evening? The strong and silent type is also the boring type, and you won't make any points with Eden that way."

Nick smiled, but didn't comment.

"Come on, brother-in-law. Ease up," Annie persisted with a laugh.

Eden felt her heart go out to Nick even as Annie teased him. She knew precisely what he was doing. It was simply easier to disguise the vulnerability that came from caring under a mantle of silence. Nick was capable of every feat of raw courage and pure male strength that there was. Yet *she* was his one vulnerability. The realization made her pulse start beating wildly.

"Hey, this might be useful," Annie said, bringing out a small photo album. "The snapshots inside are of people and scenes that obviously held some special meaning for Saya. It looks like this was your mother's personal photo album," Annie said, looking at Jake, then Nick.

As she turned the page, Annie saw a photo of Saya and another woman. "The writing at the bottom says that this is Isabel, and the photo was taken during a Harvest Festival."

Eden took the snapshot that Annie handed her. Seeing her mother's face so clearly again brought back a kaleidoscope of memories. She looked up, ready to comment, when she saw Jake brush his hand against Annie's cheek, then lead his brother to the decanter of brandy. Annie, Jake, and Nick were a real family, and love and blood bound them. More than anything, she wanted Chris to be part of them, accepted fully and loved.

Yet, although the man trying to run her off the pueblo had been caught and the threat he'd posed neutralized, there were still matters to resolve before she could tell anyone

about Chris. Nick stood to lose too much if she failed at
what she'd set out to do. Despite his stoicism, Nick was
proud of being a Black Raven. She wouldn't take away that
source of family pride by pulling him into her world—one
of shame and dishonor.

As the twin brothers moved off, studying a framed, aerial
photo of the ranch on the far wall, Annie came over to sit
with Eden.

"Look at this photo of the boys as babies," she said,
pulling out the snapshot from the album. "We both know
how hard it is to take care of one baby. Can you imagine
Jake and Nick as kids?" she said.

Hearing footsteps, they turned and saw Mrs. Chino holding the babies. "They came to say good-night," she said,
handing each to their mother.

Annie and Jake kissed Noelle, then handed her back to
Mrs. Chino. Chris was fussing, so Eden offered to keep
him a few minutes longer while Mrs. Chino put Noelle in
bed.

Annie returned to the couch but as she picked up the
photo of the twin babies, her gaze fixed on a detail she'd
missed before. She stared at the photo, then looked up
quickly at Chris, who lay quietly in Eden's arms.

Eden's heart stopped. She knew that Annie had noticed
the small strawberry birthmark on Chris's cheek and was
comparing it to the one on Nick's baby picture. All the
other similarities between father and son suddenly seemed
to scream out at them—everything from the way the babies
smiled, to their habit of leaning into objects with one hand
while trying to balance. Chris was doing it right now. Having scooted off Eden's lap, he was trying to slide down
onto the floor by holding on to the cushion with only one
hand.

Annie looked at Eden, but Eden remained silent, praying

Annie wouldn't say a word. Annie touched the birthmark on Chris's face, then looked at Nick. The birthmark on his cheek had all but faded over the years, but a faint trace of it still remained.

Eden knew that Nick had forgotten the birthmark, but she was certain that he'd remember it, if he saw the photo. Then, her secret would be out, whether she was ready or not.

As the men started coming back, Annie closed the book quickly. "These are mostly baby pictures. They won't do us much good."

From the look on Annie's face, Eden knew for sure that the secret she'd guarded was no longer strictly her own. But, for her own reasons, Annie had chosen not to say anything. Puzzled, but undeniably grateful, she let the matter drop.

"I think I better take Chris home. He's tired," Eden said, "and so am I. It's been a very long day."

"I'll drive you back," Nick said.

After saying goodbye to Annie and Jake, they walked outside to Nick's Jeep. "I wish you'd move to the ranch. You'd be completely safe here. One of the arguments against you is that you're claiming land here and you're half-white. But, if you stayed at Black Raven Ranch, no one would have anything to say."

"I can't do that, Nick. What you're offering me is only a temporary solution, but I won't leave my home. I have a right to stay there."

He nodded once, as if he'd expected that to be her answer. "What about the farmhouse? We never did get there to search because of what happened with Torres." He paused then added, "We should go back soon, but we'll have to make sure we do it without telling anyone."

Eden clearly sensed his hesitancy. "What's bothering

you, Nick? Are you afraid that someone else will come after me if it ever gets out that I'm actually searching for the artifacts?''

"There is that," he conceded. "But what's worrying me goes beyond that, too. Have you ever considered the possibility that the people who set up your mother are probably dead by now, but that their descendants aren't, and they'll be the ones to pay?"

She started to speak, then fell silent, thinking about it a bit longer. "They'll have to go through what I did, I suppose," she said at last. "I don't like it, Nick, but I've paid for this long enough already, and I want to spare my son all the years of pain."

"You're right to pursue it, Eden." Nick took a deep breath, then let it out again. "We have to see this through to the end. The truth has been hidden for too many years."

They rode in silence to her home. When they arrived, Nick took Chris, carrying him for Eden. But, as they reached the door, Chris began to get restless and she took him back.

Nick drew her and the baby she held against her chest, toward him, then dipped his head to kiss her.

"No." Eden moved away from him suddenly. "What we're feeling right now—relief, excitement, the aftermath of fear, isn't enough reason for us to throw common sense aside."

"I want you badly, Eden," Nick said, his voice a raw whisper. "But you're wrong about the rest. I'm not after a few hours of passion. I'll help you find the truth about your past, but until that's said and done, I won't pursue something that may not be mine to keep." He touched Christopher's face lightly. "He deserves more than that from both of us."

Eden knew she should let it go, but the fire in his eyes

was mesmerizing. "It's all or nothing from now on," she said, her voice unsteady. "Is that what you're saying?"

"Yes. I want everything you can give me, everything I can coax you to surrender, and then more. I want all that, because if the day comes when we make love, that's exactly what I'll be giving you."

Without another word, he turned and walked back to his Jeep. Eden's hands were shaking as she opened the door and went inside.

She stood at the window and watched the red taillights until they disappeared from view. Sometimes it felt as if their entire lives had been lived in preparation for what was happening now. "We'll each do what we have to, my love," she said, knowing he'd never hear, "and in the end that may be what rips us apart. May the gods be kind to us both."

IT WAS SHORTLY after nine the following morning when Eden heard a knock at her door. She went to answer it, determined not to ask him inside if it was Nick. No woman could ever hope to endure the temptation this Black Raven posed forever. She'd thought of little else but him all night, lying awake, staring at the ceiling.

When she opened the door, she found Annie standing there. Eden just stared at her, uncertain if she should be relieved or alarmed.

"May I come in?" Annie asked.

"Oh, of course! I'm sorry. It's just…"

"You're surprised to see me, and you want to know what I'm doing here. Or, more importantly, you're wondering if I plan to tell anyone your secret," Annie said, finishing Eden's unspoken thoughts.

"I know it must have been a shock for you, Annie," Eden admitted. "But I'm glad you didn't say anything."

"I needed time to think things through. Now that I'm here, I'm not sure how to say what I came to tell you," Annie admitted after a pause.

Eden's heart flew to her throat. "Just tell me straight out," she said, afraid that Annie had already told Jake, and it would only be a matter of hours before Nick also learned the truth.

"I know that Chris is Nick's son, Eden, but I just can't imagine why you haven't told him. He deserves to know."

"I've wanted to tell him many times, but there was always a reason for keeping quiet. When I met Nick in Arizona, when Chris was conceived, Nick was very sure he didn't want anything to do with a family—his own or anyone else's. He also swore never to come back to the pueblo, and I knew I had to return."

"But all that's changed now, Eden. The proof is that you're both here."

"I've tried to tell him, Annie, but it's not easy for me. I want to protect Chris. That's more important to me than anything else, and I haven't been able to get past my own memories of what it was like to grow up with a dad who was in law enforcement."

"But he has to know. It's his right," Annie insisted gently.

Eden paused then added, "But it's more than that. I need to clear my family's name first. By searching for the missing artifacts and the real thieves, something I intend to do now even more intensely than I have been, I'm taking a huge risk. Although it's possible that the real thief or thieves are long dead, I suspect their families will go to great lengths to keep the disgrace that has shrouded my family from tainting theirs. Anything can happen. Unless I can prove my parents' innocence, it's possible I'll be framed in some way just like they were, or create even more trouble for myself somehow. I could lose this battle, and if I do, Christopher and I will be banned from the pueblo forever. I don't want Nick to get caught up in that. I can start a new life with my son, but Nick's life is here. He's proud of being a Black Raven. I don't want to pull him into my world—one filled with dishonor and shame.''

"But, Eden, you have no way of knowing who the real thief's family is. They may not care, or even be a part of this pueblo anymore.''

"In the letter I was given along with my grandmother's personal property, she said that the person behind the frame might have been a man nicknamed Tall Shadow.''

Annie inhaled sharply. "That can't be true. That was a nickname a few of the old-timers gave Paul because he was a man of great influence.''

Eden stared at Annie, now at a loss for words. Nick had never mentioned that, yet he'd helped her knowing about his father's possible involvement and what it could cost him. Now she understood what he'd meant when he'd spoken of not reaching for something he couldn't keep. If he and his family lost everything, Nick would have gone on alone, never asking her to share his exile from the pueblo or his shame. She'd tried to protect him by doing the same thing.

"Paul wasn't guilty,'' Annie repeated. "And Nick knows it. He's trying to find the truth for our sakes as well as for yours.''

Eden nodded. "I think you're right.'' Nick's determination to find the truth undoubtedly matched her own because he would never believe his father was involved, no more than she'd accepted her parents' guilt.

"Annie, do you understand what this means? It's even more important now that Nick not know Chris is his son. If by clearing my parents I end up inadvertently implicating his father, I'll be the one who ruins the Black Ravens. You know what will happen, Annie. The tribe will put sanctions in place and not allow Paul's family to occupy land here at all. Jake and Nick will be ruined, and Black Raven Ranch will be lost. And he'll hate me for it—me and Christopher. His own son.''

Annie nodded slowly, the terrible impact of what was happening dawning over her. ''All right. I'll keep your secret for a while longer, Eden, but talk to Nick about Tall Shadow. I knew Paul, probably better than most people. Even in the old days, Paul Black Raven lived by his own code of honor and there's no way anyone will ever convince me that he was capable of something like that.'' Annie stood up. ''Tell Nick what you know and talk it over with him. He's helped you all along, though he knew what it could cost him. He deserves this much from you,'' Annie finished.

''All right. I'll talk to him.''

Annie handed Eden the close-up photo of Jake and Nick when they were babies. ''In the meantime, you better keep this,'' she said.

''Thanks.''

Annie stood and walked to the phone. Picking up the receiver, she held it out to Eden. ''Call Nick now, before you change your mind.''

Eden did as she asked, and when Nick answered the phone, she asked him to come by, her heart heavy.

''Are you all right?'' Nick asked, as if he'd sensed something was wrong.

''I'm not sure if anything will ever be all right again.''

NICK ARRIVED only a few minutes after Annie had left. He stood at the doorway, wearing his uniform, and gazed down on her. "What's going on? You sounded really upset on the phone."

Eden showed him in, but before sitting down, Nick stopped to pick up Christopher and give him a kiss.

Eden watched her son and his father, her chest tight. They belonged together, but the more she wished it were so the more obstacles got in their way.

"We have to talk," she said. Eden blurted out what Annie had told her about Paul Black Raven, hardly stopping for a breath. "Nick, why didn't you tell me you knew who Tall Shadow was?"

He said nothing for several moments, weighing his answer carefully. "I wanted to help you, Eden. I...care what happens to you. Besides, I'm a cop, and it's my job to get at the truth."

"Nick, don't you see that by helping me clear my parents, you could end up ruining your own family? We can't work together now. I'm not even sure I want to find the truth anymore. This whole thing scares me witless. I never counted on this. I have no desire to hurt you, Jake or Annie. You spoke of the cost before. Well, this is the one price I'm *not* willing to pay."

"After coming this far, you can't back off and neither can I," he said firmly.

His strong tone surprised her, and she looked up quickly. "I don't understand."

"All this time you've said that you knew your parents were framed. To you, there was no other explanation possible. It's the same for me. I spent many years thinking that my father was nothing to me, but after his death I learned more about the man than I ever did when he was alive. My father was many things, but he wouldn't have destroyed a family in this way. I know with everything in me that my father isn't guilty. He's been framed too, and I'll do what it takes to get to the truth.''

''But the letter—''

''I believe your grandmother was told that my father was involved, and that she believed those stories. But I'm also convinced that she was being misled. Someone wanted to make sure your grandmother didn't take up the investigation. My father was a powerful man and not many people went up against him. I believe the real thieves started the rumor to intimidate and control her.''

''If you're wrong…''

''I'm not. This isn't just an emotional response, or loyalty. I'm basing my belief on my knowledge of my father, just as you are on your knowledge of your parents.''

She couldn't fault him for that. She took a deep breath, then continued. ''Okay. We'll keep digging. But I want you to keep something in mind. We don't necessarily have to make everything we learn public. If we find evidence that *won't* serve justice, we'll keep it to ourselves,'' Eden said. She was capable of many things, but not destroying her child's father, or hurting other innocent people.

He shook his head. ''That's not the way I work, but let's cross that bridge when we get to it. For now, we'll work from the standpoint of what we believe—that this isn't an either/or situation. That there's a third answer, the truth.''

''Nick, I don't know…''

''I do. And by the way, I need your help. I have to go on duty later today, so we won't have time to search the farmhouse. That building is in poor shape and we'll have to go slow. I don't want portions of it falling in on us. What I thought we could do instead was check out the photos Martin told us about at the special collections section of the university library. I have a feeling we'll be able to find quite a bit of information there, but it's been a long time since I did any research at a university. I have a feeling you can cut my time there by at least half.''

"I'll have to ask Mrs. Chino if she can baby-sit. At least it's Saturday, and she doesn't have the daycare kids.''

Nick grinned. "I saw her on the way here, and stopped and asked her. She should be over in a few minutes.''

"That sure of me, are you?'' she said with a wry smile.

"When it comes to this, yes,'' he answered somberly.

They were underway less than ten minutes later. They drove south through Santa Fe, then on toward Albuquerque. Though her heart still felt like a rock inside her, she tried hard to keep her tone light.

They arrived at the large university campus in Albuquerque over forty-five minutes later. Finding a parking spot was nearly impossible, and they had a long walk across campus before reaching the library.

Once there, they realized that recent renovations had only made the facility more confusing. Finally after ten minutes of going up and down stairs, and from east wing to west, they were sequestered in a large, windowless room lined with ceiling-high metal bookshelves. The entire area was ventilated by one small ceiling fan and a trace of air-conditioning that came from a tiny vent in the ceiling thirty feet away.

Yet, despite the musty air and stifling temperature in the room, Eden still had to struggle with a different kind of heat as she sat next to Nick. Eden could feel his hard thigh next to hers and as their eyes met, she had to suppress a wistful sigh.

With a struggle, they shifted their chairs a little farther apart, though the space between the bookshelves didn't allow them much maneuvering room. Trying to pretend that neither was bothered by their proximity, they got down to work and began searching through volumes of books that were as old as the artifacts themselves.

An hour passed and they made progress, finding sketches of the missing artifacts in an old anthropology manual that had been handwritten by a professor in the early 1900s. Unfortunately, the sketches were too crude to give them any real visual images, although the descriptions were far more detailed than any they'd found so far.

Eden stood and stretched slowly. Catching a glimpse of Nick out of the corner of her eye, she saw his gaze searing over her, taking in every curve with undisguised hunger.

She was suddenly aware of everything about him. Prickles danced along her skin as they looked at each other for one endless moment. Each could sense the other's needs, yet neither spoke of it.

Too unsettled to sit down, she began to walk around the room, feigning great interest in everything and anything, except him. As she passed the row of bookshelves that blocked their view of the rest of the room by acting as a divider, she suddenly froze in midstep.

Noiselessly, she returned to their table. "You won't believe who's here," she whispered. "I just saw Patrick Korman. He's researching, just like us, from the looks of it. But why would a bookkeeper find that necessary?"

"Good question." He stood up quietly. "Did he see you?"

"No, I don't think so."

"Good. We may yet be able to turn this trip into something more than a marginal waste of time. Did you happen to notice what he was reading?"

"No. I couldn't tell from where I was standing."

Hearing a chair being pushed back noisily, they exchanged a quick glance. "I'm going to follow him out," Nick whispered.

"I'll go with you."

He shook his head. "I'll have a better chance of not getting spotted if I'm alone. Try to find out what he was reading instead."

She waited, then after hearing the door open and close twice, came out into the aisle and walked to where Patrick had been working. The books on the shelf next to the small table were tomes on Tewa religious practices, but there was no telling which of the books Patrick had been studying or, more importantly, why.

She rapidly searched through all the books, looking for a sign that would indicate which one he'd been studying so intently. Then, as she leafed through the pages, she saw the remainder of a small notepad he'd left behind. There was an impression on the top sheet, so she used a pencil from her purse and rubbed the side of the point on the paper, hoping the indentations would show clearly enough to give her an idea what he'd written down. What she un-covered was a sketch of the missing *Tsave Yoh* mask, taken from a description in that text.

It was better than anything she'd seen so far. The mask was conical in shape and tiny slits were cut for the eyes. The facial features were simple but a bit intimidating.

Now she knew what he'd been doing. But Patrick would have been about twelve years old at the time of the theft. It was unlikely that he'd been involved in any way. His interest in the relics puzzled her.

As usual, instead of answers, all she'd found were more questions. Placing the paper in her purse, she left the room and went outside to wait for Nick.

Eden sat on a bench beside the southern entrance to the library. As the minutes ticked by, her thoughts wandered back to Annie and the secret they now shared. Eden reached into her wallet and flipped it open to the photo Annie had given her of Nick and Jake as babies. The similarity between father and son was remarkable. They had the same eyes and mouth and identical mischievous smiles.

Hearing footsteps behind her, she turned her head quickly, nearly dropping her wallet.

"Relax, it's just me," Nick said.

"Did you find out anything interesting?"

He shook his head. "No. I lost him out in the mall when some classes let out." He glanced down at her wallet, but by then she was already putting it back in her purse. "What were you looking at so intently?"

"Oh, just an old family photo. Should we head back now?" she said, quickly changing the subject.

"Sure. By the way, did you ever figure out what Patrick Korman was researching?"

She filled him in as they walked, showing him the paper from the notepad. "Unfortunately we don't know why he did this—whether it was curiosity or something more."

"The theft is a sore spot with his stepmother, I know that," Nick said thoughtfully.

They were walking down the sidewalk toward the east end lot where Nick's Jeep was parked, when she noticed that Nick was slowing down imperceptibly, and stopping at odd moments to look toward the tennis courts, or one of the dorms. She let it go at first, hoping he'd tell her what he was doing without being prompted, but finally her curiosity got the best of her. "Okay, you're starting to make me nervous. What's going on?"

"Someone's tailing us. I wasn't sure at first, but I am now."

"Deputy Torres again?"

"No, this is too sloppy. Torres would have been more careful." Nick considered it for a moment. "Whoever's back there is an amateur, and I'm sure he won't make a move on us in a place this public. But I'd like to push it and find out who we're dealing with. You game?''

"You bet I am. If someone else wants to scare me away, then I want to know who I'm up against as soon as possible.''

Eden knew they were in this together now, and her courage would have to match his own every step of the way. It was no longer a matter of Nick trying to protect her. From now on, they'd have to protect each other, or what they were facing could end up destroying everything and everyone they loved.

Chapter Twelve

They worked quickly, trying to turn the tables on their pursuer by reversing course and heading back west toward most of the lecture halls. But whoever was following them anticipated their moves.

Nick muttered a curse. "This guy is crafty." He looked around, trying to come up with another plan. "I wish I'd brought my handheld radio. I could have recruited a couple of campus cops and gotten to the bottom of this fast."

"You think it's Patrick Korman?"

"No. I only caught a glimpse of the person when he was turned away, but I think I know who it is."

She waited but when he didn't volunteer any more information, she pressed him. "Do you plan to share this information with me, or do I have to drag it out of you?"

Nick grinned. "I have to admit, it would be a lot of fun to have you try." Seeing the flush of anger on her face, he laughed. "Ease up. I think it's my uncle."

"Thomas? Why would he follow us?"

Nick thought about it for a while, trying to reason it out. "I believe that Thomas is the one who stole my mother's diary," he said at last. "My guess is that Thomas took the diary hoping to find the stolen artifacts. As you know, he's in a jam with some of the casinos and I think he needs a large sum to bail himself out—the kind of money the tribe's always offered as a reward for the return of the stolen religious items.''

''Do you think he's hoping we'll lead him to a clue he can put together with what's in the diary? Depending on how much of an edge that gives him, it's possible he could find the mask and the fetish long before we do. And if he does, are you sure he wouldn't just sell them to the highest bidder?''

''I think that what Thomas wants most right now is some peace in his life. Dealing with fences and trying to pass stolen merchandise would only bring more trouble down on him, and he knows that. He's always been one to look for the easy way out and, in this case, that's the tribe.''

Nick led her into a two-story lecture hall, down a long hallway, and then ducked into an empty classroom. Crossing the room, they went out the opposite hall in a new direction. By the time they were back on the street, there was no sign of their tail. ''Okay, we've lost him,'' he said, his expression veiled, his shoulders rigid. ''At least for now.''

''I thought you wanted to catch him.''

''I do, and we will, but he anticipated me last time so I needed to come up with an alternate way of catching him. One thing's for sure. My uncle didn't walk from San Esteban or take a bus, and I know he doesn't have a parking sticker. So we're going to drive through the visitor parking areas until we spot his pickup. Then, we stake it out.''

Within minutes they were in Nick's Jeep, backing out of the slot, ready to search the campus parking lots. ''I don't believe this,'' Nick said suddenly. ''He parked in the same lot we did.''

He gestured to his left. Thomas was climbing into a beat-up old pickup several cars down from them. ''Hang on.''

Nick drove quickly down the row, then pulled up and stopped inches behind his uncle's truck, effectively pinning him in. The concrete barrier in front of his uncle's truck prevented him from heading out the front, and vehicles were parked on both sides.

"Stay here," Nick growled, jumping out of the Jeep, then grabbing his uncle as Thomas climbed out of his own vehicle.

Thomas laughed, though Nick was rough with him as he half dragged his uncle back to where Eden stood waiting.

"I figured you two would turn the tables on me sooner or later," Thomas said, winking at Eden. "But I had you there for a while."

"This isn't a school yard game," Nick said coldly.

"Oh, sure it is. All of life is one cruel game, nephew, and you better get used to that."

"You just don't know when to quit, do you? Tell me the truth for once. Why were you following us?" Nick demanded.

"I think you've guessed already. But would you like me to make up a believable lie instead?" His smile suddenly faded as a late-model sedan stopped in the lot just a few spaces behind Nick's truck. Two men were inside, staring in their direction.

Nick automatically put himself between Eden and them. From their slicked-back haircuts, sunglasses, and their obvious interest in his uncle, he knew immediately who they were. "That's casino muscle again, maybe the same guys that beat you up before. You want to tell me what's going on now?" Guessing that his uncle was about to deny everything, he held up his hand. "Don't waste my time with evasions."

Eden looked at Thomas. "You're going to need help against those men, and we need your help. Work with us."

"I'm not going to keep Eden here for nothing," Nick said. "Talk to me, or I'm taking off."

"You want information," Thomas said thoughtfully. "Well, as it happens, I do have something to trade. You're still going crazy trying to find that diary, aren't you? Well, here's a flash. It was like you and Jake thought. I took it—right off the shelf."

"My brother put a phoney book jacket over it. How did you know?"

"I watched him carefully, biding my time. Binoculars are very handy. Every evening when he went to his study, the curtain was still open. It took me about ten days but eventually I found his hiding place. The day of Noelle's naming ritual, I took the opportunity to make my move."

"So, if you have it, why are you following us now?"

"Saya's diary has many secrets, but it's also very cryptic. My sister was a clever woman, and much better educated than I am. I really can't make heads or tails out of what she wrote most of the time. But you seemed to be on the trail, even without the diary. So, I figured that you might find a lead that I could use. But I really didn't expect you to be so alert when you're off duty."

"I want that diary back," Nick snapped.

Thomas went back to his truck, reached under the seat and brought out a brown paper bag. "It's in here."

Nick blinked, but otherwise tried to keep his expression neutral. Something was very wrong here. Why would his uncle be carrying the diary around, and why would he hand it over without hesitation?

He pulled the diary out from the bag, verifying it was the genuine article, then looked at his uncle, who was watching the goons circling the lot slowly. Suddenly he understood. Thomas had undoubtedly made at least one copy of it already. The original diary itself was of no interest to him—just the information it contained.

Nick motioned with his head toward the casino's muscle. Their vehicle was coming down their row again. "Is that the reason you had this with you? Were you planning to use it as leverage, pointing out its blackmail potential, if you had to buy your way out of another beating?"

"Trading it wouldn't have been my first option," Thomas said, avoiding a direct answer.

Nick went to where Eden stood, Thomas following. "Wait here," Nick growled, handing the diary to Eden. Leaving her and his uncle standing by the truck, he strode over to where the sedan was positioned, one car length behind his Jeep.

Even the thought of his mother's diary in the hands of those men made him want to punch something—or someone.

Nick stopped just out of arms reach from the driver's window, his feet slightly apart, and his body braced for a fight, just in case it came to that. "Boys, I'm having a bad day, and I'm just not in a patient mood. Why don't you let my uncle drive away this time?" Nick's voice was calm, yet held a lethal edge.

"You're out of your jurisdiction, deputy," the driver spat out.

"True, but as I'm sure you've figured out, it wouldn't take long for any cop to get back up here." He waved a hand around, indicating a hundred or more students coming onto campus or just leaving classrooms. "Half of those kids seem to have cell phones. If you ignore that and try to lean on us, there's going to be a lot of witnesses who can also get help in a hurry."

"You misjudge us. We're not looking for trouble here,"

the man said with a shrug. "We're only here trolling for college girls."

"You're harassing my uncle," he said, dismissing their lie. "Do you really want me to start making out official reports? The regulatory commission doesn't like strong-arm tactics, and the casinos hate it when they get bad press. Before you know it, you'd be dealing with the Feds."

The driver put the car in gear. "Relax. We're going. But tell your uncle that this isn't over."

"Really? Well here's a bit of news for you. I catch you on the pueblo, harassing anyone at all, I'll haul your sorry butts in. Count on it."

The other man laughed. "Thomas won't press charges, and you know it. Don't make meaningless threats. We're not impressed."

Nick fought the urge to take a step forward and smash the man's nose with a quick jab. "I may not be able to hold you overnight, but I can and will take you in. Just think of how your bosses would react to that news. Seems to me, they'd want to keep the type of activity you boys are engaged in very low profile."

Nick's gaze locked with the driver's and neither man backed down. After several tense moments, the passenger slipped a tape into the car's stereo. "This is getting boring. Let's go."

Nick remained where he was until they disappeared down Central Avenue. Those men were trouble that wouldn't go away easily. Despite what he'd said, there really wasn't much he could do about it, not if his uncle refused to press charges.

He walked back to where Eden and Thomas stood beside his uncle's pickup. This was the second time his uncle had put Eden in the middle of serious danger. As he looked at her now, he could see the shadow of fear in her eyes. Anger sliced through him.

Nick gave Thomas a lethal glare. "They're gone, but not for long. I want you to follow me back to the pueblo's police station. We'll talk there. You've been holding out on me for a very long time and that's going to stop."

"I've told you everything—"

Nick held up a hand. "Save it." He gestured down the street. "Those guys are probably just circling the block. They'll be back. Eden and I are leaving now, so I suggest you stick with us. Once we're back at the station, we'll discuss this further. If I don't get the complete truth, and enough details so I can verify that you're not playing games, I'm going to turn you over to Captain Mora for the next round of questions. Everyone knows how he feels about gamblers and keeping the pueblo safe. After a conversation with the tribal leaders, he may take you over to their casinos himself to face the music."

"No, wait. Those choices give *me* no choice."

"Now you're getting the picture. I'm tired of playing hide-and-seek with the truth. Come clean now and I'll see what I can do for you. Otherwise you're on your own."

Thomas expelled his breath in a rush. "Look, Nick, talking about the past isn't as easy for me as you might think. I'll tell you whatever you want to know, but let's talk out here, in the open. Its more private than at the station."

"I'm listening."

"Your mother and I were never close," he began. "She had her own way of doing things and I had mine. But when she got sick, things changed between us. Both of us knew that there wasn't much time left and all the arguments we'd had just didn't seem to amount to a hill of beans. Then, toward the end, she did what she'd never done in her life. She asked for my help. She told me that she'd kept a secret for her friend Isabel who had passed away two years before, and now she had to tell someone or the truth would die with her."

"I wondered if my mother had confided in her. I guess that answers it," Eden said softly.

Thomas nodded. "Saya told me that on the days following the theft, while Isabel had been on the run, she'd called a few times and even paid Saya one hurried visit. Though she'd been rushed and very cryptic, she'd told Saya where the artifacts were hidden. She'd wanted someone to know in case something happened to her. After Isabel's death, Saya tried several times to find the artifacts. She'd wanted to retrieve them and turn them over to the head of their religious society. But she was never able to do that. Saya told me that she'd written down all the information she'd gotten from Isabel and she wanted to have that account in the hope that I would be able to succeed where she hadn't. I promised I'd give it my best shot. Saya then told me to come back in a few days and she'd give me everything I'd need. But I was drinking a lot back in those days, and didn't get back to her. A week later when I sobered up, I learned she'd died."

Thomas lapsed into a heavy silence, and, unable to look Nick in the face, continued. "It took me a long time to come to terms with her death. I knew that I'd let her down badly. Eventually, I put a few things together and figured out that Saya had been talking about giving me her diary, but when I failed to show up, she decided to have it burned. She knew the diary contained too many secrets and she was afraid it would be used to hurt her friends someday. Without family to turn to, she decided to trust an old friend. But he ended up betraying the Black Ravens."

"So twenty years after her death—*that's* when you decided to make good on your promise to Mom?'' Nick scoffed.

"Time slipped by, nephew, but I always intended to do right by her."

"So your search for the diary started when?'' Nick pressed.

"Right before you and your brother got sent away to make it on your own," he answered. "I'd seen you and Eden together by the old cottonwood about a mile from the river. You could have gotten yourselves in no end of trouble, but I saw how you held back and how gentle you were with her. I knew then that what you two had was real and that by not following up on my word, I'd not only let Saya down, but you and Eden as well. It's one thing to let the past slide, but it's another when you realize that the past has become part of the present."

"So you started breaking into the ranch right after my brother and I left home?'' he asked.

He nodded. "I was risking a lot, mind you. Paul would have pressed charges and had me thrown in jail had he caught me."

"But you never found it back then,'' Nick said, verifying what he already knew.

"True, but it wasn't for lack of trying."

Nick saw the compassion in Eden's eyes, and realized that she was buying his uncle's story. Of course there was no denying that Thomas had certainly sounded convincing.

Nick captured her gaze and shook his head slightly, giving her a silent warning to reserve judgment a little longer.

"Then a few weeks ago, I overheard Eden at the pueblo questioning some of her mother's former friends,'' Thomas continued. "That's when I realized she was fighting for her son, not just herself. A whole new generation was now being affected by what I'd failed to do for Saya."

Thomas took a deep breath, then let it out slowly. "I knew the time had come for me to act. I started spying on Jake until I found out what he'd done with the diary. But then, after I had it, I discovered that all the passages that pertained to Isabel were written down in double-talk, riddles and codes that would take forever to figure out."

"And you expect me to believe that stealing the diary had nothing to do with the fact that the casino's muscle was leaning on you? It never even occurred to you that if you found the artifacts, the tribe would pay handsomely?"

Thomas looked at the ground, kicking at stones with his boot, but didn't answer him. Instead, he continued. "I've been trying to get Theresa Redwing to help me uncover the truth behind the theft. She was an administrative assistant at the Center during that time. But so far she refuses to get involved. She's afraid she'll lose her job."

"There's another possibility," Eden said. "Maybe she was involved in the theft, and the last thing she wants is for any of us to uncover the truth."

"You're way off base with that one," Thomas said sharply. "Theresa is an honest woman. It's just not in her nature to steal."

"It's *your* nature that bothers me," Nick said roughly. "The real question is how much money do you owe the casinos, and how far you'd be willing to go to get yourself off the hook."

"Look, nephew, it's true that I've never been a model citizen, but there's one thing I wish you'd believe. I stole that diary to right a wrong. Of course if in the process I ended up earning some extra cash from the tribe, you shouldn't begrudge it. Everyone has an angle, nephew. *Everyone,* even the missionaries at the pueblo."

Based on everything he knew about his uncle, the man wouldn't have recognized the truth if it came up and bit him on the nose. Yet, despite all that, this time Nick believed him.

"We need to talk some more, but not out here," Thomas said, cocking his head toward the men who'd returned and were driving slowly past the lot on a parallel campus road. "There are passages in that diary I'd like to point out to you. Let's go to Black Raven Ranch. That's where the diary belongs anyway."

"Plus, you know that they wouldn't trespass onto our ranch. Our name carries a lot of clout at the pueblo."

"There's that, too. What do you say, nephew? You wash my back and I'll wash yours."

Nick glanced at Eden and saw her nod. He knew she wanted to be in on this, too. And she deserved to be. Her courage had never faltered, nor her loyalty to the people she cared about.

"Let's head back to the pueblo," Nick told Thomas. "You lead the way. You'll be safer with us behind you." He'd watch their backs. It was what he did best.

He glanced at Eden and gave her a nod of encouragement. He would take care of her. Keeping Eden from harm had become as vital to him as the beat of his own heart.

Chapter Thirteen

As they drove north up the interstate, Eden found her gaze continually drawn back to Nick. He was moody right now and silent, but it was the kind of silence that held no peace, only disquiet. His face was hard and cold, like a statue made of bronze.

"I know you believe everything my uncle told us, but be careful, Eden. He can't be trusted."

"Are you warning me, or reminding yourself?" she asked gently.

"Both," he admitted after a pause. "He's my uncle and although I'd like to hate him, I can't. He's blood, Eden, and that's a tie I respect."

"Your uncle has hurt you badly with all his lies, but you still want to believe him," she observed.

"So I guess that makes me a fool," he answered wearily.

His eyes were strangely vulnerable as they settled on her for a moment. He was reaching out to her in the only way he knew, not admitting a need for her, but letting her sense it. Nick wanted her comfort, and everything feminine in her responded.

She reached for his hand. "You're not a fool, Nick. You're a man who cares deeply and relies on his instincts to guide him. That's a winning combination."

He shook his head. "I've learned one thing as a cop. Hope only distorts reality."

Eden felt the loneliness that bled outward from his wounded soul. She wanted to touch the core of emptiness that lay at the center of his heart, soothe it, and ultimately heal it. But their love held the power to destroy them both and demanded she hold back. The ultimate proof of her feelings for Nick wouldn't require surrender, but strength to build walls between them so they could survive what lay ahead.

AT BLACK RAVEN Ranch, Thomas honored his word, showing them the passages that he'd spoken about. They were as difficult to understand as he'd predicted.

After Thomas left, Nick sat alone with Eden in the den, studying the passages. "One thing's clear. My mother was heartbroken when your mother died. She felt that she should have done something more for her, and that somehow, she should have protected Isabel."

"But she never says from whom."

Nick knew what she was thinking. Eden was wondering what part his father had played in everything, and if his mother had believed that Isabel had needed protection from him. But he couldn't accept that as the truth. "I think the sentences farther down the page refer to where Isabel hid the artifacts, but it's impossible to know for sure."

Eden read them aloud. "'In a forgotten land, the heart of the forgotten dwells.' That doesn't tell us anything. It could simply be your mom's way of referring to the pueblo and my mother."

"Maybe," Nick admitted. "But I suspect it's more than that. Have you noticed that Mom generally used that stylized language whenever she wrote about Isabel's troubles?"

"Do you think she was afraid that your father would find and read her journal? Maybe that was why she was deliberately vague."

Nick exhaled softly. He didn't like to admit it, but that was precisely the sort of thing his father would have done. His jealousy was legendary. Yet, even though he had nothing to go on except his gut feeling, he was just as sure that his mother had written in code simply to keep her word and protect Isabel's secret.

Before Nick could speak again, Jake came into the room. "I saw your Jeep outside, brother."

Annie followed him in, then placed Noelle in the playpen. "What's going on, you two?"

"We got the diary back," Nick said, and explained. "Thomas had it. Now the trick will be deciphering it. Take a look at the passages Thomas marked and see if you can make anything out of them."

Jake studied the earmarked pages. "Not all the passages are cryptic. Some are pretty straightforward. Here she mentions that Isabel telephoned, asking about Eden." He continued reading, then looked at Eden. "I never knew that your father was told to produce the artifacts by a certain date or the tribal council would press the BIA to suspend him. And they were going to expel him from the pueblo, too. That must have practically ripped his gut out because he had a wife and you, his daughter, to think about. Without a job or a place to live, things would have been really rough."

"It wasn't long after that entry that my parents were found dead," Eden said in a strained voice. "Nobody ever found out who'd shot them."

An uneasy silence descended over them as they each weighed the information in their own minds.

Jake finally spoke, his voice strong. "I don't know if this

aspect had occurred to you Eden, but some of your enemies may pressure the council to give you the same ultimatum that was given to your father. Either find the artifacts by a certain time, or leave the pueblo with your son forever.''

''I'd never considered that, but I've got to admit I wouldn't put that past Samuel Runningwater. He wants me out.'' Eden shook her head. ''If that did happen, I'm not sure how I'd cope with it. That would mean that by coming back here, I robbed my son of his birthright, and destroyed the very thing I wanted to preserve—our ties to this pueblo.''

As Nick glanced at Eden, the look on her face nearly destroyed him. Her pain was real, but there seemed to be nothing he could do to help her.

As they stepped off the porch, they heard the crackling of breaking glass. Looking toward the sound, they both saw a figure darting away from Nick's Jeep and into the shadows of the adjacent brush.

''Stop right there!'' Nick sprang after the man, but by the time he reached his Jeep, the person had disappeared completely, running down an arroyo.

Jake came charging out the front door, yelling at Annie to stay in the house. ''What's going on?''

Nick's face was cold and hard. ''Someone came onto our ranch to deliver a message,'' he growled. Brushing the glass away from the shattered driver's-side window, he reached in and picked up the note that had been left on the seat. Nick held the paper by the edges as he unfolded it, then opened the door so the dome light came on. ''If even one print can be lifted off this, and we can match it, I'll arrest the scumbag.''

''What's it say?'' Eden asked, her voice taut. ''Is it about Thomas?''

Nick considered lying and telling her that it was, but then

decided that it would only make things worse. He glanced at Jake, then read it out loud. "If you value your life, stay out of the teacher's way. Let her find the artifacts or face the consequences. If she fails, she'll have to answer to us."

Eden drew in a breath. "Do you think it's Torres again?"

Nick shook his head. "This isn't about running you off the pueblo, Eden. This is about the artifacts. They want you here, and from what I'm getting, they want you to find the artifacts for them."

"But who are these people?" Jake demanded. "Who would risk coming here to issue a threat?"

"I don't know, but I'm sure going to find out," Nick snarled. Anger raged inside him. They'd brought the battle here to him and challenged him right in his own home. He looked at his brother and saw the same outrage etched on his features. "They won't get away with this."

Jake nodded once. "See that they don't."

"Eden, I want you to move into Black Raven Ranch with Christopher," Nick said. "There are others here all the time. You'll never be left alone again."

She considered it, then shook her head. "No, Nick. There are people living around my home, too. This isn't a matter of a person who wants to run me off the pueblo anymore. They've concluded that they need me to find the artifacts. That means they won't harm me, not unless I stop searching."

Nick's black eyes swung to her. "If you change your mind, let me know. The offer will stay open." He checked his watch. "I'm going to see if Torres will take my shift this afternoon. I'd like to check the farmhouse today. Things are heating up too fast not to actively pursue that lead right away."

As soon as Nick made the necessary arrangements, they

got underway. Nick could feel her desperation and her need to find answers. It drove him as well. His job was to protect the innocent but, so far, he'd only been able to barely avert disaster. He was itching for a fight—the kind where only one man would remain standing.

As he looked at Eden, his determination to find answers grew. This wasn't about his duty as a cop. This battle was personal.

It didn't take long before they arrived at the farmhouse. Once there, it took them almost three hours of searching through crumbling walls and loose flooring before it was evident to both of them that nothing was there.

"Take me home, Nick," she said, dejected.

Failure echoed in her voice and ripped a hole through him. "Don't give up, Eden," he said. "The fight's far from over."

Yet when he looked at her, he saw naked sorrow in her eyes. The need to turn the tide in their favor drummed through him.

Silence hung between them like an oppressive veil as he drove across the pueblo back to her home. He prided himself on being tough but, when it came to Eden, he was anything but that.

More than anything he wanted to give free rein to his feelings and pursue this woman that was meant to be his, but too many things made that impossible. He still firmly believed his dad was innocent but, if he was wrong, then he'd have nothing to offer Eden or her son except the same shame that she was fighting so hard to erase from her life. He wouldn't gamble with their futures. Before he could offer his love to her, he had to make sure that he'd be giving her something worth taking.

AS THEY PASSED the Cultural Center on the way to Eden's home, Nick caught a glimpse of movement out of the corner of his eye. He slowed down and parked under the shadow of one of the big cottonwood trees lining the Plaza.

"What did you see?" Eden asked, realizing there was trouble.

"The Center's been closed for a few hours now, but I just saw my uncle talking to Rita Korman and her brother Wayne outside on the veranda. I'm going to circle around on foot and try to find out what's going on."

As he was speaking, Eden saw Rita lead the two men inside the Cultural Center, locking the door behind them. "I'll go too. We'll split up and go to each of the outside windows. We'll need to work quickly to find out which room they're in, or we'll never get a chance to listen in on their conversation."

Nick and Eden circled the building, listening each step of the way. After several minutes they were forced to give up.

"They're obviously talking someplace where their conversation can't be overheard. I don't think that's by accident either. Something's going on," Nick said.

"You could ask your uncle directly," Eden said.

Nick shook his head. "That won't work. But trust me, Eden, I *will* find out."

"At least we have some other leads we can follow up on right now. Are you going to process that note for prints tonight?"

"Yes," he clipped. "But you can't help me with that. Lifting a print, if there is one, won't be difficult, but matching it will be unless the vandal has a criminal or military record."

"Seeing Rita just now gave me an idea. I'd really like to know which of the Cultural Center's employees reported the theft of the mask and fetish to the police. Can you find out? If we can establish the sequence of events that day, we may uncover another lead."

"I think that's information I can access through the computer. The department hired some part-time data processors to transfer all the open case files into the system. Of course I'm not sure how far they've gotten. Information on the theft at the Cultural Center may not have been entered yet. But let's go check it out."

IT WAS LATE, and only the dispatcher was still at the station as Eden and Nick walked inside. Angelina looked up from her romance novel, said hello, then began reading again, ignoring them after that.

Eden sat in the main office waiting as Nick processed the note for prints, but the results were disappointing. Whoever had handled it had made sure to keep his prints off both sides.

Nick then went to the computer terminal at his desk. "Did your father ever read the police files on the case?" Nick asked.

"He wasn't allowed to do that. No one at the police department trusted him. They refused to even talk to him, much less let him see official documents."

After about ten minutes Nick turned off his computer. "That case isn't part of the records that have been entered into our database. That means that all the paperwork pertaining to it is in the portable building out back. That place is a zoo, but we should go now if you're not too tired. If Captain Mora was here, he wouldn't let you go inside, but I really could use your help to find the right files. I think it's high time we both get a look at the official report."

"Let's do it. I called Mrs. Chino already and told her it would be a while longer before I could get home."

Borrowing the key from Angelina, he led the way outside.

Inside the trailerlike building the air was stagnant. "Don't they ever open the windows in here? Your records are going to be trashed without ventilation," Eden said.

"The captain used to hire people to come in and clean, but lately funds have been running low. We can't afford air-conditioning either."

Working together, they began sorting through the boxes of file folders. Every time Nick bent down to move a box of folders, Eden did her best to avoid looking at him, but world-class buns like his were hard to resist.

"Had enough of a look?" he asked, after placing another box down on the floor.

She coughed. "I was only trying to read the dates on the other cartons back there."

"Don't look now, but your nose is growing."

Feeling her cheeks burning, Eden avoided his gaze.

With a throaty chuckle, Nick bent down again. He then lifted another heavy box and placed it on the floor before her. "These boxes with the blue labels are for the time period we're interested in. All the case files inside them are listed under the name of the person who contacted our department or filed a complaint," Nick said. "It's a form of duplication we used before we had computers that can do searches using a variety of criteria. Let's see what's under *K*."

They searched the files together, and soon found what they were looking for.

"Marc Korman reported the theft, but he's not very involved with the Center these days. He only helps out during the busy season. I don't think he's a good suspect," Nick said.

Hearing footsteps in the gravel leading toward the portable building, Nick stood and walked to the window.

"Captain Mora's on his way over," he said with a grimace. "I don't know what he's doing here, but there's going to be hell to pay."

As they stepped outside, Mora came up to them. His black eyes were blazing as he pulled Nick aside. "What do you think you're doing bringing a civilian in here? You know the rules."

"The only cases in here are old ones, and I didn't think there was any harm—"

He held up a hand, stopping Nick's explanation cold. "Our department has rules, and all my deputies *will* follow them. Is there anything that's unclear to you about that?"

"No, sir." Realizing that his captain wasn't in the mood for explanations, he decided that one-syllable answers were his best chance of avoiding even more trouble.

"If you ever pull a stunt like this with an active case, I'll have your badge."

"Yes, sir."

Mora gaze locked with Nick's. "Now that we understand each other, tell me what you were looking for."

"Facts, information, witness accounts. Anything that would give us a clear idea about what happened between the time the theft occurred and the deaths of Isabel and James Maes."

Captain Mora nodded. "I know why this is important to you, Deputy. I was talking to some old-timers today and I finally learned who Tall Shadow was. But you've known from the moment I showed you the letter, haven't you?" He didn't wait for a reply. "Now you're in this because you can't stand the questions this case has raised about your father's integrity. But you may do a lot of harm to yourself and your family if you don't back off."

"I don't believe my father played any part in what happened to Eden's family and his name deserves to be cleared."

"My father was the investigating officer on this case and I can tell you that he worked on it day and night. Back then, I was thinking about following in his footsteps, and I paid attention to everything he did or said. Father hammered at every detail, but he never got anywhere."

"I *will* find the truth," Nick said.

"It may not be as freeing as you think."

Nick left Mora beside the portable building and went back to join Eden. She'd moved away and was waiting for him under the covered back porch of the station. Seeing the fear and concern etched on her features made him want to take her into his arms, but this wasn't the time or the place. Danger lay everywhere now and he couldn't afford to forget that for one second.

EDEN WATCHED Nick as they climbed into his Jeep and got underway. More than anything she wished there was something she could do to protect him, but she knew he wouldn't walk away now.

Nick drove her home and walked her to the door, but didn't go inside. "I'll say good-night here," he said.

There was something dangerous in his eyes, a new resolve that she couldn't understand. It frightened her.

The look remained as he brushed his knuckles on her cheek gently. The tenderness of the gesture had a sadness in it that nearly brought tears to her eyes.

"If you can't prove your family's innocence, what will you do?" he asked. "Have you thought about that?"

"I'll have made so many enemies on this pueblo by that point, my only choice will be to leave."

"So you'd just walk away from me again?"

Her throat tightened. "Eventually you'd find someone else."

"I haven't in all these years. That should tell you something."

Without giving her a chance to answer, Nick turned and walked back to his vehicle. He'd never spoken of love. It was one of the things that Nick never did, no matter how much she might have wanted to hear the words. But perhaps he was right not to. She just didn't know anymore. Maybe if no words of love were ever said between them, their parting, when it finally came, would hurt a little less.

Chapter Fourteen

It was still the weekend, so Eden decided that the time had come to take a new direction in her search for the truth. Although she'd spoken to a lot of people, she hadn't tried Maria Lassiter yet.

The elderly woman had spent the last twenty-five years or so living in virtual seclusion. Maria had left her home along the river valley where most of the pueblo's residences were located and moved to an old house in the forest near the sacred lake. No one ever mentioned her by name or had anything to do with her because many believed she was a witch. But Eden remembered her mother telling her that Maria was simply a woman who'd experienced too much heartbreak in her life. She'd lost her husband and only son in a car accident off the pueblo, and the tragedy had destroyed her spirit.

Her mother had often said that Maria knew more about the secrets of the pueblo than anyone else. People were used to ignoring her during her supply trips to the pueblo and they often continued private conversations around Maria, oblivious to the fact that she was there.

Maria would be an ideal person to question since she'd been around during her mother's time—but, of course, there was no guarantee Maria would even want to talk to her. She'd heard stories that Maria would run off most visitors with a shotgun.

After dropping Christopher off at Mrs. Chino's, Eden headed out. That section of pueblo land, one the villagers usually only visited for firewood and herbs, had always seemed inhospitable to her. She didn't know how anyone managed to survive so far away from roads, stores and electricity.

Eden was driving up a nearly indistinguishable dirt trail when she heard a siren click on and off behind her. Looking in her rearview mirror, she saw it was Nick behind her. She stopped, but there was no place to pull over.

As he came up to her car, she stepped out to meet him. "What on earth are you doing all the way out here?" he asked.

The heat from his gaze made a shiver course up her spine. "I might ask you the same question! You're the last person I expected to run into."

"I'm patrolling the outer areas today. And you?"

She tried to peer ahead through the thick growth of tall pines. "I'm looking for Maria Lassiter's house."

"Are you nuts?" he roared. "She may just shoot you if she's not in the mood for visitors."

"I've heard the stories. But she won't hurt me." She saw the skepticism on his face. "I'm not turning back, Nick. But you should get out of the area as soon as possible. Seeing a cop isn't going to put her at ease."

"True," he admitted, "but if you're going, so am I."

Instinct told her nothing she could do or say was going to get him to change his mind. "If you won't go, then at least ride with me. If she sees the tribal unit, she won't even come to the door."

"How do you know?"

"Call it woman's intuition."

"Why? 'Cause I can't argue with it?"

"That's one reason," she admitted. The other was the promise of trouble in his eyes. He wasn't a man used to proceeding slowly and with patient gentleness when someone opposed him and that was exactly the tactic they'd need to use. If they stayed together, she could at least try to influence him and get him to hang back a bit.

She stayed at the wheel, and they rode together to the end of the track. As she saw the house for the first time, a long shudder ran through her. "Dear heaven, I never expected it to be like this!"

The paint on the trim around the windows was nothing more than a memory and the logs stacked upon each other looked like they were ready to roll away. Mud had been applied by hand to cover the joints between the crooked timbers, but it had crumbled away in several spots already.

"People have come out and tried to help her, but she won't tolerate any interference with her life. This is her choice," he said softly.

"How can you truly try to help someone you're afraid of? My guess is that, at best, they were just going through the motions."

"Maybe, but she's always said no. Every time. Some say that she's finally gone insane."

"If she has, I can't say I blame her," Eden snapped. She didn't believe in witches, and she hated the injustice that had been done to this woman. Maybe it took one outcast to really understand the plight of another, but whatever kept Maria out here was only partly due to choice.

Eden parked fifty feet away from the gray weathered front door, then turned to Nick. "Wait for me here."

"No." He left her car before she'd even opened her door, then walked up to the door and knocked loudly.

Eden sighed. If he yelled out 'police,' she'd sock him

herself. "Go easy, will ya?" she whispered, catching up to him.

He gave her an unblinking look. "I am."

Catching a glimpse of a stooped figure moving just beyond the paper-thin curtain, Eden stood by the window. "Miss Lassiter, we don't want to bother you, but I really do need your help. I'm Isabel Maes's daughter."

There was a long silence, then finally the door opened. "Last time I went down for supplies, I heard you were back, asking around about your past." She looked at Nick, as if trying to decide what to do about him.

"He only came—" Eden started.

"Because he's involved, too," Maria finished, then with a nod invited them inside. "I hear people talking when I go to the pueblo for supplies," she added.

Eden looked at Maria, studying the woman that was part legend, part enigma. Maria had to be in her eighties now. Her face was a road map of deep furrows that attested to a life of hardship and sorrow. She wore a long dress made of simple blue cotton that had been darned and patched in many places. Although she couldn't quite stand up straight, her dark eyes were so bright and alert that they captured Eden's attention instantly. This woman was as sane as she was, perhaps even more so.

"I wondered if you'd come talk to me, or if you'd be too afraid," Maria said.

"I'm not at all afraid of you," Eden said gently. "I don't believe in witches."

"That's not very sensible of you. There *are* such things," she said, then when Eden shook her head, smiled. "But I'm not a witch. If I were, I would have cast some very big spells on certain annoying people a long time ago. But, being thought a witch serves me, so don't tell anyone

I'm not. As long as they believe it, they'll stay away, and that's what I really want.''

''But why? It's got to be so lonely out here!''

She graced Eden with a rare smile. The gesture was kind, and softened her features. ''What you see as lonely I see as peaceful. Out here, I don't have to worry about anyone except myself. I have all I need.'' Maria gestured for Eden and Nick to take a seat on a simple cot covered with several quilts.

Nick remained standing near one of the windows, his face as inscrutable as a sphinx.

Eden could tell Nick was uncomfortable in the nearly empty house, as if the silence and the loneliness had seemed familiar to him.

''Your alliance seems an unlikely one,'' Maria said, looking at Nick, then back to Eden. ''There were rumors that Paul Black Raven played a part in your family's troubles,'' she added, making it a point then not to look at Nick.

''Do you think that's true?'' Nick asked, pressing her.

Maria stared at the floor a long time before replying. ''Paul was a man who had a lot of power and wasn't afraid to use it. And he *did* want James Maes to take his wife and child and move away from the pueblo. But I don't believe Paul would have framed anyone. He would have seen a scheme like that as beneath him.''

Nick seemed to relax marginally, but Eden could sense that this woman's determination to let no one get close to her, and the price she was paying for that decision had struck a chord with him. Perhaps he saw a bit of himself in her. Nick protected himself well. There was a barrier around his heart he allowed no one, even her, to get past. Yet if anyone could understand that, she could. It was a survival skill that life had taught them both.

''Can you tell me anything that will help me find the real

thieves?'' Eden asked. ''My mother's not guilty of anything, but I have to prove that before others will believe me.''

''Be very careful what you do. The real thieves have spent years covering their tracks. The more you push to find them, the greater the threat you become, and that makes every day more dangerous than the last.''

''I can't turn back now. It's too late for that.''

Maria nodded. ''Then keep a close watch on your enemies. Men like Samuel Runningwater will never give up trying to run you off pueblo land. Don't underestimate him, though his daughter takes care of your son. Runningwater will incite the people against you every chance he gets. To him, you're a reminder of a scandal he wants the people to forget. He may not have been part of the daily business of the Center, but he was the one who suggested to the religious societies that they store their treasures in that building. He promised everyone that it was the safest place in this pueblo. Now that you're back, he's afraid people will remember that and it'll cost him the election for pueblo governor.''

''Can you tell us anything about the other employees at the Cultural Center? Who hated my mother enough to do this to her?''

''Isabel had many enemies. Although she was a good woman, she was an Anglo who married one of our own. Lots of people didn't approve of her but, at the top of that list, I'd have to put Theresa Redwing. She loved James and hated your mother because James left her for Isabel.''

''I never knew that,'' Eden said.

''Isabel didn't know either,'' she answered. ''If I were you, I wouldn't trust Theresa. Years have gone by, but the heart has a long memory.''

"Do you think she framed my mother out of jealousy or revenge?"

"No. It's more likely that Theresa knows who did and has never said, because it served her purposes. But to actually plan something like that and carry it through, is beyond her. Theresa has never been much of a thinker."

"What about the Kormans?" Nick asked.

Maria shook her head. "Marc's sense of duty would have prevented him from doing anything against the Center. Do you know how he got his job in the first place?" Seeing Eden and Nick shake their heads, she continued. "Marc lived on land adjacent to the pueblo all his life. Jack Mora, Captain Daniel Mora's father, was our head of police at the time. One day Daniel got lost while deer hunting when a storm came up. He was gone for two days. It was bitterly cold but there was hope because Daniel was a smart boy and he knew the land. He built a snow cave and stayed warm and even managed to find something to eat, but things were looking bleak. That's when Marc Korman found him. He was the one who brought him back."

"Captain Mora never said anything to me about that," Nick said thoughtfully.

"I think he prefers to forget the debt he owes the Anglo, but he won't. He'll honor that." Maria continued. "Months later when the pueblo council decided that they needed to find someone who knew our arts and crafts to operate the Center, the council offered Marc the job. He's been associated with it ever since then."

"Sounds like Mora owes Korman, but what would have stopped Korman from stealing from the tribe?" Nick pressed.

"Pride. He always managed the Center like it was his own business, and liked the sense of power it gave him. A man like that is not after wealth. He simply wants to feel important."

"What about his wife?" Eden asked.

"His first wife was a beautiful woman. She died giving birth to Patrick. But the second wife, Rita, along with that lazy brother of hers, are too self-absorbed to plan out a theft like that. Twenty years ago Rita spent most of the time she wasn't working, outside playing, taking part in white-water rafting and hot air balloon rides, that sort of thing. She desperately wanted her white friends to see her as a free spirit. Of course that was the last thing she was. She cared too much what everyone thought of her."

Maria stood up slowly. "Now I've told you all I know. I've done so in payment for the kindness your mother Isabel showed me many years ago. When no one else spoke to me, she did. And every holiday, she always came with a basket of food. I never had the chance to do much for her, but now I've helped her daughter. That balances things."

Eden stood up. "Thank you for the help you've given us."

"I would like to ask something of you two in return."

Eden glanced at Nick who nodded. "Name it," she said.

"Never tell anyone that you talked to me today."

"Why?" Eden asked, suddenly worried about Maria. "Are you afraid that people will come after you?"

She laughed. "Not in the way you think. They're afraid of me, remember?" She paused then grew serious. "But if people find out that I've helped you, they'll start taking notice of me when I come into town. Many of the younger women, the ones who don't believe in witchcraft and such, will take it upon themselves to come and visit. After that, they'll want to fix this and that around here and, before I know it, my life will not be my own. I'll either have to spend the last of my days arguing with them, or having do-gooders underfoot all the time.''

Eden smiled. Maria had a point and her mind was crystal clear. She'd never really met anyone more capable of looking after herself. ''We'll keep our visit to ourselves. Promise.''

As Nick received a call on his handheld radio, he stepped outside. Eden started to follow him, but Maria pulled her back.

''One more thing,'' she said in a whisper-soft voice. ''I've watched Nick Black Raven's face when he looks at you. He feels deeply for you, but you have to trust in that. You've both seen firsthand what lies and secrets can do. They poison everything. Don't let it happen to you two. Fight for what you want and let the blood ties between you guide you right back into each other's hearts.''

Eden stared at her. By blood ties, had she meant Christopher? Surely there was no way this woman could know that Christopher was Nick's son. ''Everyone has secrets,'' Eden said softly.

''You have one chance left, if your love is strong enough.''

Eden stared at Maria, trying to figure out if, by some miracle, the woman had managed to guess the truth. But there was no way of finding out without tipping her own hand. ''Thanks again for seeing us, Maria.''

Eden met Nick by her car and drove him back to his tribal unit. A shiver of longing passed through her as he captured her gaze. The invisible boundaries between them seemed to melt away into nothingness whenever he looked at her like that. There was an intensity in his eyes as if nothing in his world was more important than she was. Aching for him in a way she never would have believed possible, she forced herself to look away, shattering the magic of the moment.

Nick got out of her car. "I have to get back to work," he said. "Will you be all right?"

She would have been if only she could have stepped into his arms, if she could have kissed him and forgotten everything else... But those were only wishes. "I'll be fine, Nick."

A powerful yearning ripped through her as he drove off. Someday she'd have to learn that every dream came at a price, and the cost of loving was the highest of all.

AS EDEN PULLED into the driveway of her home, she saw a group of three tribal officials waiting at her door. One of them was Samuel Runningwater. After the warning Maria had given her, she was curious to see what had brought him here. She suddenly had a feeling that Maria had managed to get advance warning of this visit. As she walked up to meet them, she braced herself for trouble.

"Gentlemen," she said, unlocking her door, and ushering them inside. "What brings you here?"

"Business. Tribal business," Runningwater said.

She didn't trust the coldness in his gaze. It was like looking into the eyes of a rattler about to strike.

After they'd all sat down, refusing her offer of soft drinks, she studied them. Samuel was obviously the leader, though she recognized the lieutenant governor of the pueblo, Manuel Peña, and Francisco Serna, the governor's counselor. Peña was restless, as if sitting on an ant hill. Serna was a thin, observant man in his forties. His thoughtful eyes seemed to weigh everything about her.

"We have come to reason with you," Samuel Runningwater said. "Your recent activities are creating a lot of unrest here. People remember your mother's betrayal too clearly for you to be safe on this pueblo.''

"There are many kinds of betrayals, sir," she said quietly, holding his gaze.

Runningwater looked away. Clearing his throat, he continued. "Many in the council, and many of the leaders of our religious societies have requested that you be asked to leave the pueblo for the good of everyone. The tone of the talk makes us all believe that you may be in a great deal of danger."

"My parents suffered a grave injustice. I'm here to right that wrong."

"Your motives are commendable, but the longer you persist with this, the worse things are bound to get," Runningwater said. "Consider what you're doing carefully. You're a single mother. If something happened to you, what will become of your son?" He didn't wait for an answer. "Don't let stubbornness and misplaced pride keep you from doing the only sane thing."

She stood up. This was not an argument she intended to have with a man who was clearly her enemy. "Thank you for stopping by."

Runningwater, Serna and Peña started for the door, but Peña stopped and turned to face her. "Maybe we didn't put things too well, but we really are worried about what you're stirring up. Nothing good will come of it. Let go of the past, Ms. Maes. You'll be a lot better off."

She stood by the open door. "Thank you for your concern," she said.

She watched the men go back to their truck, a lump the size of a large rock in the middle of her stomach. Why was it so difficult for others to believe that one couldn't let go of the past until it was resolved? She wished people would stop thinking of her as a troublemaker and try to understand. But she knew that she wouldn't have any peace until she cleared her parents and the objects were returned.

Restless, Eden paced around the room and then finally stopped by the rear window staring pensively at *Tsin*, the mesa that overlooked her backyard. Memories of the past danced through her mind, and she remembered the stories about the *Tsave Yoh*. The supernatural beings were said to make their home in the caves that wound through the belly of the mountain like labyrinths.

Slowly an idea began to form in her mind. It was her mother who had told her many of the legends associated with those tunnels and piqued her curiosity until she'd had to go take a look for herself. She'd never told anyone of her visits there, knowing it was considered sacred ground, but now a thought began to niggle at the back of her mind.

Her mother had wanted to keep the *Tsave Yoh* mask and fetish safe, and there was no better hiding place than the home of the *Tsave Yoh* themselves. No Tewa would ever venture inside the tunnels, since they were reputed to be protected by the enforcers of the gods.

A plan took shape in her mind and she suddenly knew what she had to do. For the first time since she'd arrived, a sense of hope filled her. Maybe luck was with her at last.

Chapter Fifteen

After making sure that Mrs. Chino would keep Chris a few hours longer, Eden headed out to explore the secret caves. As she drove past the Plaza, she saw Nick patrolling on foot and nearly stopped to tell him where she was going. Deciding against it, she continued down the road.

This time, being half white had its advantages. Tewa beliefs were a part of Nick and the sacred site would not be one he'd broach easily. There was also the undeniable fact that if someone saw *her* going in there, they'd shake their heads and blame it on her Anglo blood. For Nick, there'd be serious repercussions.

Eden was traveling slowly past the Kiva when she saw several men in line going down into the subterranean chamber. Noting that they were carrying different bundles, she suddenly realized that the finishing ceremony was just about to begin. Nick would have his hands full tonight.

A moment later, she saw Nick's vehicle parked near the Trading Post. She pulled over to the side of the road, thinking. Now that they both had something at stake, it seemed wrong not to let him in on her plans. She would go alone. That was the right thing to do. But if she left him a note in his car telling him where she was going and when, approximately, she expected to return, maybe he'd be able to stop by her home later after the finishing and they could discuss what, if anything, she'd found.

Eden first confirmed it was Nick's patrol unit instead of Torres's by checking the vehicle tag. She then slipped a handwritten note through the crack at the top of the window where he'd rolled it down slightly.

She was back on her way a minute later. As she left the developed section of the pueblo and headed toward the mountain, Eden glanced in her rearview mirror and saw a set of headlights off in the distance. A niggling sense of uneasiness wound through her, but she concentrated on what she had to do. No one would be able to tail her where she was going. The ground and the surrounding area were too rugged a place and afforded too much cover, and she was going someplace no one would anticipate.

As she drew closer to the sacred mountain, Eden tried to remember everything she knew about the caves there. As a kid, the stories about the *Tsave Yoh's* hiding places and the labyrinths had fascinated her. The adults had been fond of telling the kids that the *Tsave Yoh* would kidnap bad children and take them into those caves as their prisoners. Envisioning herself as a heroine attempting a daring rescue, she'd explored every inch of the subterranean labyrinths.

She smiled. As a kid, her imagination had been second to none, but now the knowledge she'd gained back then would serve her.

She arrived at her destination at the base of the mesa within twenty-five minutes. Leaving her car beside a dry arroyo, she started hiking uphill across the rocky terrain toward the limestone caves, located just above the base of the cliffs.

Dusk had settled over the land, and the uneven ground was treacherous here. Remembering there was the possibility of snakes coming out to hunt, she chose her path carefully, intent on avoiding the many hazards the desert posed during this time of day.

Eden soon located the main entrance to the caves. The opening was nearly blocked with weeds and spiderwebs. Although she hated spiders with a passion, in this case they afforded her some useful information. No one had been here in quite a long while. The webs were simply too numerous and elaborate.

Switching on the flashlight she'd brought from her car, she swept aside the cobwebs and stepped inside. The tunnel branched in several places as it extended back into the mountain. Some of the pathways led uphill, and others down at steep angles. It was easy to get lost in here. She'd scared herself silly once, long ago, by venturing too far and then having to work really hard to find the way out.

Moving carefully, she looked through each passage, but there weren't many places here where things could be hidden. The low corridors reminded her of mining shafts, except they usually led back to each other or narrowed to dead ends where the original water that had carved them had seeped from inside the mountain. She spent the better part of an hour searching the labyrinth, but at long last realized that she wasn't going to find anything there.

As she made her way to the cave entrance, she discovered it was now pitch black outside. The moon was hidden behind a thick layer of clouds. Then she saw the flicker of another flashlight downhill, coming up the slope toward the cave. Quickly turning off her own light before it could be seen, she stared into the darkness. She was sure Nick would have called out to her, but this person remained silent, as if he were trying to hide his approach.

Several heartbeats later, she saw the vague outline of a man silhouetted against the skyline. Surprised, she pulled back into the cave, hoping he wouldn't be able to find the entrance. She still wasn't sure how he'd tracked her, but from his halting steps, she had a feeling he wasn't exactly sure where the caves were, though he must have heard of them.

Eden stayed hidden behind a large rock and waited. The man hesitated, shining the light past the spot where she was hiding. Then, from farther down the hillside, she heard Nick's voice calling her.

The beam from the man's flashlight went out instantly, then she heard a metallic click that sounded like a gun being cocked. Eden knew that unless she acted fast, Nick would walk into an ambush.

Peeking out as the moon appeared from behind the clouds, she saw the man's outline. He stood a few feet away from the mouth of the cave, facing in the other direction, waiting for Nick to come up. Eden reached down for the large rock beside her foot, took careful aim, and threw it as hard as she could.

Hearing a dull thump and a groan, she quickly ducked behind cover. She'd barely moved out of sight when the man fired two shots into the cave. The bullets ricocheted, impacting on the rock wall behind and above her. But Nick had been warned now.

Eden huddled down as low as she could get, knowing that the gunman couldn't see her without using his flashlight and coming closer, and he wouldn't risk it with Nick nearby.

Then Eden heard Nick's voice clearly. "I'm a deputy sheriff. Put down your weapon and come out with your hands above your head," he ordered.

The man in the shadows bolted, firing rapidly behind him as he ran, forcing Nick to seek cover. Eden heard Nick's two answering shots, but then there was only silence.

Eden waited as long as she could, then finally shouted. "Nick, are you okay?"

"Yeah. Where are you? Are you hurt?"

"No. Did you see who it was?" she called out, moving toward the cave opening.

"No, but I'm going after him right now. I'll be back."

She heard him run off. "Be careful," she said, but her words were nothing more than a whispered prayer in the desert night.

NICK COULD SEE the vague outline of the man against the terrain. He followed cautiously, wary of an ambush. Then, a moment later, he heard the roar of a car engine. Risking the use of his flashlight, Nick swept the area below. All he saw was a trail of dust that filled the cone of his flashlight beam. It was too late.

Nick jogged back to where he'd left Eden. Taking one look at her pale, frightened face, he hauled her against him. "If you ever go off alone like this again, I'll shoot you myself."

His lips suddenly crushed hers with a fierceness that sealed out any answer she might have given him and bound her to him. His breath rasping through his lungs, he ravaged the moist recesses of her mouth with a kiss so intimate it left no room for anything except total surrender.

"You're safe, you're safe," he murmured, for his own benefit as much as for hers.

He felt the softening of her body as he held her and the victory was sweet. But it wasn't enough. He wanted more. He wanted forever and beyond.

He stepped away, fighting something primitive and masculine that urged him to keep her in his arms until her surrender was complete. "Why did you come out here alone? What if he hurt you—'' He couldn't even bring himself to complete the sentence.

Nick faced her, wanting to make her understand how much he cared, and how he hadn't felt anything but terror from the moment he'd learned she'd come out here alone. Yet, when he opened his mouth and spoke, what came out was entirely different.

''What you did tonight was totally crazy. That guy could have killed you if I hadn't showed up.''

''I know, but he probably wouldn't have fired if I hadn't tried to protect you,'' she said, explaining. ''So I saved you as much as you saved me.'' Seeing the exasperation on his face, she softened her tone. ''Were you really worried about me?''

''How can you possibly doubt that?'' His voice was as brittle as broken glass. ''Why do you think I raced out here?''

''I don't know. And you still haven't said. As much as I'd like to, I still can't read your mind.''

''Be grateful you can't. At least not right now,'' he snapped, frustration flowing through him. ''Come on. Let's head back. We've both been through enough for one night.''

Nick insisted on following her car as they drove back to the pueblo. It was a good thing they'd come separately. He couldn't have stood sitting beside her tonight, taking in the sweet scent of her perfume and feeling her with everything male in him, while she remained out of his reach.

He needed time to get himself together. He couldn't allow himself to love or even think of the future until all the questions about his father were settled. A man needed something to offer a woman, and, although perhaps that wasn't politically correct in the Anglo world, it was still a part of his own beliefs and the way he looked at life.

They stopped by Mrs. Chino's so she could pick up Christopher, then continued to her house. Nick stayed behind her, guarding her all the way.

When they reached her house, he walked her to the door. "I'm going to have to say good-night, Eden," he said, trying not to be swayed by the disappointment in her eyes. "I'm on call because the ceremonies are under way."

"Okay. I'll see you tomorrow," she said quietly, stepping into the living room, holding Christopher.

Nick returned to his vehicle and, seeing that Chris and Eden were safe, drove off without looking back. A man with a questionable future had no right to a woman like Eden and a little boy who would depend on the adults in his life.

Although he was sure his father was innocent, he needed to prove it first. Then, once that was settled, he'd make Eden see that they belonged together. Pretty words were beyond him but, somehow, he'd show her that a man of action was worth far more than a man of words.

Chapter Sixteen

Eden arrived at school a few minutes earlier than usual Monday morning. Instead of the normal greetings from the other staff gathered in the office, all she got were cold shoulders and suspicious stares.

Something was clearly wrong. Checking her mailbox, she saw a note from Principal Puye. It said simply, "Come see me right away."

Eden walked across the room to his office and knocked on the open door.

Mr. Puye looked up from the papers before him and waved for her to step inside. "Close the door behind you, Miss Maes, then have a seat. We need to talk."

There was something in his tone that spelled trouble. Fear undermined her confidence, but she sat quietly, scarcely moving a muscle.

"I had a group of parents waiting for me in the parking lot this morning. They're asking for your suspension."

"On what grounds? My contract spells out the circumstances under which I can be suspended, and I haven't violated any laws, or behaved unprofessionally with any students, parents, or staff."

"According to more than one parent, you've become a negative role model for the kids. They believe that your behavior here and in the community has been inappropriate.''

"How so? I've done nothing wrong."

"The parents are complaining that you're all the kids talk about when they get home. They're curious about your past and all the events surrounding the theft of our artifacts. The parents are afraid that you're not a suitable teacher anymore. Their children are more interested in an old crime and its repercussions than in school-related things.''

"I have no control over what the kids talk about outside my class, or what they do after hours. But at school, we follow the curriculum. Come and observe my classes if you don't believe me."

"I'll be doing that from now on. And, if there's any hint of impropriety, or if I discover that you've allowed discussions pertaining to the crime to go on in your classes, I *will* suspend you.''

Eden left the principal's office and walked back to the classroom. She had a feeling this was all tied to Runningwater's visit. Since the tribal officials clearly wanted her out, the pressure would not let up unless she let them win and left. But that was the one thing she'd never do.

The morning proceeded slowly. The kids, sensing something was wrong, seemed better than usual, but Mr. Puye dropped in unannounced several times. By the time the morning ended and she left school, the tension had taken its toll and she felt exhausted.

Eden picked up Chris and went straight home. At least her little boy was in a calm mood, content to play in his activities chair after she had sung a few songs to him.

Sitting on the sofa, she glanced through some of the free publications she usually picked up at the local grocery stores. Living on a part-time teacher's salary meant that she was always in need of bargains, and these were the next best thing to finding a good garage sale. Suddenly one classified header caught her eye. It advertised "Southwestern Religious Art" in bold, oversized letters.

As she read the smaller text below it, she felt her heart freeze. The seller warned that all prospective buyers would be screened and showings would be by appointment only. The items were listed as one of a kind original work that would be sold to "individual collectors only."

Serious warning bells went off in her brain. No legitimate collector or merchant would advertise in a free pulp flyer of this sort. This practically screamed "fakes" or stolen merchandise.

Taking Chris, Eden dropped him off at Mrs. Chino's again and drove straight to the police station. They'd know where she could find Nick.

Moments later, she went inside the building and, to her surprise, saw Nick at his desk.

Nick glanced up and walked over to meet her. "I'm caught up on my paperwork, and was about to go on a lunch break. What brings you here?"

She showed him the advertising newspaper and pointed out the ad. "I think we should look into this. It sounds strange."

Nick read it quickly, then shook his head. "I know what you're thinking. But the odds are astronomical that these will turn out to be the artifacts. What's more likely is that someone is hoping to trick people into forking over some money."

"You're probably right. But don't you think we should still look into it?"

Captain Mora came out of his office just then, and joined them. Nick filled him in on what Eden had found, and showed him the ad.

"Look into it, Deputy," Mora said, his face suddenly

hard. "The telephone number listed has a local prefix. If one of ours is trying to pull a scam, I want him hauled in. I'll try and get a court order to get the name of the person who placed the ad or a reverse directory listing on that telephone number, but I doubt I'll have much luck. We don't have enough to go on. So the fastest way to get answers is for you to set up an appointment with this joker."

"You've got it, Captain." Nick nodded, then led Eden out of the station.

"Shall I call and arrange for a meeting?" Eden asked, eager to do anything that might advance her search.

"No. If it's someone from the pueblo, chances are they'll know you and me. I'll get Rick—Martin's nephew, who also works for Black Raven Ranch—to make the call," he said, heading toward his police vehicle.

"Let me ride with you, then. That way, if the guy wants to meet right away, I'll be ready."

"No, Eden," he said firmly. "I appreciate you bringing this to our attention, but now it's official police business and you've got to trust me to follow through on it."

"But you'll at least let me know if you schedule a meet with this person, won't you? Fair's fair, Nick. I gave you the tip."

"Okay. I'll make sure to call you."

Eden watched him go to his unit. Nick may not have wanted her along on this operation, but she had no intention of staying behind. This was her business, too, and she wouldn't be brushed aside.

By the time he drove away, she was already busy making her own plans.

HOURS PASSED. Eden had just put Christopher to bed when the phone rang. The moment she picked up the receiver and heard Nick's low, deep voice, desire stirred within her.

With effort, Eden brushed the sensations firmly aside and concentrated on what he was saying.

"This seller's got a line even a three-year-old wouldn't buy," Nick said. "He asked me to meet him by the Anasazi ruins outside the pueblo, across the highway on the west side."

"That's not a bad deal for you. He won't be able to ambush you in open territory like that."

"Yeah, but he'll see me coming for miles. If he decides the meet is off, that'll be it."

"Nick, you need me on this. If his intent is to check out who he's dealing with, he'll recognize you for sure. I can at least wear a wig and disguise myself."

"I'll be out of uniform and wear a hat low on my face. Don't worry."

"You're not going to use your own Jeep, are you?"

"No, I'm taking Rick's truck. It's already parked here at the bunkhouse. I'll set out tomorrow at daybreak."

"Good luck," she said, trying to sound disappointed so he wouldn't get suspicious. But the truth was she had all the information she needed to carry out her plan now. "And be careful."

"I always am."

Eden sensed he wanted to talk for a while longer, but there was nothing more to say. Wishing him good-night, she got to work. She had a lot to do before daybreak.

NICK SET OUT in Rick's truck the following morning. The air was brisk, and that helped him stay alert. He'd need to stay sharp today, too. He was on his own out here. Mora couldn't back him up because the sting was taking place just outside their jurisdiction. The state police had been notified, but the patrolman assigned to this sector was responding to a traffic accident and would be indefinitely delayed. Although Mora had wanted to call everything off, Nick had insisted on seeing it through. He owed Eden, the tribe he served, and himself that much.

He drove slowly, aware of everything around him. He was really surprised that Eden hadn't been more insistent about coming along with him. He half expected to see her car somewhere behind him, but he'd looked in his rearview mirror several times and there had been no signs of anyone tailing him.

Arriving at the crossroads that led to the ruins a short time later, he slowed down, and parked. From here, he'd have to go on foot. The ruins were ahead, but only a motorcycle or horse could make it across the rutted, boulder-strewn ground.

He'd just stepped out of the truck when he heard the camper shell's door swing open. Spotting a mass of red hair out of the corner of his eye, he drew his weapon and pressed against the side of the truck, using it for cover.

"Come around to my side of the truck. Slowly, and with your hands empty."

Eden stepped into view, smiling. "See? Even you didn't recognize me with this wig. Now put that gun away before anyone else sees it."

Nick glared at her, trying to process what he was seeing. The flaming red hair looked like a prop from a hair dye commercial. "What the hell do you think you're doing here? I could have shot you."

"I knew you wouldn't. You'd make sure of your target first." She smiled. "You didn't want me to come on my own so I went to your bunkhouse before daybreak, broke the camper's lock, and stowed away."

"Don't you have to teach this morning?"

"I took the day off."

"You still can't come with me," he growled. "I'm on duty."

"So I'll stay behind you and be your backup."

Until that very second, he hadn't thought that the situation could possibly get worse. He muttered a curse under his breath. "I can't leave you behind. He may have already seen you and you'd be an easy mark, unarmed." He looked at the wig pensively and winced. "You're right about one thing, though. No one would recognize you in that. Why did you ever get something so...bright?"

"It was for a skit I was in during college. I was playing a Hollywood starlet. Since then, I've only used it for Halloween dress-up days at the school where I taught before coming here."

He remained lost in thought for a moment, considering everything that had happened. "This may yet work to our advantage," Nick said at last. "Let's go. The seller's eyes will certainly be on you, so maybe that'll cut me some slack," he said, pulling his black felt cowboy hat down low over his eyes. Reaching back into the truck cab, he brought out an envelope filled with phoney money he'd run off on a color copier. "Here's the fake money for the payoff. You get to carry it so I can free up my hands. Just stay sharp. If you spot anything that doesn't look right, let me know."

They started walking toward the ruined adobe structure ahead. It had been a two-story multifamily dwelling several hundred years ago, but now all that remained was the remnants of a high wall. Beyond that were a series of trenches and pits where archaeologists had unearthed anything they could find, then carted it off to museums. It wasn't exactly a tourist attraction anymore, and the historical marker had been vandalized beyond recognition.

"This place is deserted," she said, disappointed. "Unless he's hiding in one of the holes that the university people dug, there's no one around except us.''

"He's here. Listen to what the land's telling you.''

"I don't hear anything.''

"Exactly. You can't even hear birds. It's deathly quiet and that's not natural.''

They stood at their agreed upon meeting spot on the north side of the adobe wall for a full ten minutes, looking and listening, but no one approached. Nothing moved except the insects. Then, Nick heard the faint sound of footsteps along the opposite side of the wall, on the south side.

"Don't move. And don't try to look over the wall,'' a harsh muffled voice said through a small crack in the adobes. "We are going to do this my way. The objects are close by, but first I want to know if you have the money to deal.''

Nick signaled for Eden to answer. There was something vaguely familiar about the voice, though he couldn't place it.

"It's here.'' She held up the envelope with the copied fifty dollar bills inside. "But we're not handing even a dollar over until we see the goods.''

"I'll stay here while you go drop the money through the small break in the wall, halfway down.''

"Not until I see what you've got for sale.''

Nick glanced at the spot the man had mentioned. The opening, where an adobe had been moved, was twenty or so feet away, and about three feet above the ground. It would be safe enough for Eden as long as the guy didn't follow her.

"The things you want are right in front of you. They're in a hole underneath that knocked-over No Trespassing sign. Put the money where I told you as your partner goes to take a look. I'll stay here until we finish.''

Nick nodded to Eden. As soon as she'd placed the phony money where the man had instructed, Nick moved off to check out the merchandise.

Cautious for traps, he walked over and picked up the sign slowly. Underneath, in a scooped out hollow, was a mask and a small paper bag. Nick studied the mask first. If it was a fake, it was a good one.

Suddenly a shot rang out from behind him. The bullet struck metal somewhere with a clang. A quick, second shot struck one of the top adobes, showering Eden with chunks of hardened earth.

Nick ran back and yanked Eden down to the ground against the wall. Shielding her with his body, he drew his weapon and fired back over the top of the wall. He suspected that the shots had come from behind an outcropping of rocks a few hundred yards from their position. Nick fired six times in rapid succession, hoping only to force the sniper back. Scoring a direct hit with a pistol was all but impossible at this range and he knew it.

An uneasy silence descended as the shooting stopped. Then, over the stillness, they heard a soft groan.

Nick dove over the wall and into a shallow trench scientists had dug while examining the foundation. As he rolled to one side, he nearly hit his uncle, who was lying face up in the ditch, contorted in pain.

Nick didn't bother hiding his surprise. No wonder the voice had sounded familiar.

Thomas stared at him for a moment. "I was hoping to flush out the real thieves with my ad. I never expected you to show up."

"You flushed them out, all right, but it nearly cost you your life."

"Go after him, nephew. I'll just lay here, safe and out of sight. I'm fine," he said, trying to catch his breath. "I was prepared. When you make yourself a target by letting desperate thieves know you've got what they want, precautions like wearing a vest are necessary. The bullet still caused a considerable impact, but it didn't penetrate.''

Nick studied Thomas for a moment. There were no signs of blood and that left him free to act. "I'll be back."

Eden scrambled over as he finished speaking, and crouched down in the trench beside the men. She took in the situation with one glance. "I'll take care of your uncle," she assured, taking off her wig and shaking her hair free.

With a nod, Nick ran down the shallow ditch, then leaped out and found cover farther away.

Eden watched him disappear from view, then looked down at Thomas. "This is a very dangerous game you've chosen to involve yourself in."

"I can look after myself," he said, finally managing to sit up. Opening his shirt, Thomas revealed two heavy make-shift armor plates he'd worn in the front and back beneath his shirt. The one in front was actually two layers thick. "An aluminum griddle and cast iron from an old wood stove. They're not exactly bullet proof vest material, and they really slowed me down, but they did the job today." He showed her a bullet still imbedded in the cast iron after passing through the aluminum griddle completely.

A few minutes later Nick returned. "The sniper's long gone."

Eden and Thomas stood up, climbing out of the trench. Seeing his uncle on his feet, Nick came closer, trying to figure out exactly what had happened.

"Did you see who it was?" Thomas asked before Nick could speak.

"No. He had a partner waiting and they were gone before I was able to catch up to them." He looked at the bullet flattened into the cast iron, and the penetrated aluminum plate. "Having two layers was the only thing that saved your life. What exactly were you trying to do here today? Cheat somebody out of their money?" Nick demanded.

"I'm offended by that suggestion, nephew. Actually, I was hoping the real thieves would come after me. I wanted them to assume that Isabel had given the artifacts to me, and I was finally willing to make a deal to raise some much needed cash. Most people at the pueblo know that I'm in a jam with the casinos, so I had a good chance of pulling it off. If I'd have been able to complete a deal, I could have given you a good lead as to who you should look for. In the meantime, I'd have scored a handful of cash."

"Not to mention getting shot. The real thief would have probably taken you out of the picture completely. He must have been able to see the artifacts from his vantage point when I removed the sign. He was using a rifle scope. I guess he figured he didn't need you anymore."

"No one followed *us* here," Eden said, then seeing the surprised look on Nick's face added, "I kept watch from the camper shell on the way here." She looked at Thomas. "The sniper must have tailed you."

He gave her a weary half smile. "It was a calculated risk."

"I'm bringing you in," Nick said. "But first I want to take another look at that mask you brought. I expected a fake, but if that's what it is, it's a good one." Seeing hope flicker in Eden's eyes, he shook his head. "It's not the one we're after. I didn't recognize it. My guess is that it belongs to one of our secret religious societies."

"That's exactly right. But it's just a practice mask, not the real thing. My group made it so that we could work out certain ceremonial steps without giving offense to the gods.'' Thomas looked at Eden then explained. ''It's really difficult to keep from bumping into each other when we're all wearing masks that only have tiny slits for eyes.''

''And they gave you permission to sell it?'' Disbelief was etched clearly on Nick's face.

''Not exactly, but I didn't steal it, either. They asked me to burn it, along with two others, years ago. I kept them because I suspected I might find a better use for them someday.''

Nick glowered at his uncle. ''We'll sort this out at the station. I'm through giving you any breaks.''

''You have no case against me. Nothing was stolen and my religious society won't press charges.''

Nick scowled, knowing his uncle had a valid point.

''Whether you believe me or not, I really *am* on your side. I've been doing everything in my power to get information you can use. I've even tried to talk to Rita Korman a few times, hoping to find out a little more about the theft,'' Thomas said.

As Nick glanced at Eden, he knew she remembered having seen Thomas with Rita. That answered one question at least—providing his uncle wasn't playing mind games again. Knowing that taking Thomas to the station was a waste of time, Nick recanted.

''Let's head back. I'll follow you home and make sure you stay out of trouble,'' he said. ''But I'm going to take that,'' he added, indicating the makeshift armor Thomas still wore. ''That's evidence I intend to log in and follow up on. We'll try to get a caliber and weight on that bullet.''

They were underway several minutes later. Nick could feel Eden's gaze on him as keenly as he felt the breeze blowing in through his open window. ''Nothing is ever simple these days. Have you noticed?'' he commented.

She nodded and gave him a tiny smile. ''But that

shouldn't come as a surprise. Whenever you and I get together, life always becomes very complicated.''

"True. But some things are worth the price,'' he said, his voice low, but loud enough for her to hear.

She didn't reply, and maybe that was for the best. There wasn't anything more either of them could say. He'd always been a realist, and he knew that this case could blow up in their faces at any given moment. Yet, despite that, he couldn't seem to let go of the one hope that kept him going—that compelled him to fight to hold on to what they had together even when logic cautioned against it.

Maybe that was what made love one of the strongest forces in the universe. It gave a man the power to believe in a dream, despite the odds against him.

Chapter Seventeen

Nick followed Thomas home, staying about five car lengths behind. There wasn't much traffic at this hour on the highway that led back to the pueblo, and it would be difficult for anyone to tail them without giving themselves away.

Silence stretched out between him and Eden. He saw the worried frown on her face and had to fight the urge to reach for her hand and hold it like he had so often as a teen. But they weren't kids anymore, and what he wanted seldom stopped with holding her hand.

He took a deep breath and forced himself to think of what he had to do next as they crossed into pueblo land. Ten minutes later they pulled up in front of his uncle's house. Thomas, who'd arrived just before them, got out of his car, and waved for them to come inside.

Nick turned to Eden. "I want to take a look around and make sure there isn't someone hiding around here, waiting for him to return. Do you mind waiting?"

"No, not at all. But, once we're done here, I need to stop by the school. I have a conference this afternoon with one of the other teachers and a parent."

Nick walked around the property, then came back to where Eden stood with Thomas. "There are no signs of an intruder."

"You help me today, nephew. There's something I'd like to give you as thanks." He led the way to a shed in the back. "The other two masks are here. You can have all three now to dispose of as you see fit."

As Thomas opened the door, Nick grabbed his arm, holding him back. "Someone broke in here. This place is a mess."

Thomas smiled and shook his head. "No, it always looks like this." He walked to one corner, kicking some old tools out of his way, then pulled off a canvas tarp. There was nothing beneath or around it. "They were here someplace," he muttered, continuing to search.

Finally he walked to the other end of the shed, pulling a wool blanket off a large cardboard box. With a curse, he kicked the empty box aside. "Someone stole my stash! I had important things here, too."

"Did you have other pieces hidden here besides the ones you mentioned?" Nick's voice was cold. "Think hard before you answer."

Thomas hesitated, then nodded. "I kept two small things for my religious society. They weren't copies. They were the real thing and sacred." He looked around shaking his head. "Everyone said that no thief would ever come here. I guess they were wrong."

"What's missing, besides the copies of the masks?" Nick demanded.

"A medicine bowl and pouch."

"When's the last time you actually saw them?" Nick asked.

Again, Thomas hesitated. "That's a hard question, nephew. It wasn't the kind of thing I checked regularly."

"Did you see them when you came here to get the mask you intended to sell today?" Eden asked, trying to help jog his memory.

"I saw the two other masks, but not the bowl and the pouch," he said. "I kept the real items below that blanket."

"We know you were being watched and followed earlier today, so someone must have discovered you were the one who placed the ad," Eden said. "Once they saw you take the practice mask out of here, they must have decided to see what else you had."

"But there's no way for us to prove when the real artifacts were taken," Nick said, then looked at Thomas. "Who else knew that you had religious objects stored here?"

Thomas shrugged. "The members of my society, of course."

"Who is in your society? I need names."

Thomas shook his head. "You know better than to ask me that. That's something that you'll have to put together on your own. Since some of us are the keepers of certain objects, our families generally know which group we belong to. But by and large, identities are kept secret."

Nick expelled his breath in a hiss. "You're right. Forget the question."

After getting Thomas's promise to stop by the station and make a statement, they left.

Nick lapsed into a thoughtful silence, then continued speaking after a moment. "You realize that people will probably blame you when they learn that religious objects are missing again."

She nodded slowly. "The same thought occurred to me, but there's nothing I can do about gossip. The only thing I can do now is stick to the truth and, eventually, things will bear me out."

The doubt in her voice wouldn't have been evident to anyone who didn't know her as well as he did. Hearing it made him want to find the ones who were doing this to her and break them into little pieces. But their enemy remained faceless and in the shadows. Frustration gnawed at him.

He dropped her off by the front door of the school, and was almost out of the parking lot when he glanced in his rearview mirror and saw Mr. Puye, the principal, standing in the gravel and waving his arms, trying to flag him down.

Nick circled around the parking area and pulled into a visitor's slot. By then, the principal had walked over to meet him.

"Deputy, if you don't mind, we need you inside."

As Nick entered the building, he saw Eden standing in the hallway, her expression somber. Mr. Puye led him through Eden's classroom, out a rear door, and into a small common storage area that separated her classroom from that of the next teacher's.

"This is the storage area the school designates for Ms. Maes and the teacher in the adjoining room. Ms. Maes's substitute teacher was looking for some supplies earlier today when she came across this," he said, then pointed to two crude leather masks and a small pouch inside an old-looking pottery bowl. "I don't know if those are genuine or fakes, but I do know one thing—they don't belong here."

Even without taking a closer look Nick knew where the artifacts had come from. He was looking at Thomas's missing stash.

EDEN SAT IN the interview room at the station, wondering how things had gone so wrong for her. The principal hadn't been interested in the truth, or her theories. The school administration had been looking for a reason to run her out, and whoever was after her had handed it to them.

Nick had been supportive, but Mora had taken over the interview, sending Nick away on investigative tasks.

"If you're absolutely sure you don't want an attorney, let's get started," Mora said. "You claim you've never seen the items found in the storage room?"

"I haven't, but I'll wager they're the items that were stolen from Thomas Ray's storage shed."

"Deputy Black Raven will verify that. He's gone to show the pieces to Thomas right now."

Nick entered a moment later. "They're my uncle's, Captain."

"Any fingerprints that will give us a lead to the thief?" Mora asked.

"I dusted the masks, the medicine bowl, and the pouch. I also took the substitute teacher's prints for comparison and exclusion. There's only one set of prints on those objects, and a quick match-up indicated they belong to the substitute teacher."

"But don't you see?" Eden protested. "Had I stolen those items, I wouldn't have put them in plain sight in an area frequented by at least one other teacher. And if I had hidden them in a place that would have easily incriminated me, why would I have bothered to wipe my fingerprints off them? What would be the point?"

"It could have been a very smart thing to do—in case you got caught. You could argue your case from that exact standpoint."

"And you would believe me? You don't sound like you do now, so it wouldn't have been a very smart plan, would it? Face it, Captain. I'm being framed—just like my parents."

"If that's true, then someone's going to a lot of trouble to ruin you. Any idea who that might be?"

At that moment Deputy Torres appeared in the doorway. Eden glanced over, but without saying a word, he shook his head, then walked away.

"Several people have wanted me off the pueblo and others who believe I can find the artifacts probably want to make sure I need money badly enough to deal. What better way to create that need than to take away my only source of income?"

"I want to know the names of the people who have threatened you."

She exhaled softly. "I only know of one for sure, but I gave him my word that the matter would stay between us as long as he stopped his harassment," she answered. "And I believe he has, so far. But you might talk to Samuel Runningwater. He came to my house with two other politicians to warn me that people wanted me out, and I should leave for my own safety."

"He threatened you?" Nick asked suddenly.

"No, it wasn't like that. I was more like a statement of fact. The lieutenant governor and a tribal council member came over with him, so they were witnesses."

"The real problem is that we can't narrow down who knew the artifacts were in my uncle's shed," Nick told Mora. "He thinks he may have mentioned it to Runningwater, but he's not sure. He also can't swear that he didn't tell Theresa at one point or another."

"If we find out who framed my parents, I think we'll find out who's framing me," Eden concluded.

Mora stood. "These items will go back to the head of the appropriate religious society as soon as possible. In the meantime, Eden, I suggest you keep a low profile and let us look into this. After what happened today you're going to be more of a target than ever. People will quickly condemn you based on the circumstantial evidence alone."

She nodded. "Am I free to leave?"

"Yes. No charges were pressed against you. Thomas spoke to the people involved, and now that the items are back they'd rather forget the whole thing. As you know, our religion derives its power from the secrecy that surrounds it. So the last thing they want is to have their religious objects become part of a police investigation. Since everything's back where it belongs, everyone's eager to get back to business as usual.''

Eden picked up her purse and with a nod, started toward the door. Without a job, things would get very difficult for her from this point on. Of course, now that the charges had been dropped, she could probably push the matter and get her suspension upgraded to ''with pay.'' But her future here as a teacher was gone. Her contract would never be renewed.

It was early evening, about dinnertime for most, and the Plaza was nearly deserted. She got about twenty yards from the station when Nick called out her name and jogged up.

''Wait a minute. I'd like to walk you home.''

''Shouldn't you be returning Rick's truck? Oh, and that reminds me, tell him I'll pay to fix the lock. I forced it open with a screwdriver to get inside.''

''Don't worry about it. I already told him what happened, and he thought it was funny. He said he was thinking of putting a better lock on it anyway, and you just convinced him it's a good idea.''

''I'd still like to cover his expenses. It's important to me.''

Nick nodded. ''Are you going to be okay?''

She shrugged. ''The house is paid for, so I don't have to worry about that, and I've got some savings. Providing I don't have any large, unexpected expenses, I can hold out. But I'll need to get to the truth of who framed my parents, and now me, quickly. Time isn't on my side.''

''I'll do my best to help you, Eden, you know that.''

''I trust you, Nick,'' she said, ''but I'll keep digging on

my own, too. The truth is that it's really hard for me to let go and put myself in another person's hands all the way.'' She looked up at him. ''But if anyone can understand that, it's you. You don't trust easily either. That's why you're so closed and no one can ever figure out what you're thinking.''

''That's not true,'' he said, surprised. ''I take people at face value and I'm pretty open. That's the one thing that makes me a good cop.''

''You're open only to a point. No one gets too close to you, Nick. There's a barrier you won't let *anyone* cross. You've always protected yourself well.''

''Is that really the way you see me?'' he asked, surprised.

''It's the truth. You work to solve crimes and help people, but you keep those very people at a distance. You keep a wall up that's meant to protect you from any emotion that can cut you too deeply. I think everyone is that way to one extent or another, but you and I have perfected that art,'' she said sadly. ''We've taken it on the chin too many times not to put boundaries around our feelings.''

He considered it for a long moment. ''You may be right about me,'' he admitted reluctantly.

What she'd said was particularly true when it came to his feelings for her and Chris. He loved them, but he couldn't quite let go and give his heart free rein. Deep down, he was afraid that what they had would never last.

Nick knew he'd hurt Eden badly when he was forced out of his home at the age of eighteen and hadn't taken her with him. Then she almost destroyed him when they reunited as adults. He wasn't sure what the third time would bring, but he did know that if things didn't work out this time, they'd both end up feeling the pain.

AFTER LEAVING Christopher with Mrs. Chino, Eden spent the next morning at a meeting with the principal and members of the school board. She'd had to push the matter of suspension with pay because she hadn't had a choice, but she'd never realized just how difficult the fight would become.

They continued to press her, insisting that she was becoming a corrupting influence on the kids, and their assaults on her integrity were merciless, despite the lack of proof to back up their charges. The hours stretched out to eternity, but she tried to remain composed and not allow her temper to come to the surface.

Then the school secretary knocked lightly on the door and came in. "Ms. Maes has an emergency call," she said, looking at Mr. Puye, then at Eden.

Only one person would have called her here with an emergency—Mrs. Chino. Suddenly the meeting and the outcome meant very little to her.

She stood up, not caring about anything now except her son. "What phone should I use?"

"The one on my desk," the secretary said, pointing directly ahead. "Line one."

Eden's hands were shaking as she picked up the receiver and identified herself.

"I'm really sorry to call you at work, but I didn't know what else to do," Mrs. Chino said.

"What's wrong?" Eden managed through clenched teeth. She had to stop shaking. She had to be able to think clearly and control her fears.

"I think two men are watching my house. I saw some figures behind a tree in the orchard across the street. They haven't made any move against me or the kids, but I can just feel them out there."

"Why didn't you call the police?"

"I did, but there was a big accident on the road leading

out of the pueblo and all of the available deputies are there. They'll send someone as soon as they can, but it'll be at least twenty minutes before they get here. I was hoping a couple of the male teachers could come by.''

''No. They can't leave their classes unattended.'' Fear gnawed through her. There was no way for her to tell if this was a threat against her son, or something as simple as Mrs. Chino's imagination working overtime. But she'd never known her to have flights of fancy. Mrs. Chino was the most down-to-earth, practical person Eden had ever met.

''I'll take care of this, one way or another.'' Eden hung up, not taking time to explain. She had only one option now. Black Raven Ranch was just a few minutes away from Mrs. Chino's—if someone took the shortcut.

She called Nick and had her call patched through to his radio. ''Nick, you've got to help us,'' she said, explaining. ''I don't know why those men are there or if this has anything to do with Christopher, but I'm really scared.''

''Hang tight. I'll send my brother and the wranglers over right now, then I'll join them as soon as I tell my boss.''

A glimmer of hope warmed the coldness that had spread through her. Nick wouldn't allow anyone to hurt Christopher or the other children.

Her unfinished meeting with the principal and the board was suddenly a low priority. Without giving it another thought, she ran out of the office and got into her car.

NICK CALLED his brother, then explained the situation to Captain Mora, who immediately released him from the accident scene. The injured had already been taken away, and there was no work left there at the site that Mora and Deputy Torres couldn't finish.

Nick raced down the main road, his hands tightly

wrapped around the wheel. At the speed he was traveling, he would arrive before Jake did.

Less than seven minutes later, he reached the small stucco home and, turning the corner, saw that a window in the back had been smashed. A thin wisp of white smoke was billowing out.

Slamming on his brakes, he jumped out of the Jeep and radioed the fire department on his handheld as he ran around back. He'd known fear before and he was sure he would again, but nothing in his experience prepared him for the cold hand he felt squeezing his heart now.

Nick climbed through the damaged window into a bedroom, then moved forward quickly through the increasing haze. There were no sounds, and that was enough to fill him with dread. A house with children in it should not have been silent.

As he opened the door into the hall, he saw two men wearing stocking masks standing in front of a closed door off the kitchen. They'd set a large trash can filled with paper on fire, and were trying to smoke out the ones behind the locked door.

"We know you're in there," the tallest of the two yelled. "Open the door and give us the boy, or you'll burn alive." Then he started banging on the door with his gloved fist.

The terrified cries of the children inside were the worst sounds he'd ever heard in his life.

Nick ran forward, reluctant to draw his weapon with the children and Mrs. Chino somewhere around. "Get away from that door!"

The men turned and the larger one picked up the fiery trash can and threw it directly at him. Nick tried to dodge, but the hall was too narrow, and the can struck him in the knees, knocking him down. Flaming debris flew out of the can in every direction.

While Nick was still down, the other man threw a kitchen stepladder at him. Then, as Nick blocked it away with his arms, the pair ran into one of the bedrooms, closing the door behind them.

Nick didn't give chase. He had more important problems to take care of now. The pantry door and wood frame had caught fire, and the smoke had reduced visibility in the kitchen to almost zero. Mrs. Chino was yelling for help, and the rest of the children were either crying or yelling along with her.

"It's Nick Black Raven, Mrs. Chino," he shouted, trying to be heard over their cries. "Can you open the door?"

"I jammed it shut by wedging the bottom of the door." She shouted back. "Now I can't get it open and the door handle is too hot to touch."

"Then move everyone away from the door. I'll have to break it down." He heard Mrs. Chino yelling at the children to get behind her and quiet down.

Waiting only a few more seconds, Nick kicked the door with everything he had. It took two tries, but he smashed through and kicked away the burning wood. As he forced his way into the tiny, smoke-filled room, he could see Mrs. Chino cowering in the corner, with two little children tucked under her arms. All were coughing from the smoke.

Then he heard shouts out in the hall. Nick spun around, and saw Jake step into the kitchen, a handkerchief over his mouth. "I'm here, brother and I've got two men with me."

"Grab the kids," Nick said, grabbing the two toddlers Mrs. Chino pushed in his direction. Jake helped Mrs. Chino stand, and Rick came in, moving her out of the kitchen as Jake scooped up another child.

They got outside quickly, but as Mrs. Chino counted heads, Nick's worst nightmare suddenly became alarmingly real. Christopher wasn't among the kids they'd rescued.

"I'm going back in," Nick said, heading for the front door quickly.

"No!" Jake tried to grab his brother by the arm. "The fire's spread all over the hall, and into the front room. The smoke and heat are too much. Wait for the fire department."

"Christopher can't wait, and neither can I," Nick said, pulling free of his brother. As he stepped through the doors, he made himself one promise. Either he'd come back out with Christopher or they'd be carrying him out, too.

Chapter Eighteen

The air was hot and thick as Nick entered the house. The fire was spreading, but most of the problems were still in the kitchen area. Breathing through his handkerchief, he moved into the living room and then the hall.

Nick squinted, trying to see through the dark gray haze that stung his eyes, keeping in a crouch and searching for movement. Nick ignored those rooms with closed doors and worked his way back to the pantry. The smoke was thickest there.

Working on instinct fueled by hope, he dropped to his knees and continued to search around the perimeter of the room. The air was better down here, and he could see more clearly. Still, Christopher was nowhere in sight. Fear ripped at him, pushing him to the edge.

He called out Christopher's name, but all he heard were the sharp snaps of burning wood and crackle of flames licking new tinder. He was just about to leave the pantry again and check the bedrooms when he heard a soft shuffling noise.

Closing in on the sound, he hurried toward a shelf of canned goods and, as he drew near, he saw that the space below the bottom shelf and the floor was occupied. Christopher sat between a gallon jug of apple juice and an empty plastic waste paper bucket, chewing on a small stuffed dinosaur.

"Come here, buddy. We have to get out of here."

Taking off his jacket, Nick wrapped the baby in it. Instead of protesting loudly, something he'd fully expected, the baby was soothed by the cool satin lining.

Nick began to feel his way out of the house, now so thick with smoke he couldn't see more than a foot in front of him. As he was forced back into the hall, he heard the firemen breaking a window somewhere ahead, and felt the cool water from the spray of a fire hose.

As light streamed through the smoke, he found the opening he needed. Nick ran through the pocket of smoke, sure of the safety on the other side. In a few seconds, he was outside, the baby squirming in his arms. As he opened the jacket Chris suddenly squealed, and tried to cover his eyes with his arm.

"Too bright, huh guy?"

Hearing his name, Nick looked up and saw Eden running toward him. In a heartbeat, she threw her arms around his neck. "I knew you'd find him and bring him back to me." Her eyes were shimmering with tears as she looked down at her son then back at him.

"I *had* to find him," he answered truthfully. "He's your little boy, but he's gotten under my skin, too. I can't explain it any better than that."

"For once, those are the only words I need to hear." Eden cupped his face and pulled him down to her.

Her kiss was soft and exquisitely tender. It sent its shock waves spiraling all through him. Nick reached out and pulled her close to his side. Holding Eden against him with one arm, and the baby with the other, he felt complete.

A heartbeat later a paramedic came up. "Deputy. We need to check you and the baby out. Will you step over here?'' he asked, leading them toward the back of the emergency vehicle.

Nick saw that Eden stayed with Chris and him, unwilling to be separated from either of them for even a short time. The realization pleased him. The bond that had always existed between Eden and him was now even stronger. As she looked up at him, she seemed less guarded and more vulnerable. The impact of that soft look slammed all through him.

"We have to talk," she said.

"Yes, we do," he answered.

"But not right now, folks," the paramedic interrupted. "We need to have everyone transported to the clinic so they can be checked out again by the medical staff. The deputy and the baby have to ride with us. The mother will want to take her own car, or get a ride. With the attendants and all the patients, there's just not enough room for another adult."

Nick's gaze never left Eden's. "Will you trust me with Chris a little while longer?" he asked, holding the baby as he climbed into the ambulance.

"For as long as forever takes," she answered.

Her words touched him deeply. But before he could answer, the paramedic shut the ambulance door, and she disappeared from his sight.

Nick glanced down at Chris, who was now holding on to his little finger with a tiny grip. "If hard work and determination count for anything in this investigation, little guy, then someday you, your mom and I will be a family."

AN HOUR LATER, they were all discharged from the clinic. Before they could leave, however, Captain Mora questioned every one of the adults who'd been at the crime scene.

Despite what both Mora and Nick had hoped, there

wasn't much to go on. They knew that the kidnapping suspects had escaped out one of the bedroom windows, but had only vague descriptions to work with because the perps had both worn masks. The pueblo was being searched for strangers, and Torres was interviewing each outsider he found before allowing them to go on their way. But, so far, they were coming out empty-handed.

Finally, after all the questions had been asked and answered, Eden and Nick, who was holding Christopher, walked to the side doors. There, they waited for Jake to bring the Jeep around.

Eden's eyes misted as she looked at their son, then at Nick. Today, Nick had risked everything, including his own life to come and help them. When she'd needed him he'd been there, saving the baby from kidnappers and the fire.

She owed him everything and, from that moment on, she would never again hold anything back. She'd already given him her heart, but, now, the time for the truth had come. No matter what the cost, even if Nick never found it in his heart to forgive her, tonight he'd know that Chris was his son.

As Jake pulled up, Nick reached for Eden's hand. "I want you and Christopher to move to Black Raven Ranch. It's just too dangerous elsewhere for you."

She nodded slowly. She wouldn't deny him anything now, not after all he'd done without even knowing the truth. "But we have to talk. I've got something important to tell you."

"We'll have time—and privacy—once we're home. Can it wait till then?" he asked, then waved at Jake, who was approaching.

She nodded. She wanted no distractions when she spoke to Nick.

On the ride back they all agreed that she and Chris would

use Nick's old bedroom in the main house, and Nick would remain in the bunkhouse. For the first time Eden let go, allowing Nick to make the decisions for her. If only for now, she wanted to let him take care of her. Most of her life she'd fought hard for everything, and, at the moment, all she felt was tired.

Almost as if sensing her thoughts, Nick pulled her against his side, letting her lean on him. With his strong arm draped over her as she held Christopher, Eden felt loved and protected.

Nick tilted her chin up and gave her a light kiss. "You belong here in my arms," he whispered.

Love filled her heart. She didn't want to think about tomorrow. She didn't even want to think about what the next hour would bring. Fate had given her this one perfect moment, and no matter what else happened, she'd always have this memory.

"Would you have someone go to Eden's house and pick up some of her things as well as Christopher's?" Nick asked Jake. "I'm going to help her get settled in."

"I'll go with Annie. Another woman is more likely to pick up the things she and the baby will need."

Once at the ranch, Nick led Eden to his room upstairs, then brought in an extra crib from the nursery.

Chris was already fast asleep as she set him down. "Poor baby. He's had quite a day. He's exhausted."

Christopher barely stirred as she covered him with a blanket, kissed him lightly, and moved away.

"What about me?" Nick said with a smile as he reached for her arm, drawing her back to him. "I've had quite a day, too. Do I get a kiss?"

Eden wrapped her arms around his neck, pressing her body to his. He was a tall man, all muscle and sinewy strength. His large hands pressed on the small of her back, pulling her into him, letting her feel his manhood. The gathering of heat stoked new fires inside her.

"You were meant to be mine, Eden," he said, his voice a raw, dark whisper.

Heat and desire coiled around her, making it difficult for her to think. Following the leadings of her heart, she drew his face down toward hers and kissed him deeply, filling his mouth with her tongue and letting him taste her.

His grip tightened as shock waves traveled over him. Her aggressiveness sparked every male instinct he possessed. He wanted to take her now, hard and fast, until all she could do was cry out his name in helpless surrender.

Then suddenly Christopher woke up, his loud wail filling the room.

"He's hungry," she said, stepping out of Nick's embrace. "I was hoping he'd sleep through the night, but I guess he has other plans."

"I'll see if Annie has a bottle we can use," Nick said and hurried out.

It took several minutes to find the right formula, warm the milk, and bring it back to Eden. By the time he returned, Eden had placed the baby next to her on his bed. Her shirt was open, and the baby was suckling on her breast. Nick almost groaned at the rightness of it.

Eden took the bottle. "He's been weaned for a while, but he still likes the extra attention." Christopher fussed at taking the bottle, but then settled down as Nick sat beside him.

As Eden started to button up her blouse, Nick reached out and stopped her. "Don't. It's just the three of us."

Nick ran the tip of his finger down her breast and smiled as a shiver coursed through her. "We belong together, you, me and Christopher. Someday, after the investigation clears our families, he could be the son I never had."

"No." Seeing the pain that flashed in his eyes, Eden reached for Nick's hand. "You don't understand. Chris is the son you *did* have. He's yours, Nick."

He stared at her, a stunned look on his face. "But you said I wasn't..." He looked down at Christopher.

A lump formed at the back of her throat as Nick touched the baby's soft skin almost in awe. Eden saw the emotions playing on his face. Surprise had turned to wonder, and now to a gentle love that all but tore her breath away.

"Why didn't you tell me the truth before?" He carried Christopher, who was once again asleep, to his crib, then sat on the easy chair, facing the bed.

Eden saw the savage battle taking place behind his dark eyes as he struggled to understand. The news she'd just given him had redefined his world.

"I want the whole story, Eden."

She nodded. "I left you that day in Arizona because I knew I had to return here. Then, later, when I discovered I was pregnant, I wanted to tell you, but you'd been very specific about never wanting a family, Nick. I didn't think it was fair for me to rope you into becoming a father, and then force you to come back to the pueblo, a place you hated at the time. And, truthfully, I wanted far more for my child than a dad who'd only see him as an unwelcome responsibility."

"Back then, because of the circumstances, I may have seen it in that light, too," he admitted slowly. "To be honest, I would have done my best to keep you and my son from returning here also, and I would have never agreed to come back myself." He paused then added, "But time has a way of changing everything. After we both found ourselves at the pueblo, why didn't you tell me then?"

"Many things had changed by then, Nick, but you still seemed glad to be a bachelor. And then there was the fact

that you'd become a deputy for the tribal police. I knew
what I'd gone through in my life because *my* dad was a
cop. Dad missed almost every function that was important
to mom and me, from birthdays to anniversaries. He was
never really there for either of us until it was too late, and
then he got himself killed, and Mom, too.''

He nodded thoughtfully but didn't say anything.

''I remembered crying myself to sleep after being kept
awake for hours hearing their bitter arguments. I always
felt torn between wanting to side with one or the other.
You can't imagine what that's like. It cuts you up into
ribbons. I just couldn't risk putting Christopher through
anything even close to that. I wanted him to have a daddy
who would put him first, and I wasn't sure any cop could
do that.''

''I remember talking to you about your dad when you
were growing up, and I know what you went through. I
know you, Eden, and I know what you need and what you
fear. But I can't make you crazy promises and tell you that
you'll never be disappointed in me. What I can tell you is
that nothing will ever be more important to me than you
and my son.''

Nick hadn't spoken of love, but she could see it in his
eyes. He wanted them together and, in her heart, there was
nothing she wanted more.

Nick crossed the room and offering her his hand, pulled
her to her feet. With a tenderness that made her weak at
the knees, he began to slowly undress her.

''This is how I want you,'' he said in a husky voice.
''Naked and vulnerable. For me.'' His hands swept down
over her breasts, loving the way she responded to him and
the little shudders that rippled over her.

''Your clothes…take them off…I need to see you,'' she
whispered.

"In time. For now, just *feel*," he growled.

As his mouth closed over her breast, her thoughts became jagged and she couldn't speak.

Nick was relentless, murmuring dark promises as he caressed her, but never voicing the words she longed for most. Eden desperately wanted to hear his whispered words of love but, deep down, knew it wasn't something Nick would give her. To him, actions had always spoken louder than words and, now, with his every touch, he was showing her what was in his heart.

Moving with infinite care, he rained soft, moist kisses along the length of her body. Then, kneeling before her, he found and kissed the center of her being. She came apart, shattering into a million stars. As her knees gave, he picked her up in his arms and laid her gently down on the bed.

Nick stripped off his clothes, casting them aside in a heap on the floor. He then stood by the bed, needing her, but wanting her to reach out to him first. Her surrender had to be complete—body and soul—because that was what he'd be giving her. He waited as Eden's gaze seared over him intimately, making his body impossibly hard. At long last, she reached out to him and he lay beside her.

Eden ran her hands over his smooth, hard body, needing to know him in every way. Raw, male strength was there in every flat plane and muscled contour. And, yet, her touch alone was enough to make tremors shoot through him. "I don't want to hold back anymore, Nick. Tonight, I want everything you can give me."

"And you'll have it," he said, his voice unsteady for the first time.

Eden pressed her hand to his chest, feeling his heart beating wildly beneath her palm. Holding her gaze, he wound his fingers through hers. He was speaking to her again, though he hadn't said a word. Letting love guide her, she caressed him, fueling his need until the pleasure became too intense for him to bear.

Nick shifted over her, pressing her down into the cool linens. Blood thundered through his veins as he entered her in one long, bold stroke. The many sensations that held her captive became like a kaleidoscope of great beauty that revealed a startling new facet with each caress.

"Look at me," he said. "I want to see your thoughts and your needs."

She cried out time and time again in helpless pleasure as he taught her about passion's darkness and the wildness of the light.

At long last, he satisfied her with that final welcome release. The trembling started deep within her, exploding outward. Surrounded by her warmth, he cried out in triumph and followed her over the edge.

She opened her eyes slowly. Nick lay over her and, enjoying the feel of his body on hers, she remained still. "It was perfect," she said.

He nuzzled her neck then rolled onto his back, taking her with him. "Yeah, but it's going to get even better," he said in a low, guttural voice. "There are many ways a man can love his woman and we're only at the beginning, sweetheart."

"His woman." The words wrapped themselves around her heart. They weren't the words of love she'd longed to hear, but right now was not the time to ask for anything more. It was enough to enjoy the magic she'd found in his arms.

NICK WAS UP at daybreak, happy and completely at peace. Eden and his son were still sleeping and everything seemed very right. Today, he'd talk to her about getting married. After what they'd shared last night, saying goodbye to her and Chris seemed unthinkable. They'd face whatever lay ahead, no matter what it was, together.

Hearing a light knock, Nick pulled on his jeans and, shirtless, answered it. Annie came in holding a bottle. "You'll need this," she said, and laughed as Chris began to cry. "Just in time."

As Eden sat up, the sheet wrapped around her, Annie waved. "Mrs. Chino is here. Since her home will be under repair for a while, she agreed to be Noelle's nanny. If you'll let me have Chris, she'll take care of both babies and then put them downstairs in the playpen."

Nick glanced back at Eden, who nodded.

"That would be great," Eden said, "but I wonder what Mrs. Chino will say once she finds out I'm here this early."

"Don't worry about that. You and Chris belong here now," Annie said flatly, then took Chris, giving him his bottle at the same time. "See you two later."

As the door closed, Eden got up. "I should have been up sooner," she said, avoiding Nick's gaze.

Instead of the soft light of love he'd hoped to see in her eyes this morning, there was a faraway, worried look that cut through him and filled him with uneasiness.

"Nick, I need to ask you to do one thing for me," she said, dressing quickly.

"Anything," he answered.

"Don't tell anyone Christopher is your son, at least not yet."

The words knifed into his heart. Making love to her last night, he'd bared his soul to her in a way that, to him, had transcended anything they'd ever shared in the past. By pulling away from him now, and asking him to deny his own son, she was showing him clearly that it hadn't meant the same thing to her.

He looked away from her and remained silent, gathering himself. Finally, he turned to face her.

"Understand one thing, Eden. Christopher is my son, too, and I intend to play a big part in his life. I have that right."

"I'd always hoped you'd feel that way," Eden said gently.

He looked at her in confusion. "Then why are you asking me to keep this a secret?"

"Because of what's happened. Until we settle the past, letting people know that Chris is your son may carry a very high price."

Nick stared at her, the words seeping into his mind slowly, and tearing him up every step of the way. "You're thinking that no one will allow me to work on an investigation that involves both my father and my son," he said.

"Yes and it's absolutely imperative that you stay on the case. That'll be the only way we can suppress any evidence we might find incriminating your father. No matter what happens, Nick, I won't allow Jake, Annie and you to pay for something that happened long ago."

"I won't suppress evidence," he said flatly. "I believe in my father's innocence and I'll prove it. And, if I'm wrong, I'll face the consequences," he added. "But I won't put the weight of that shame on my son's shoulders, even if it means never claiming him as mine."

"If you weren't welcome at the pueblo, we'd leave also," Eden said. "Once things are settled, I won't hide the fact that you're Chris's father forever."

"No. You've worked too hard to give Christopher a life free from shame. He deserves that."

"He needs his family—one that sticks together. I want you to put us first, but that works both ways."

"We'll both do whatever it takes to give our son a good

life," he said. Yet even as he spoke, he could sense that she would never allow him to do what he had to. She wasn't a teenager anymore. This time, if he left, she'd go after him. She would never force herself and Christopher on him, but she'd follow him and let his own heart lead him back to her.

Without another word, he pulled on his shirt and left the room. Determination filled him as he strode back downstairs. He knew what he had to do. Somehow, he had to find the proof they needed to clear his father and her family.

Nothing had ever stopped a Black Raven and he wouldn't fail now. Eden and his son were the most important things in his life and he wouldn't lose them without one hell of a fight.

Chapter Nineteen

Eden met Nick, Jake and Annie downstairs in the den. A somber mood had settled over all of them.

Jake held his mother's diary in his hands, staring at it lost in thought.

Eden spoke first. "Yesterday somebody tried to kidnap Christopher, and almost killed a half-dozen children in the process. The would-be kidnappers probably planned to use my son as leverage. My guess is that they wanted me to pull out all the stops and find the mask and fetish, then hand over the artifacts to them in exchange for Chris."

"For some reason they're getting desperate. Maybe they're afraid we're getting too close and we'll find out who they are before we locate the artifacts," Nick said, his hands curling into fists. Someone had tried to hurt his child and the woman he loved. It didn't get more personal than this. And no matter what it cost him, he'd bring them in. They'd pay for this.

Jake held up the diary. "If the key to finding those thieves or the stolen artifacts lies here, then let's make use of it. But I've got to tell you, I've read those passages time and time again and I can't make heads or tails out of them. Neither can Annie." Jake handed Nick the diary. "Here. Maybe you two can."

Eden sat next to Nick. "Here she speaks clearly," Eden said, reading one of the passages. "She talks about my mother needing help. But then it goes cryptic again."

"'Isabel's answers are written in the winds of the past. When the barren land gives up its secrets, and the rocks tell their story, she will find peace,'" Nick read out loud.

Jake shrugged. "I have no idea what the heck that means."

Eden read the passage again silently. "She's obviously talking about the artifacts, but the rest..."

Nick stood up. "We're not getting anywhere. There's got to be another way."

Eden closed the diary and, contemplating what she'd just read, ran her fingers over the binding. The leather was smooth, worn with age and the dryness of the New Mexican desert. Yet there was an elegance to the volume that she'd never seen in the more modern hardcover books. As she admired the reddish-brown binding, a slight imperfection caught her eye. There was a small tear in the leather near the spine. It had been skillfully repaired, but the glue had discolored slightly over the years. If the light hadn't been just right, she would have never seen it.

She pressed against it and felt a raised section. "I may have something here," she said slowly, holding the book out to Nick. "I think there's something inside the tear."

Nick took the journal from her and pressed against the repaired section lightly with the tips of his fingers. "You're right," he said, then showed it to Jake.

Jake reached for his pocket knife and as Nick steadied the journal, cut through the glue. "Let's find out what's here." Reaching inside the pocket made by the tear, he pulled out a thin piece of paper and read what it said. "My heart is bound to the land that is no more, a prisoner of the piece that fits."

"Great. Another riddle," Nick grumbled.

Eden, looking up from her seat on the couch, saw it from another perspective. "That's my mother's handwriting. She must have left this with Saya right before she went into hiding. And there's something on the back."

"It's a map of sorts," Nick said, "indicating some landmarks, but it's still very generic. That mountain can be any of four, and the high spot marked as the starting off point from which to take fifty paces, can be any of a hundred hills, mesas, ridges or mounds on pueblo land." Nick expelled his breath in a hiss. "So we still have nothing."

"No, that's not so," Eden said slowly. "We've all read the passages and figured that your mother was waxing poetic. But this map, drawn by my mother, makes me think Saya was more literal in her clues than any of us realized." She paused, and studied the simple sketch. "There's a section of land on our pueblo that is consistent with the markings on the map, and where nothing much ever grows—the alkali flats. That might be the barren land she mentioned."

"Good point," Nick agreed. "But we're still talking about a fairly large area that runs for a mile or two along the south end of the pueblo. We need to narrow our search a little more."

Eden said nothing for a long time. "What we have to do is get inside my mother's head. She was obviously scared and getting ready to go on the run when she met with Saya. The two never had much time to discuss things. If I can make myself think like she did, maybe I can see that stretch of desert with new eyes." She paused for a moment. "I need to go back to my house and look through my mother's things. I have a box of her personal treasures, and although nothing in there is valuable, they meant something to her. If I reacquaint myself with her in that way, maybe we can make sense out of the map together."

"I wouldn't stay there for long, if I were you," Jake warned.

"It's broad daylight, and I won't be alone. No one's going to try and threaten me there, not with Nick along," Eden said.

"She's got that right," Nick growled.

Eden kissed Christopher goodbye, leaving him in Mrs. Chino's care. With Jake, Martin, Annie, and several ranch hands around, Chris would be safe.

Nick led Eden to his tribal unit, and drove her home. He insisted on going inside the house first and taking a look around. "Okay. Everything's as it should be."

Eden went directly to her office, then pulled two small, decorative boxes from the far shelf. Next to them, lying on its side, was an old photo album.

"Do the photos in that book date back to your parents' time as well?" he asked.

She nodded. "Mom usually slipped the snapshots loosely in there between the covers. That's why it's bulging so much. I mounted a lot of the photos myself, but it was hard facing all those memories, so I never got around to finishing the job."

"I think we should look through it now," he said gently.

"Okay." She handed him the boxes, and carefully carried the album herself.

As Eden sat down on the sofa next to him and began to sort through the photos, an undeniable sadness settled over her.

Noting it, Nick stopped her. "Why don't you let me take a look. If there are any photos of people or things I don't recognize, I can show those to you."

She nodded. "I'd appreciate that. Looking through things like this just hurts too much, particularly since I haven't accomplished what I came to do—proving their innocence.'' She stood up. "Let me go to the bedroom and get a few more things to take back to Black Raven Ranch.''

By the time she returned to the living room, Nick was holding what appeared to be half of a photograph. "What's that?'' she asked.

"I'm not sure. It's hard to make out. I found it deliberately lodged near the spine of the album, beneath twenty or thirty other photos.'' He held it out to her. "It appears to be a piece of a photo taken with an instant camera. All you can see are three faces, and just barely, at that.''

Eden picked it up carefully, though she doubted she could have damaged it any more than it already was. The lighting had been bad, and now there were so many scratches on the photo itself, it was hard to make anything out clearly.

"Do you happen to have a magnifying glass?'' Nick asked.

"Sort of,'' she said. She went to her desk drawer and pulled out a tiny device that was used to inspect mineral samples. "This is a hand lens. Its viewing field is much smaller, but in this case, it should do nicely.''

Nick held it near the faces for a long moment. "I think that's Rita Korman and her brother, Wayne. Boy, did he have long hair back then. But I don't know that third person. Do you?'' He handed the small magnifying device to her.

She tried to study the man's face, but finally shook her head. "It's hard to say, the photo quality is zilch, but I don't think that's anyone I know.''

Nick stared pensively at the photo, then looked up at her. "Do you have a computer I can use?''

"Sure, but I don't have scanners and fancy equipment,'' she warned.

"I don't need that as long as you have a modem hooked

up. What I'm going to do is log into the police data banks from here."

"The modem came with the computer, and I've used it to get information for my classes from the Internet." Eden led him to her worktable and switched the computer on for him.

After gaining access to her Internet provider, Nick entered the police department's site address. Using his password, he logged in a moment later. "I'm going to follow a hunch and check to see who the known fences were at the time of the thefts."

He began pulling up rap sheets and studying the accompanying photos. Ten minutes later, he struck pay dirt. "This looks like it could be the same guy."

Eden looked over his shoulder. "There *are* similarities," she conceded.

"This guy was pretty well known around here twenty years ago, from what I can tell. He went to prison just before your parents' murder, but it was for an unrelated crime."

"I can think of only one reason why Rita and Wayne would have met with this man," Eden said slowly.

"Me, too. But this isn't proof Eden. Not by a long shot. From a legal standpoint, the most we can call this is an interesting coincidence."

"I know. But it does suggest that my mom and dad believed Rita and Wayne were the thieves. They must have been trying to gather evidence against them. Remember, Dad was a cop. He would have gone after them, one way or another."

"I'll tell you one thing. If Rita and Wayne were dealing with this guy, they were playing in the big leagues. A guy with a rap sheet this long wouldn't have taken it kindly if Rita and Wayne failed to deliver what they'd promised. My guess is that when Isabel kept the artifacts from them, Rita and Wayne found themselves in danger of losing their lives.''

"I know my mom and dad wouldn't have handed over something they knew belonged to the tribe. They would have gone down fighting," she said, her voice trembling. "And that's exactly what happened."

He tried to take her hand, but she pulled away. "No. I need to stay focused. If those two animals are the ones who killed my parents and tried to take Christopher, I want to nail them."

"And we will," he growled. "I give you my word."

He gestured to the keepsake boxes she'd brought out. "Let's look through those. Maybe we'll find something else that'll help us."

Eden set the first one upon the table. "My grandmother threw out or gave away a lot of Mom and Dad's things, but these keepsake boxes contained their personal effects, and I held on to them." She opened the lid carefully. Nestled inside was a faded rose encased in plastic. She took it out carefully, her voice thoughtful as she spoke. "My father gave this to Mom on their first anniversary, and she always kept it. Even after they started having problems, she'd often go into the bedroom, take it out and look at it. I saw her holding it one time when Dad had to go back to work though it was late at night. She told me then never to marry a cop unless I wanted to have my heart broken," she said sadly.

"It doesn't have to be that way, Eden," he said.

"I know," she said simply, but didn't continue. She couldn't bring herself to talk about anything that had to do with their own future, not while looking at her mother's things and remembering.

Eden laid the other trinkets inside the box out on the

table. There was a small Apache tear pendant made from volcanic glass, a silver four-leaf clover, and a blue-and-white feather she'd found on a hike one day. "Mom noticed and valued the simple things most people overlooked. She had no desire for wealth. That's why it was so incredibly painful for her when people branded her a thief. The theft was an affront to everything she stood for and believed in."

Eden opened the second box. "I have to admit, I've only looked inside this one once before. The things my father kept were a lot different from my mother's. See?" She pulled out a stuffed pig wearing a badge. She squeezed it and it squealed loudly. There was also a turquoise-and-silver ring. Eden picked it up. "That'll be Christopher's someday."

Eden then picked up a large, reddish-brown rock. "Ugly, isn't it?"

"Why the rock?" Nick asked.

"I have no idea. Near as I can figure, it's just a piece of volcanic rock from one of the lava flows. Had I found this in my mother's box, I would have thought it was something she picked up where Dad first kissed her, or something along those lines. But Dad wasn't the sentimental type."

"He must have kept it for a reason," Nick said, taking the heavy stone from her and studying it. "One edge is less weathered, and look at these metallic, silver scrapes. It's as if someone used a steel tool, like a hammer, to break this piece off a larger chunk."

Eden drew in a breath. "Wait a minute. Remember my mother's map and her clue? She said something about 'prisoner of the piece that fits.' This may be what she was talking about. I can't think of any other reason why someone who lives in the desert would keep a piece of volcanic rock. They're found in almost every part of the state."

"If it really is a clue, it's not a very good one. Do you

have any idea how many of those rocks there are out in the alkali flats and the surrounding mesas? Looking for one with a piece missing is going to be all but impossible. One whole layer of those mesas comes from an old lava flow."

"I didn't say it would be easy," she answered with a thin smile. "I only said we had a clue."

He mulled it over. "We only have one choice left."

"We have to go out there and look around," she finished for him.

"It's a rugged hike. To get to the flats we have to cross an escarpment filled with hiding places for rattlers. And they love to sit out on the rocks and get warm this time of year. Or I should say, if we're lucky, that's where they'll be. Better the rattler you see than the one you don't. Take it from me, they don't like to be disturbed."

"I'll wear boots," she said. "But we have to go. If we take the map my mom gave your mother, we may also recognize other landmarks once we're both out there. Then we'll have to search for a large reddish-brown rock with a chunk missing, and see if it matches the piece from my father's box."

"I hate to put a damper on things, but to find one particular rock, we might have to stay out there for days. And even then, there are no guarantees. Remember that after twenty years, weathering will have discolored the main piece some more, and maybe even worn away some of the broken edges."

"What other alternative do we have?" she said simply. "I'm not going to wait for the kidnappers to come after our son again."

Anger rose up inside him as he thought of what had almost been taken from him. The thought of his only son, and the woman he loved being harmed in any way— No. He could never allow that to happen.

"Agreed. We'll go out there," he said brusquely. "But I'll need to make a stop first. I want to get some bird shot in case we have a problem with snakes, and some other supplies. Would you consider staying at Black Raven Ranch and letting my brother and me hike out there?"

She gave him an incredulous look. "I've been in on this from the beginning. Do you honestly think I'm going to step aside now?"

"No," he muttered, "but it was worth a try."

Chapter Twenty

Back at Black Raven Ranch, Nick spoke to Jake, filling him in on their plans.

"I sure wish I could go along with you," Jake said, "but I've just hired extra hands to help repair fences and round up horses. Are you sure you can't wait a few days?"

"The sooner we get there, the better off we'll all be."

"I'd tell you to take the cell phone so you can reach me, but it's pretty unreliable out there," Jake said.

"Same with police radios. I've heard that the iron from the old lava flows causes the problem."

"When do you expect to be back?" Jake asked.

"A couple of hours, all day. Who knows? You'll see me when I get back," Nick said.

"Good luck, brother. I hope it doesn't end up being a wild-goose chase."

"So do I."

Saying goodbye, Nick went out to join Eden, who was already waiting in his old Jeep.

TWO HOURS LATER after Mrs. Chino had left to have lunch with her daughter, Annie sat with Christopher and Noelle in the *sala,* the big family room. Annie had two babies to take care of now and she was loving every moment of it.

Sitting on the rug, she played with them, enjoying their smiles and the sound of their laughter. She thought of how different things were for her this fall as compared to last winter when she'd been a pregnant widow trying to make ends meet. Now she was part of a wonderful family.

Hearing the phone ring, she picked up the receiver, not moving far from the babies.

"Annie, this is Thomas," a familiar voice said. "We have a problem. There's been an accident just at the end of Sage Canyon. Two Black Raven Ranch horses spooked and collided, and we need you to bring the horse trailer so we can get them to a vet. Can you do that?"

"Sure, but I'll have to bring the kids. Mrs. Chino left."

"Just put them in their car seats and get here as quickly as you can. You'll be able to see us once you arrive at the stop sign across from the northwest gate."

"I'll be there as fast as possible."

Worried about the horses, Annie got the kids ready quickly. Any injuries could be disastrous to the animals unless treated right away.

As she strapped the kids into their car seats inside the extended cab of the pickup, she thought about Nick and Jake's uncle. She was a bit surprised that Thomas had been hired on. Ranching certainly wasn't in his blood, and he didn't seem the type to go in for hard physical labor. Maybe he'd finally decided to start trying to pay off his gambling debts.

Working efficiently, Annie hitched up the horse trailer and got underway. She headed north up the main ranch road, glancing in the rearview mirror for the umpteenth time. Both kids seemed perfectly happy. Chris was chewing on a teething ring, while Noelle contented herself by waving her stuffed bear in the air.

As Annie pulled up to the stop sign across from the

northwest gate, she caught a glimpse of another vehicle parked just behind a cluster of pines. Suddenly two men wearing stocking masks jumped out from the brush bordering the road and leaped onto the running board on both sides of the truck. The one on the driver's side pointed a gun directly at her face.

"Turn off the engine and give me the keys. Then hand me your cell phone and pop the hood open," he growled.

Shaking badly, she did as the man requested, handing him the keys and phone. "Pop the hood…. Why?"

"Just do it."

She obeyed, knowing she had no other choice with a pistol just two feet from her. The second man jumped off the passenger side and moved around front, doing something to the engine.

"Now I need the boy," the gunman snapped.

Annie knew then that these were the kidnappers. The knowledge filled her with fear so intense she could barely draw in a breath. "What do you want with Chris?" she managed, her heart drumming at her throat.

The man pointed the barrel of his gun directly at Noelle. He knew she was the older of the two. "I don't need that one. She's your daughter, isn't she?"

Annie began to shake even more than before. She wasn't sure if anyone could actually shoot a baby, but she couldn't take a chance. She opened the door and went around to the other side of the truck, the man with the gun right behind her. As she unfastened Chris's car seat, she desperately tried to think of a way to save both babies.

The man's partner returned with a van a moment later. The gunman suddenly pushed Annie aside hard, knocking her to the ground and grabbed the car seat with Chris in it. As his partner opened the side doors of the vehicle, Annie saw Thomas inside, bound hand and foot, and gagged.

Terror shot through her. If there had been any doubt in her mind before, there wasn't any now. She knew that these men were going after Nick and Eden, and were going to use Chris as leverage.

It was Noelle's crying that pushed her to get back to her feet. She'd injured her knee, but there wasn't time to worry about it. As the van roared away, Annie limped back to the truck. Though she suspected it was useless, she tried to start the engine, but it wouldn't make a sound.

Biting back the pain, Annie reached into the backseat, grabbed her daughter and started walking down the road as fast as she could. There was a farmhouse about a mile away. She'd use the phone there, and warn the police and Jake.

EDEN PICKED her way carefully across the rocky terrain. Footing was precarious here, and the sharp edges of the lava flow could cut through the soles of shoes. Though she was wearing boots, one wrong move could mean a nasty cut. If that wasn't bad enough, there was also the danger of snakes. Twice now she'd heard an ominous dry rattle as she stepped too close to where one lay in a drift of sand beneath a rock, sheltered from the sun.

Nick guided her across the worst of the stretch. His strong hand at times became the only point of safety in one of the most forbidding sections of land she'd ever been.

Below the escarpment they were now climbing down was a natural basin, devoid of most plant and animal life except for a few hardy tufts of salt-tolerant grass and the ever-resilient insects. Poor drainage had resulted in the buildup of alkali that was so thick in places it formed a crust that crackled beneath a hiker's shoes. Even the small tendrils of the old lava flow extending out into the flatlands had a white ring around them, indicating how high the water level could rise during the rainy season.

It was a depressing place. As the sun rose in the sky she moved carefully, always searching for that particular rock that was missing the chunk she carried in her knapsack.

Time passed slowly, and it seemed like they'd been out there forever. Finally, tired and discouraged, she sat down on a relatively smooth rock formation that looked like a lump of black taffy poured over an earlier lava flow. "It's like looking for a needle in a haystack. No wonder your mother couldn't find the spot either."

Nick's gaze drifted over the terrain. "My mother was no outdoors person. She wouldn't have stayed out here as long as we have."

"Come to think of it, my mom got lost even in Santa Fe. What we need to do is find a landmark she could have depended on to orient herself no matter when she chose to come back here—day or night. If we do that, we'll be able to find the other landmarks on her map."

He looked around. "There *is* something that remains constant, despite the season. The low spot at the center of the basin. And there are only a few big rocks down there."

They hurried down into the lowest spot in the basin, and Eden climbed up onto the largest boulder there, which was about the size of a large tree stump.

"If we imagine that this is the high spot she indicated on her drawing," Eden said looking north, "then that rock out by itself straight ahead is the one. It's about fifty paces away, wouldn't you say?"

Together, they crossed to where the basketball-sized rock lay and rolled the boulder over. "I think this is what we've been searching for," Eden said, barely able to contain her excitement.

Eden reached into her backpack and fished out the rock

she'd found among her father's things. Moving it around like a piece of a puzzle, she finally felt it fall into place, fitting against one corner almost perfectly.

"That's a match," Nick said grimly. "Now we dig." He reached for the folding shovels he'd strapped to his backpack and handed one to her.

As the sun pounded down on them, they moved the rock marker aside and began digging. It was hot, sweaty work. Before long, Nick stopped and stripped off his shirt. Perspiration covered his chest, making his bronzed muscles glisten in the sun. He was all steel and hard planes. Desire rocked her, unexpected and fierce.

With effort, she tore her gaze away but, as she tried to grip the shovel, she realized her hands were trembling.

"Do you plan on just staring at me, or will you actually start moving some dirt?" he teased.

"I'll work, but you've got the advantage. You can cool off by removing your shirt."

"Feel free to take off yours. I'm fair."

The slow grin he gave her made her tongue wedge in her mouth. Her pulse raced out of control. Eden made herself take a long, deep breath. Then, when she looked back at him and saw his eyes bright with mischief, she realized just how much he was enjoying baiting her.

She matched his smile. "And if I took off my shirt, would you be able to work?" Her breath caught in her throat as she saw the dark passion that suddenly flickered in his eyes.

He captured her gaze and held it. "Let's save that particular game for another time," he said, his voice low and seductive.

A shiver raced up her spine, but she didn't dare look back at him. Instead, she forced herself to concentrate on digging.

A few minutes later the tip of Nick's shovel touched something metallic and hard. He began to move the sand away with his hands, trying to uncover what lay beneath. "Be careful. We don't want to damage anything."

Working together, they managed to free a metal box the size and shape of a small suitcase. The lock was in place, but the case was rusted and swollen from water damage. "I'd like to carry just the contents back with us. It'll be easier and I can always come back for the box later."

Nick smashed the lock, hitting it hard with a rock, then pulled open the lid. Aluminum foil was wrapped in thick layers around a smaller, cylindrical container inside.

Peeling some of it away, Eden laughed when she saw a blue ceramic jar with a matching lid. "It's Mom's old cookie jar."

Nick took off the rest of the foil, then removed the lid, which had been sealed shut with freezer tape. The canvas, conical-shaped mask was inside, safe and dry. On top of it lay the fetish that belonged to that *Tsave Yoh*.

"The artifacts," she whispered, her throat constricting with emotion. "Now the rituals can be held as they'd been meant to be."

"With these things back, our tribe will finally be able to put the past behind them," Nick said. "But it's not over yet. We still need to bring in Rita and her brother. We know that they're at the bottom of everything, including spreading the lie that my father was involved."

"But we still don't have enough against them, do we?" Eden asked.

"This evidence may give us an edge. There's technology available now that wasn't around when the crime took place. The fact that this mask and the fetish weren't part of any display may really help us. Remember that these artifacts were stored at the Center because it was supposed to be the safest place in town. Rita and her brother may have known something was being stored for the tribe in the vault, but they wouldn't have been told what it was, and they wouldn't have been allowed to touch any of it. We'd expect your mother's fingerprints to be on these artifacts, but if the FBI lab can lift their fingerprints from these items as well, then we'll be a step closer to proving that they were the ones who took them out of the vault, intending to steal them.''

Eden looked around to verify that they were still alone. "Let's hurry back to the pueblo. We need to get these things in a safe place."

Nick noted her apprehension. "Don't worry. No one can sneak up on us out here. There's not enough cover." He placed the mask and fetish inside his backpack.

Carefully Eden put the cookie jar in her own backpack. She intended on bringing it back unbroken. "I'm going to keep this to remember my mom and everything she went through. Not that I'd ever forget."

They hurried across the basin and climbed to the top of the escarpment, reversing the route they'd taken before. Picking their way across the treacherous rocks, they finally reached normal terrain, the piñon pine-dotted upland desert that rimmed much of the pueblo's land.

They'd stopped for a moment to drink some water from a canteen, when suddenly they heard a clear voice from behind the brush directly ahead.

"Don't make another move. We've been watching you through binoculars since you went down below, and we know you've found the mask and the fetish. Put both backpacks on the ground, and walk away."

Nick instantly jerked Eden down behind the tall sagebrush.

"No deal," he yelled back taking his pistol out of its holster.

Eden nodded in approval. "They're not going to take this from us. We've worked too hard for it," she whispered.

"We have hostages," the man said, his voice cold. "Wanna see?"

As they peered out from their cover, they saw someone being pushed out from behind a low, wide piñon. It was Thomas, his hands tied, and a piece of duct tape over his mouth. Nick cursed.

"And we have more!" the man's voice added.

Eden heard the sound of a baby crying and her heart suddenly froze. "That's Christopher."

A masked figure carried out Christopher in his car seat and set him down out in the open, then quickly disappeared.

Eden reached for Nick's backpack. "That's it, they win. I'll give them what they want."

"No, wait," he said, holding on to her.

"Stop playing games," the woman ordered simultaneously. "Toss your gun out into the open, Deputy, then the backpacks. If you don't, I'll shoot the hostages."

Though he hated the thought of relinquishing his weapon, Nick knew he didn't have a clear line of fire and couldn't have risked a shot. All he could do now was buy time.

Nick unloaded his pistol, then tossed the clip and the weapon in separate directions. "Rita Korman, we know it's you, and so does Captain Mora," Nick said. "And your accomplice is your brother, Wayne. The game's up. You can't play this out and win."

The sound of her laughter reached them. "Sure we can. And we will. But you can try to save some lives unless you want me to shoot your uncle and the baby. Just keep in mind what happened to Isabel and James Maes when they decided to fight us. James came to us with replicas of the artifacts, pretending to be ready to deal in exchange for his wife. We saw that all he'd brought were copies and refused to deal. That's when he went for my gun. Isabel tried to help him and, by the time it was all over, they were both dead. We didn't want to kill them, but in a gunfight things have a way of going very wrong. Play things smart. Don't push this and end up making the same mistake they did.''

"Please don't hurt anyone else," Eden cried. She tried to go to her son, but Nick tightened his grip on her arm and held her back.

"Then do as I say. Now!" Rita shouted. "All we want are the artifacts. By the time you get to civilization, we'll be gone from this God-forsaken pueblo forever."

"What assurance do we have that you won't start shooting once we put the artifacts on the ground?" Nick looked over at a nearby tree, where a piñon jay had just screeched, then grabbed Eden even tighter.

"None at all. But if you stay where you are, I'll kill the baby and old man while you watch."

Nick heard the cry that was wrenched from Eden's throat and pulled her closer to his side. "Trust me," he mouthed.

Hearing a rustle to their right, Nick turned and grinned at his brother as he came through the brush. "You took your sweet time. I heard your birdcall."

"Are you alone?" Eden asked Jake quickly.

"For now. I came ahead, figuring you might need someone in your corner right away," Jake said, tightening his grip on the rifle in his hand. "Martin is getting the men together, and Captain Mora is already on his way here."

"We can't use that. Not yet," Nick said, pointing to the weapon. "But I have an idea. Change shirts with me and take my badge. Wear it on your shirt pocket to give them something more to think about. Let them see you, and stall any way you can. While they're busy keeping an eye on you two, I'll go around and take Wayne out first, then Rita.''

Jake handed him the rifle.

Nick took it. ''I'll use it only as a last resort. No way I'm risking a fire fight with Christopher and our uncle out there.''

''Then maybe I should go. I'm a better fighter,'' Jake said, ''and they owe me.'' He told them about how Annie had been ambushed earlier. ''I'd love the chance to tear that cocky guy's head off.''

''I'll do it for you. I'm trained in hand-to-hand. I have some moves even you wouldn't see coming,'' he said, then saw Jake nod. ''When you let them see you,'' Nick added, ''don't give them a clear shot, and always hold the artifacts directly in front of you. They'll hesitate to shoot, knowing that they might damage what they've waited all these years to get.''

''You've got it,'' Jake said. ''Just watch yourself out there, brother.''

Nick nodded, then took Eden's hand in his. ''I *will* be back with Christopher. I swear it.''

Before she could do more than blink back her tears, he'd slipped away.

Nick moved as quietly as he could over the landscape, using every instinct and skill he possessed. As he circled, he heard his brother and Eden suddenly start arguing. Their voices were loud and carried easily. He froze, wondering what had happened. Then he heard what they were saying, and smiled, understanding. It would be just one more diversion to confuse Rita and Wayne.

''We have the artifacts,'' Eden said, staying in the shadows, but holding the mask out so they could see it clearly.

"But I swear that I will rip the mask apart and shatter the fetish against a rock unless I get my son back *now*."

"If you destroy those artifacts, your son *will* die," Rita yelled. "Don't be stupid. Just put them down on the ground. There's no reason for anyone to get shot."

"Give me my son!" Eden yelled out, her voice hysterical.

Nick knew that her acting had been no stretch.

"Give me a moment with her," Jake yelled to Rita. "I can get her to listen to reason."

"Do it!" Rita screamed at him. "This doesn't have to end up a disaster for all of us."

Their playacting kept Rita and Wayne distracted. Nick moved in close and crouched behind a bush six feet away from Christopher's carrier.

From where he was hiding, Nick could see that Thomas had been forced to get down onto his knees, and Rita was watching him, looking over toward Jake and Eden every few seconds. She held a pistol casually down by her leg.

Wayne had a pistol too, and was closer to Chris. Seeing his son's vulnerable position filled him with a fear so intense it was nearly paralyzing. One stray bullet and his son would be dead. He put the rifle down.

Then, guided by some unerring instinct for survival, Thomas turned his head. He saw Nick and nodded. A split second later, though his hands were tied behind his back, he lunged forward like a track star leaving the blocks. Thomas hurled himself into Rita, knocking her to the ground with his shoulders and head.

As Wayne scrambled to help his sister, unable to fire without hitting her, Nick tackled Wayne from behind, throwing him face forward into the sand. Twisting one of Wayne's arms painfully, he tried to get him to drop the gun. But Wayne fought with the tenacity of a madman, and his weight lifting had obviously paid off. The man was as strong as an ox. With Nick holding on to him, he still managed to lift them both to their feet.

Out of the corner of his eye, Nick saw Thomas struggling to keep Rita pinned to the ground as his brother Jake came forward to help him. Eden was somewhere behind him, headed toward Chris.

Wayne had almost managed to pull away, but Nick still held on to both wrists, forcing the gun to stay between them at eye level.

"Keep this up, Wayne, and the gun will go off. One of us will get shot right in the face. I'm willing to give up my life so that no one else gets hurt. Are you?"

They struggled a few inches from each other, eye to eye, neither flinching nor looking away. Wayne tried to knee Nick in the groin, but Nick anticipated the move, smacking Wayne's knee with his own. Wayne groaned.

Realizing it was hopeless now that he could see his sister was already captured, Wayne released his hold on the gun. "Forget it. That dumb mask isn't worth this."

"Good call." Nick stepped back, pointing the pistol at him. "On the ground, face down. And lock your hands behind your head."

"Good fight, brother," Jake said, coming over to help. He slipped a rope around Wayne's wrists, and started to tie him up. "I'll take care of him now. Our uncle has the woman under control."

Nick glanced over and saw Thomas sitting on Rita Korman's back, the barrel of the gun pressed against the side of her head. His hands were now untied, supplying the rope that was restricting Wayne. "I guess he does," Nick said with a chuckle.

Nick turned to Eden, who was holding Christopher in her arms. "He's all right!" she whispered, tears streaming down her face. "I don't know what to say. This is the second time you've risked everything for us."

"You and Chris are a part of me," he said, drawing her close and keeping Christopher between them. "You're blood of my blood. Do you understand what I'm trying to tell you?" He tilted up her head up, ready to kiss her and show her exactly what he meant.

Jake came up just then and poked him in the back. "Save it for later."

Nick turned his head and scowled at his brother, but then saw Mora's vehicle pulling up, followed by two pickup loads of newly deputized men.

Nick's gaze swept over Eden's face tenderly.

"Go," she whispered. "We can pick up where we left off later." Slowly and deliberately, she ran her fingertip down the length of his chest slowly. "And we won't have to rush."

"You're killing me, woman," he murmured, and he heard her husky laugh as he moved away.

As Deputy Torres and some of the others cuffed the prisoners, Nick filled the Captain in on what had happened.

"You did good work here today, Deputy Black Raven," Mora said as Nick finished briefing him. "But what about Marc Korman and his son, Patrick?"

"We have no evidence to indicate they were ever part of the theft or conspiracy," Nick said.

Thomas approached them, interrupting their conversation. "I have a little gift for you, nephew." Thomas looked at Mora. "It's good you're here to hear this, too" he added, then continued. "I overheard Rita and Wayne talking, and found out they were the ones who led Eden's grandmother to believe Tall Shadow was involved in framing Isabel Maes. They'd hoped that if word got around, everyone would back off. But of course, that ultimately backfired big time. Wayne was the one involved in the sniper attack on me and also took some shots at Eden and Nick near the sacred mountain.''

Nick looked over at Eden, and the love he saw shining in her eyes as she gazed at him stole the last piece of his heart. "If you don't need me right away, Captain, I'd like to take care of some personal business."

"Go. You've earned it. I'll take the artifacts back with me now."

Nick glanced at his uncle for a long moment, then looked back at Mora. "My uncle risked his life for all of us here today. Without his help, things may not have gone as well as they have. I think he deserves to be the one who turns in the artifacts and collects the reward money. Do you agree?"

"I have no problem with that, providing he goes in with a police escort," Mora said.

Nick looked back at Thomas. "But the deal only holds if you promise to use the money to square your debt with the casinos."

"Sounds fair to me," Thomas said.

Nick moved away and took Christopher from Eden's arms, but before he could say anything Captain Mora came up to him.

"If your uncle is going to return the artifacts, you're riding with him."

"Yes, sir." Giving Christopher back to Eden, he brushed her lips with a kiss. "We'll be together later," he murmured, holding her gaze, but not elaborating further.

"I'll be waiting."

BLACK RAVEN RANCH was decked out for a celebration. Nick and Jake had burned the diary in a private ceremony.

The wrongs of the past had finally been set right and it was now time to look to the future.

Lights shined brightly in all the downstairs rooms as evening settled over the land. A buffet had been set up in the patio, and family favorites such as green chile stew, horno baked breads and bread pudding lined the table.

Eden walked around the garden holding her son and watched the last rays of the fading sun dip down below the horizon. For the first time in a long time, she could be proud of who she was and of her parents. No one would ever put her or her son down again.

As a gentle rain began to fall, she moved back to the shelter of the covered porch. Hearing someone coming from inside the house, she started to turn around, but Nick never gave her a chance. Wrapping his arms securely around her, he pulled her back into him.

"Rain is a good sign. It means that the dead have found peace at last," he whispered.

"We're all finally free to start our lives fresh."

"Now all that's left is for you to say yes," he murmured.

"To what?"

"To everything," he said, nuzzling the sensitive skin below her ear. "But to getting married in particular." He turned her around in his arms. "So what do you say?"

She sighed. "Do you realize that you've never told me that you loved me?"

He cupped her face in his hands. "How can you not know that? I've showed you what's in my heart. Actions speak louder than words."

"At times, actions have definite advantages," she said with a tiny smile. "But a woman needs to hear the words, too."

"Tell her you love her and kiss her, you idiot," Jake prompted from inside the house.

Nick pulled her away from the windows into the shadows, then faced her, ignoring his brother. "I'm crazy in love with you, Eden. I figure you'll need to hear it said as often as I'll want to show you. So let's work this out." His slow grin was devastatingly sensual. "What do you say. Marry me?"

"You're a man of action. Convince me," she whispered.

As his son slept in her arms, Nick covered Eden's mouth with his own.

* * * * *

Shh!

has a secret...

September 2000

Back by popular demand are

DEBBIE MACOMBER's

MIDNIGHT SONS

Hard Luck, Alaska, is a town that needs women!
And the O'Halloran brothers are just
the fellows to fly them in.

Starting in March 2000 this beloved series returns
in special 2-in-1 collector's editions:

MAIL-ORDER MARRIAGES, featuring
Brides for Brothers and *The Marriage Risk*
On sale March 2000

FAMILY MEN, featuring
Daddy's Little Helper and *Because of the Baby*
On sale May 2000

THE LAST TWO BACHELORS, featuring
Falling for Him and *Ending in Marriage*
On sale July 2000

Collect and enjoy each MIDNIGHT SONS story!

Available at your favorite retail outlet.

HARLEQUIN®
Makes any time special ™

Your Romantic Books—find them at

www.eHarlequin.com

Visit the *Author's Alcove*

➤ Find the most complete information anywhere on your favorite author.

➤ Try your hand in the Writing Round Robin—contribute a chapter to an online book in the making.

Enter the *Reading Room*

➤ Experience an interactive novel—help determine the fate of a story being created now by one of your favorite authors.

➤ Join one of our reading groups and discuss your favorite book.

Drop into *Shop eHarlequin*

➤ Find the latest releases—read an excerpt or write a review for this month's Harlequin top sellers.

➤ Try out our amazing search feature—tell us your favorite theme, setting or time period and we'll find a book that's perfect for you.

All this and more available at

www.eHarlequin.com
on Women.com Networks

HARLEQUIN®

I N T R I G U E ®

COMING NEXT MONTH

#573 THE STRANGER NEXT DOOR by Joanna Wayne
Randolph Family Ties

First a baby was left on the family's doorstep, then a beautiful woman with no memory inherited the ranch next door. Langley Randolph wasn't sure what was going on, but he intended to find out. Danger lurked, but the passion aroused by his mysterious new neighbor, Danielle, made protecting her his duty—and having her his heart's desire.

#574 INNOCENT WITNESS by Leona Karr

After witnessing a murder, Deanna Drake's four-year-old daughter was traumatized into silence. With the help of Dr. Steve Sherman and his young son, her daughter found her voice—and incited the killer to attack again. But to get to Deanna and her daughter, the madman would have to go through Steve first....

#575 BLACKMAILED BRIDE by Sylvie Kurtz

For two weeks, Cathlynn O'Connell agreed to play the role of wife to the enigmatic researcher Jonas Shades. But alone in his secluded mansion, what began as a temporary arrangement soon spiraled into an intricate web of deceit, danger and disguised passions. Someone knew Cathlynn was an impostor. What they didn't know was that Jonas intended to make a proper bride of Cathlynn—if he could keep her alive.

#576 A MAN OF HONOR by Tina Leonard

Intuition told Cord Greer that things were not what they seemed. When two men came in search of Tessa Draper, Cord's first instinct was to protect. But now that the pregnant Tessa shared the intimacy of Cord's solitary ranch, he had to rethink his actions. Someone was out there watching, waiting to take away the only woman he'd ever loved and the child he considered his own.

Visit us at www.eHarlequin.com

CNM0600